Tacoma

PRE-EMPTIVE LOVE

How a Hiroshima Man's Story Might Save Hong Kong

By

George L. Olson

ISBN: 0-7596-9564-4 (ebook)
ISBN: 0-7596-9565-2 (softcover)

This book is printed on acid free paper.

1stBooks – rev. 4/4/02

Acknowledgments

Special thanks to Libby Grandy and the Writers' Critique Group at BORDERS in Montclair, CA, Mildred Tengbom and the Write Group at Pilgrim Place, Kimi Noda, Pastor Kiyoshi Watanabe's daughter, Shizue Marian Asai who kept pressing the author to have the manuscript published, and my computer-literate wife Miriam.

1

A Troubling Question

If anyone asked Joe Weaver whether he preferred to be called "Joe Weaver" or "Joe Orimura," he would answer, "Just call me Joe." Then with a straight face he'd add, "If you're sending me a check, make it out to 'Joe Weaver.'"

That was his birth name, the one on his U.S. passport. Joe prided himself that the Japanese in Hiroshima had given him the name of Orimura and that the famous *haiku* poet Teijo Nakamura had praised it as an excellent pen name for doing haiku poetry. Japanese rarely honored foreigners that way, so he had gradually considered Japan his adopted homeland.

Whenever he and his wife Anita left California for Japan, he'd tell his neighbors, "We're going home to Japan." That Japanese home was a rustic summer cabin atop a hill overlooking Lake Nojiri in the mountains of Nagano, 160 miles northwest of Tokyo.

In 1996 on the night of August 5, Joe was seated inside the cabin listening to the NHK classical music program. At 8:59 the announcer broke in to remind listeners that on the next day the nation would be observing the anniversary of the atomic bombing of Hiroshima.

At the 9 o'clock station break, Joe switched to shortwave in order to hear the English news over the BBC. Static made reception terrible, but he did catch the tail end of the news, something about rising tensions over Hong Kong's reverting to China.

A month earlier one of Joe's Chinese friends from Hong Kong had confided to him: "After the honeymoon with China, what then? Who can trust China's promises?"

Joe hadn't recalled those words until tonight, but why tonight? Hong Kong had been off Joe's radar screen until he'd heard that barely decipherable news. His Chinese friend had been predicting a brief honeymoon — a rosy grace period — five years, maybe seven. Then the euphoria of the post-wedding years would fade away. The marriage between Hong Kong, the wealthy freedom-loving debutante, and the Beijing lover would turn sour.

During Joe's forty years in the Orient he had learned the hard way that a Westerner could never be 100 percent certain what the Japanese or Chinese really meant.

Removing Debussy's "Afternoon of a Faun" from its portable CD-case, Joe set the disk on to play. He turned the volume down for his sleeping wife's sake,

1

then flopped onto the sofa, hoping the musical images of a deer grazing in a forest would quiet his nerves.

Around 9:30 he said to himself, *Why does the Hong Kong situation haunt me?* From experience he knew that events or people far away had a way of mysteriously linking with his own life. Anita had told him that Jung called it "Synchronicity."

Letting Debussy play on into "Clair De Lune," he turned off the light and crawled into bed. In spite of the peaceful music, Joe couldn't sleep. He tossed and turned hour after hour. Even when forcing his legs out in isometric stretches, he couldn't unwind. He even tried praying for the friends he could remember from A to Z and back again, but sleep eluded him. Giving up, he went back to the *ofuro* bathroom and swallowed two sleeping pills. Usually that would knock him out in thirty minutes, but not this time.

About 3 a.m. when a squirrel rattled across the tin roof, Joe sat straight up. A cold pre-dawn dampness had penetrated the bedding. He tiptoed over to the tea box in the corner to fetch an extra blanket because Anita soon would be shivering, too.

Outside from the woods lining the golf course, the neighborhood owl hooted with little grunting sounds: "All is well on the hill. So, go to sleep. Hong Kong can wait till morning."

An hour later, the first glimmer of dawn appeared through the doorway. Mount Madarao's black silouette jutted up out of the fog blanketing the lake below.

Joe slipped into his soft blue *tanzen* jacket and went to the kitchen to boil water for tea. To avoid the squeaky front door, he exited from the guest room in back, pushing open the screen door with his forehead, careful not to spill the tea.

When his bare feet touched the cold concrete floor of the veranda, he felt uneasy. Still too dark to read, he switched on the green paper lantern hanging from the corrugated plastic roof. Slowly he moved over to his favorite seat, a well-worn rattan chair. He tried to set his mug and tea pot on the end table, but a large manila envelope already occupied it. Since it had been forwarded from Tokyo, he concluded it was full of mail. Joe had seen it the day before but didn't want any uninvited intrusions. Today, however, he felt different. His inner antenna quivered. Picking up a bronze Korean letter opener, Joe ripped through the sealing tape. Holding the envelope up by the bottom, he dumped the contents out on the floor. He tossed aside junk mail and outdated invitations as he searched for bona-fide letters. He pulled out one important-looking note scribbled in Japanese.

He squinted at the paper. *Why can't Kawaguchi write so I can read it? It's worse than my doctor's prescriptions.*

2

Unable to make out the Japanese characters in the dawn light, Joe stood up and walked to the lantern. The brownish hair on his hands had turned seaweed green. Holding the note up to the glare, he struggled for about ten minutes to decode the message, but gave up. When it became bright enough for him to read by daylight, the significance of the message became clear. Taking a pad of lined yellow paper, he wrote down the Japanese in Roman letters and beneath them the English translation.

"Welcome back to Japan. You must be having happy days at Lake Nojiri. I look forward to seeing you before you leave for the States. Let's have lunch at Tony Roma's. Call me when you get to Tokyo."

Next came *"Sate,"* which signaled the main point was about to follow.

"A Chinese journalist by the name of Mei Li Ping telephoned for you. She was calling on behalf of a British TV producer from Hong Kong by the name of John Redone. Redone wants to meet you in Tokyo. He has heard about your efforts to produce a movie about Watanabe's years in Hong Kong. Phone her on Monday, the 5th. Redone says thirty-five years ago Pastor Watanabe made a big impression on him and many British viewers. Rare in television. Takeshi."

Stunned, Joe gazed out through the mist which had rolled in from off the lake. *What can this mean?* Pouring himself a cup of hot tea, he inhaled slowly, Japanese style. *Ping, Redone, Kawaguchi, each of them had been trying to reach me. That could explain the vibes.* Bending his head down into his hands, Joe pondered it for several minutes. Lifting his head as though he'd figured things out, he again spoke to himself and slapped the armrest. *That's why Hong Kong popped into my mind last night.*

Oh no, they wanted me to call yesterday. He re-read the note. "Great!" he exclaimed. "No telephone number. I'll have to get it from Takeshi, first thing."

When Joe pushed the rest of the mail underneath his chair, a picture postcard fell loose. The front side showed a colored photo of the Washington Monument at cherry blossom time. *Tiny handwriting, but at least it's a real letter.* Signed by Eric Gunderson, the high school student who'd stayed with them when he was checking out the Claremont colleges.

"Dear Mr. and Mrs. Weaver *(Orimura)*,

"Thanks again for your hospitality. I decided on Pepperdine for Asian and media studies. Dad is giving me a trip to Japan for graduation. Will stay at the Fairmont from Aug. 9, near our old apartment by the British Embassy.

3

Sincerely, Eric." Under the photo in minuscule letters, he'd written, "Brother Bob is posted to Bosnia."

Forgetting his bare feet, Joe jumped down into the wild flowers and wet grasses. He stared up toward the tree tops. As if addressing someone, he complained aloud, "There goes the summer. They're hijacking it."

He reached down and felt his sopping pajama bottoms and tried to squeeze the water out. He stepped back up onto the porch and for a change headed to a canvas-webbed chair. Still trying to recover from the two letters, he looked out at the lake. Fog no longer hid it. The motionless surface reflected the hills and village in the distance. Everything was quiet, and still no neighbors were stirring. The spider he'd named "Evangeline" had rolled up her web for the day and was resting under the eaves.

Although not yet 6 o'clock, much had happened already. He wondered what might come next. A certain Japanese proverb he'd learned almost always proved true.

"Nido aru koto sando aru."
"What happens twice will happen thrice."

2

Watanabe Connection

Joe sat, staring blankly toward the lake. He always had been sensitive to possible connections between events and persons. Since he had been working on his memoirs, he was more conscious than usual about patterns in the past. He had assembled a looseleaf notebook divided into twenty-eight aspects of his life. He asked himself, *Were the notes from Takeshi and Eric connected, or was it mere coincidence that he read them today?*

A British TV producer wanted to see him about Watanabe. Young Eric who was in search of a media career also was coming.

"Watanabe Sensei! What's going on?" he blurted outloud.

Joe looked around, fearing the neighbors or the newsboy might have heard him. *They'd think I'm hallucinating. Maybe I am. Absurd! Watanabe has been dead twenty years. Why does his death seem as though it happened yesterday? If I only could die like him!*

During Watanabe's final days, this little man, who had been born near seven waterfalls in the tiny Kumamoto village of Nanataki, had refused food and medical help. Gaunt and weak, he lay dying in the hospital at Oita City on the southern island of Kyushu. Several weeks earlier when he and his pastor, Noboru Ishii, were making plans for the funeral, Watanabe had requested that a recording of Handel's "Amen Chorus" be played.

All of his friends in the area knew the old shepherd was nearing death. On his final sick call, Ishii had to lean over the hospital bed to make himself heard. "Shall we pray?" he asked. But before Ishii could close his eyes for prayer, Watanabe already had begun to pray. Ishii sat open mouthed, as the dying man began gasping out his own prayer.

"O God, loving Father, hear my prayer. Bless this young pastor. Bless our church. Bless all churches. Bless our kindergartens and the orphanage at Beppu. Give hope to our young people. Forgive our failures. Give peace to your world. Release the Hong Kong prisoners from bitterness. Forgive us for destroying cities and lives. Bless my old church in Hiroshima. O God, no more Hiroshimas, please. Help us live and die in the merciful arms of Jesus. Amen."

Watanabe's voice trembled and grew silent. He forced himself to look straight into Ishii's eyes. Mustering energy from deep within, Watanabe said,

5

"Play the 'Amen Chorus.'" Pastor Ishii said it sounded like a command, not a request. Since the cassette already was set for that chorus, all he had to do was push the play button, and turn the volume on high. As the Amens in the chorus rolled in over and over again like giant waves, Watanabe's drawn face took on a pinkish hue and the corners of his mouth turned up in a gentle smile.

When the music finished, he whispered in Ishii's ear, "Once more." Not understanding, Ishii leaned closer so that his ear almost touched Watanabe's lips. "Once more. Once more," he wheezed. So, Ishii backed up the tape and played it again. During the final crescendo Watanabe closed his eyes and died. The room became unbelievably quiet, so quiet that Ishii could only compare it to what happened in Revelation when the seventh seal was broken: "there was silence in heaven about the space of half an hour."

Since then twenty years had passed, but every time Joe recalls Pastor Ishii's account of that scene, he heaves with grief as though he had heard it for the first time.

Joe's head drooped to his chest. He was desperate to link his feelings to the now. With measured slowness he lifted bleary eyes. Suddenly the connection came to him. The lake and lights on the far shore represented Hong Kong. He knew that wasn't happenstance. God was dealing with him in an uncharted way. Forces he didn't understand had been set in motion, thrusting him into an unpredictable future that must have to do with the turnover of Hong Kong to the Chinese in July, 1997, but he could not guess why.

By nature Joe liked to be in control, at least aware of the direction he was headed. A Japanese colleague had pegged him rightly when he once joked, "Orimura Sensei has to test each rock before stepping on it." He knew Joe's fears of presumptuous mistakes.

Joe sat wallowing in doubt, baffled about the future, afraid of what might be bearing down on him from around the corner. As per custom Joe turned to coffee when he was perplexed. "No big decisions before coffee," was his motto. Coffee often accompanied Joe's retreat into lateral thinking which he had picked up from a speech by Edward De Bono at an advertising convention in Tokyo. It was a simple trick, viewing an unsolved problem from the side when other answers weren't forthcoming.

That's what I need now, a big dose of lateral thinking. Back to the kitchen he went. Not for weak Chinese tea this time, but for strong black coffee. He filled his mug. Then instead of heading out the front door with it, Joe veered left, stopping in the study. He picked up some scratch paper out of the drawer and planted himself behind the desk, determined to doodle his way out of bewilderment.

He pulled back the window curtains so he could see Lake Nojiri and Mt. Madarao. Three times he tapped the desk with his pencil as though conjuring up a secret formula. First he asked himself whether the future would come toward him out of the unknown or would it evolve out of the past? His gut instinct ruled out the unknown as the answer. Whatever was coming had to come from the past. God does not throw curves from out of nowhere.

Out in the middle of the lake he spotted a swimmer being followed by a rowboat. A teenager, no doubt, was out to win the Island Swim Badge. Kids had to cross over early in the morning before the Western breezes began blowing in from the Japan Sea. That wind would make the water too choppy for a long-distance swim.

Again Joe began wondering what the day would bring. How might his past dictate the way he would cross over his own lake today? That question pushed his memories back to the first time he and Anita had crossed the Pacific, a long long time ago. It was October 7, 1950, when they arrived in Yokohama Bay aboard the SS President Cleveland. She was twenty-one, and Joe had just turned twenty-six. The Korean War was raging. U.S. Navy and transport ships jammed the harbor so that the Cleveland couldn't dock.

Having awakened that morning with the realization that the ship's engines had shut down and all movement stopped, Joe went over next to the night light to read his watch. It was 4:30. He quietly dressed and climbed up on deck. He didn't want to miss the splendor of the rising sun on their first day in Japan. Outside everything was dark, except for a few safety lights on deck. Looking westward he beheld what resembled a theater marquee with shining white lights. A woman by the guardrail called out, "Mt. Fuji! There's Mt. Fuji."

The rays of the rising sun already had reached Fuji from 14,000 feet up. The snowcapped volcano shone brightly. *What an auspicious welcome to Japan!* Weaver thought, even though during the thirteen-day passage from Los Angeles, he had been worrying about having to minister in Hiroshima. The very word *Hiroshima* had always bothered him.

On V-J Day, August 15, 1945, young Weaver had been filling in as student pastor at a parish in Menominee, Upper Michigan. When he heard the news about Emperor Hirohito's speech of surrender, he rushed to the church to plan a special thanksgiving service to celebrate the coming of peace. He entered from the back, walking up the middle aisle. When he reached the front, he impulsively threw himself down on the communion rail, thanking and praising God that the awful nightmare of war had ended. Standing up, he turned and walked over in front of the pulpit and peered out over the empty church. Surprising even himself, he began preaching an imaginary sermon to the Japanese people about reconciliation. He tried to recall his text, but wasn't sure. He thought he must have paraphrased Jesus' dying words from the cross: "Father, forgive us for we don't know what we are doing."

Little did Joe Weaver expect that five years later he would be landing in Japan, called to labor amidst the shambles of Hiroshima.

After being taken ashore in a large motorboat, they headed toward the Tokyo YMCA thirty miles away. The young Japanese driver, blaring his horn at every corner, sped them along mile after mile of rubble which once had been the Tokyo-Yokohama industrial belt. *If this looks bad, what can I expect to find in Hiroshima?* How could he, an only son who had never missed a meal in his life, identify with the people of destroyed Japan? How could he ever get inside their skins: feel what they feel, think what they think, suffer what they suffer?

The sound of a truck rumbling past the cabin shook Joe back to August 5, 1996. His trip into lateral thinking had carried him far away — almost beyond sight of his original problem. He yanked back on his thoughts, but he couldn't rein them in.

He recalled a small, handsome Japanese gentleman with sharp, but not unfriendly features. It was about ten days after Anita and he had moved into an old Japanese-style house in Denenchofu, Tokyo, overlooking the Tama River. The mission had purchased it for language students who would be required to study two years before going out on assignment.

The guest at the door bowed when he introduced himself as Pastor Kiyoshi Watanabe from Hiroshima. He reached out his hand to shake Joe's, with a confidence that showed he'd shaken hands with Westerners before. But he couldn't suppress a slight Japanese bow.

The Weavers had barely unpacked their suitcases. Only one downstairs room was tidy enough for inviting him in. By Watanabe's clean, neat appearance one would not have guessed he had been sitting up on the train for over twenty hours. He didn't waste time on polite chitchat, but spoke straight to the point.

"I've come to welcome you to Hiroshima. I need your help. Can you come soon?"

Fortunately for the Weavers, Pastor David L. Vikner, senior missionary and mentor, came through the door then and overheard the pastor's request. Vikner was too experienced to squelch Watanabe. Rather he manuevered the conversation to various neutral topics, before getting around to explaining that these two "green" missionaries had studied Japanese for only two months in a crash course at Yale. They were far from ready to go to Hiroshima. New missionaries, he explained, normally study the language two years. Then they can move to their place of work.

Hiroshima, however, was no normal place. The atomic bomb had killed Watanabe's wife and daughter and obliterated his home. He couldn't find a trace of them. He had lost everything. The explosion and spreading holocaust of fire had either killed his church members or scattered them beyond reach. Not even the church records remained.

The young Weavers listened to this story. Several times during Watanabe's accounting of it, Anita looked at Joe and wondered if they both were feeling the same call from God. When Anita grasped his hand and squeezed, Joe replied with two squeezes. No words were needed. They knew they could not let Watanabe down.

Excusing themselves for a brief word with Vikner, they came back offering a compromise. They promised to move to Hiroshima at the end of February, 1951, provided Watanabe could find a suitable language tutor for them. Before they moved, they also wanted to learn how best to prepare for living there. They would visit Hiroshima later that autumn to see what they were getting into.

Fearing those memories would bog him down in nostalgic dead-end detours, Joe from habit stuck his left thumb into his teeth, readying himself for some serious contemplation. First though he had to fill his coffee mug, then creative thinking.

3

To Hiroshima

Joe returned to the veranda carrying his mug of hot coffee. His memoir notebook lay on the table beside him.

I haven't written yet about our first trip to Hiroshima, he said to himself. *That was late autumn 1950.* Opening his records to the section labeled "Hiroshima," he began re-living that adventuresome journey.

The veteran missionary, who had driven them to Tokyo Station, pointed to the green in front of the Marunouchi entrance where the statue dedicated to *agape* stood.

"We'll need lots of that kind of love," Anita said, "selfless, sacrificial *agape* where we're going."

The American B-29s had spared Tokyo Station as a cultural treasure. Its classical nineteenth century design in red brick contrasted noticeably with the gray office buildings of the area. The only restaurant in the station was the old, stylish one near the Marunouchi wicket. They didn't need to pause at the display window to study the plastic menu samples. They knew beforehand what they wanted: chicken rice with dark-pink ginger pickles on the side.

Strange, Joe thought, *what small details stick in one's mind.* He also remembered that Anita had avoided wearing flashy clothes. She had on her honeymoon navy-blue suit, reasoning that if the weather turned hot, she could remove the jacket and still look proper enough for a minister's wife, not a bit ostentatious.

Their train of choice was the one with Hiroshima as the terminus. It bore the name *"Aki,"* after the feudal Hiroshima fiefdom of Aki.

On the platform they walked by several third-class unreserved cars, already so jammed with passengers that people were standing in the aisles. Although they weren't going first class like the Occupation personnel, they felt guilty for having splurged on second-class sleeper tickets. Since the bunks were made up, they had no choice but to crawl in and try to make themselves comfortable.

The excitement over the trip along with the swaying of the train prevented sound sleep. On top of that, at every stop boarding passengers making a commotion awoke them. Three hours later at Hamamatsu, Joe recalled that two men stumbled into the adjacent bunks. Joe peeked between the curtains and was relieved to see they were only in the happy-hour stage. Soon he fell into a deep sleep which lasted until they arrived at Okayama the next morning.

When the porter came to clear the bunks, Joe reached down and poked Anita, saying they had to get up. Returning after washing, they saw that the porter had removed the bedding and was motioning for them to sit down.

That's as far as his reminiscences took him because six deep sonorous gongs from the temple bell in nearby Kashiwabara Town announced the time to be 6:00 a.m. and for a brief moment reminded Joe where he was, but he was able quickly to return to the flash-back of their train ride to Hiroshima in 1950.

The two Japanese in their compartment had motioned for Anita and Joe to sit next to the window where they could view the scenery better. The older, baldheaded man with a black mustache could have come straight from Hollywood's central casting, perfect face and physique for the stereotyped wartime officer. The younger man acted like his orderly. Both grinned broadly, off-white teeth spotted here and there with gold and silver.

Pointing outside at the Inland Sea and mountainous islands, the older man said, "Beri naisu biu" which Joe and Anita deciphered as "Very nice view."

Just then the door at the end of the coach rattled open, letting in gusts of coal smoke and the clickityclack noise of wheels against the tracks. A girl in a light blue uniform shouted out from the doorway in a memorized monotone.

"Food and drink have come. *Obento* (box lunch), *sandoichi* (sandwiches), *rakkasei* (peanuts), *ocha* (green tea), *kohi* (coffee), *biiru* (beer), *osake* (rice liquor). Slowly she pushed her vending cart down the aisle and stopped by the Weavers' compartment. The Japanese grabbed two tall bottles of beer, then peanuts and two box lunches. Anita raised two fingers, pointing at the tea. Before peeling the covers off their box lunches, the men poured each other a cup of beer, gulping it down like orange juice. Anita stared at the inside of the men's boxes, too ashamed to bring out her own plain cheese and ham sandwiches. The Japanese-style *obento* breakfast resembled more a work of art than food: *sushi* balls, seaweed with soy sauce, pink ginger pickles, parsley and paper lettuce to keep the foods and colors separate.

Joe remembered holding his thimble-size throwaway-cup while Anita poured in hot tea. Every time she'd pick up the pot, the train jerked. Giving up, he set his cup on the windowsill and told her not to worry. "Green tea couldn't hurt anything if you spilled."

By the time the Aki reached the junction at Itozaki, the two men had downed their bottles of beer, freeing them up to try out their English again. Pushing his flushed face and bloodshot eyes up close to Joe, the older man paused a moment to pump up courage, then asked, "Where you go?"

"Hiroshima," Joe replied.

"You Americans?"

Afraid the two drunks might create a scene, Joe and Anita put on their most benign faces.

11

"Yes, next year, next year," and Joe pointed at his wife and himself, "we are going to live in Hiroshima."

"Good," the older man said, and the younger concurred with a nod, neither showing the slightest animosity.

Vengeance was what Joe and Anita feared most. They didn't want to be accused of dropping the A-bomb. These two men, even though inebriated indicated no bitterness, rather nothing but good will.

Following a brief stop at Mihara, the Aki circled south to follow the coast. At the end of a peninsula the train stopped at the former naval base and shipbuilding city of Kure. Once a bastion of Japan's naval might, Kure now was used by Australian forces to supply United Nations troops in Korea. From Kure the train turned north along the shore opposite Eta Island, the former site of Japan's Naval Academy.

Strange which scenes and conversations stuck in Joe's head. Both of them recalled that Pastor Watanabe, his teenage daughter Kimi and the badly scarred *hibakusha* (A-bomb victim) Mr. Kikkawa were waiting at Hiroshima Station to welcome them. Joe shook hands with Watanabe, but quickly stopped squeezing Kikkawa's hand when he felt rough keloid bumps. Noticing Joe's embarrassent, Watanabe explained that *Life Magazine* had made Kikkawa famous by labeling him "A-bomb Victim No.1."

After dropping off their luggage at the inn by the station, the Watanabes took Joe and Anita on a tour by streetcar. They rode through the main business district past Fukuya Department Store and up to where the memorial dome stood. Kikkawa and his wife were waiting for them in front of their souvenir stand. In contrast to her husband, Mrs. Kikkawa looked healthy for her forty years, perhaps because her scars didn't show.

Her husband reminded them of Chief Sitting Bull, dark, high cheek bones and regal. Anticipating their questions, Kikkawa explained that the steel frame of the dome on the once magnificent Industrial Arts Exhibition Building had been left as a permanent reminder of where the world's first A-bomb had been exploded in warfare.

"Across the way about 500 meters," Kikkawa was quick to point out, "was where the Japanese Fifth Army had been headquartered."

"So," Joe said, "it wasn't only civilians killed then, but still why drop it in the middle of 300,000 civilians?" The four Japanese kept silent.

All Joe remembered about the inn where they stayed was the ice-cold Western breakfast of spam and eggs, toasted white bread an inch thick and coffee diluted with milk and a tablespoon of sugar. That was the last time they ordered that. From then on they stuck to Japanese breakfasts of fermented beanpaste soup sprinkled with dried minnows, seaweed, fish and rice.

Sunday morning the Weavers rode to church in a *batanko* taxi, a three-wheeled cab powered by a motorcycle, the name coming from the drum-like pounding sound of the engine.

Watanabe's remnant of a congregation worshipped on the 9-foot by 9-foot *tatami*-mat floor of his rented quarters. Son Shinya, home from the war, and daughters Kei and Kimi lived with him.

Of the original postwar congregation of fifteen, four were *hibakusha*. Each could relate experiences of that fateful 8:15 a.m., August 6, 1945. Survivors told of air-raid sirens screeching around seven that morning, when three planes approached, sending people into the air raid shelters. Contrary to the official American report, a Japanese military expert has postulated that the fly-over was a deliberate feint to lull the people to believe no attack was iminent. When the danger appeared gone and the all-clear siren had sounded, the people came up from the shelters and out to their tasks for the day. The bomber quickly circled back and unloaded its bomb to inflict the highest possible number of casualties. Two other B-29s lurked above the suburbs, one for dropping a measuring and communication apparatus with a parachute on it and a third plane for photographing the extent of destruction.

That fateful morning at 8:15, high above the Industrial Arts Exhibition Building the heavens bleached white, followed by an ear-splitting boom. Japanese called it the *"Pikadon." Pika* means a flash of light and *don* the sound that followed. No one could have guessed the scenariio which followed.

In spite of five years of peace, Hiroshima remained a wasteland of shantytowns separated by rivers of rubble, the skyline broken only by occasional buildings resembling giant sentinels left over from an ancient ice age.

At that early stage of Joe's language study, he thought the words in the Sunday liturgy resembled a jumble of machine-gun shots. In the sermon, except for Pastor Watanabe's repetition of *ai*, the word for love, Joe understood nothing. Watanabe would follow that with *agape* and then more torrent of words. Once in a while he'd look at Weavers and burst out in English, "We were all crazy. Everybody was crazy. True peace can't come through war, but only through forgiveness and Jesus' spirit." In spite of losing his wife and a daughter in the bombing, in this little shack of a house love reigned. Watanabe embodied love and preached it. We could see that through his wounds and words people were being healed.

After worship Kei and Kimi escaped to a shallow alcove from where the aroma of curry soon came drifting in. Almost every congregation the Weavers came to know had made curry rice the staple "post-benediction" meal.

While people were finishing lunch, a young doctor by the name of Yamada asked to be excused. In broken English he explained he had to go pick up something being made special for the American guests.

13

After that, as Joe recalled, Kimi asked if Anita would sing for them. This was before Yamaha manufactured small reed organs which most congregations came to use. Since all the hymns had the words printed in phonetic *katakana*, she was able to sing in Japanese, but with no accompaniment. Anita picked out a hymn made famous in a postwar movie about an injured soldier returning home to his devastated hometown. Its English title was "God Be With You Till We Meet Again." That was the same hymn the Church members sang at the railway station when the Weavers moved in 1965. On the last stanza, Anita asked everyone to join in on the chorus.

God, that tear-jerker broke me up.

Not a few members were weeping. Anita choked and couldn't finish.

An elderly man dressed in a shabby dark-gray suit moved over to squat next to Anita and Joe. He introduced himself as Mr. Taguchi.

"How do you spell your name?" he asked, handing Joe paper and pencil.

"JOE WEAVER," he printed. Next he wrote, "ANITA WEAVER."

Taguchi-san untied the bow on his *furoshiki* cloth and pulled out a big book. It was a well-worn English-Japanese dictionary. He thumbed his way to the w-section and found *weaver*.

Pondering for a moment, he sighed, *"Saa, komatta. Orite* is no good for a name. If we write *Weaver* in phonetic *kana* letters, it becomes *Uiba*. Terrible! It means a dark, sad place. We do not need any more dark, sad people in Hiroshima."

Taguchi-san thought a moment, then exclaimed, *"Wakatta!"* I've got it. *"Orimura,"* he pronounced distinctly. "It means a weaving village, especially for silk. Good name for you. *Joe* is okay. You can say Joe in Japanese. *Anita* is a good name. Now you can be like us Japanese, with real names."

Not knowing how to take this, Joe joked to the pastor, "Maybe you should baptize us again with the new names."

He translated the joke into Japanese. Everyone howled approval and clapped their hands. *"Orimura Joe, Orimura Anita."* From that day on, among their close Japanese friends, who knew, they went by their Japanese names.

Soon afterward, Dr. Yamada returned on his bicycle carrying a gift-wrapped package. Bowing low to the Orimuras, he pronounced in a loud, clear voice, "When we were without hope, you brought us hope. Life is still worth living. On behalf of the Hiroshima Church, we present you with this gift of peace." He held the present up high and while lowering his head as far as he could, he offered the gift to the newly named Orimuras and motioned for them to unwrap it. While Joe held the package, Anita carefully removed the wrapping and lifted out a simple clay bowl, about ten inches in diameter. On the side were inscribed the characters for peace: *heiwa.*

Although close to fifty years had passed since then, Joe and Anita never were able to recover from their shame at dishonoring that love-gift by carelessness. In Tokyo when Anita opened her suitcase, she found the peace bowl crushed into irreparable fragments.

That painful recollection jarred Joe out of the past and back to 1996 on the veranda of No. 56 cabin at Lake Nojiri. "Christ," he called out, "don't let me break faith again." He pushed himself up out of the chair and lifted his eyes to heaven and pledged that no matter what the future brought, Watanabe's compassion in Hiroshima and Hong Kong would serve as his model.

He sat down, repeating over and over, *Lord, don't let me fail again, although I have no idea how to begin.* Joe didn't know which thread of the future he was supposed to take hold of first.

4

Confusion

Joe hated confusion. The fragments of his puzzle reminded him of the shattered Hiroshima peace-bowl. No amount of ingenuity could glue it back together.

The bedroom door scraped against the floor. Anita was up. She shuffled through the kitchen to the back door. The spring slammed it shut. A minute later the spring stretched open. He called to Anita.

"Ani, can you come here a second?"

Anita disliked *Ani* as a nickname. She insisted on being called, "Anita." When she was three-years old back in Geneseo, Illinois, a neighbor lady asked her if she had a nickname.

"No!" she pouted back, "no one has ever nicked my name."

But like many traditional Japanese husbands, Joe relished teasing her with *Ani*. It meant "elder brother" in Japanese. It was Joe's backhanded sign of endearment.

"What do you want?," she asked.

"That Hiroshima peace-bowl we broke. Remember how it looked?"

"In many pieces — too damaged to glue back together." She turned away from the screen door, but Joe had more to ask.

"What kind of bird is that?"

"Where?"

"Over there in the bushes beyond the porch. Can you hear it?" He knew he'd caught her. She came back to listen. Nothing could catch his wife's attention faster than a bird's song.

"I can't hear it."

"Must have flown away," he fibbed. "Say, do you remember the sleeper we took to Hiroshima in 1950? Were the seats blue felt?"

"How do you expect me to recall that?" She hesitated. "Wasn't felt. That I know. Never felt. Velvet maybe. Faded blue and threadbare. I'm going back to bed."

"One more question. How many beers did those two guys on the train down for breakfast?"

"You think I sat there counting?" Counterattacking she scolded him. "You left the toilet seat up again! Can't you ever remember to put it down? You remember two drunks fifty years ago, but..." She pursed her lips and with a final "Pfft!" started to leave.

"Sorry, it'll never happen again — at least until next time."

"Until next time?".

Changing the subject, Joe asked, "Going birdwatching this morning?"

"No, tomorrow. Vicky and I are going up to Togakushi."

"Can I bounce some ideas off you? In that packet of mail yesterday were notes from Kawaguchi and Eric Gunderson. They've got me confused. I can't tell what they mean."

"You mean how they're connected? Maybe no connection. Let me get my bathrobe. I'm chilly."

Joe fidgeted with a wooden pencil, digging his thumbnail into its soft yellow covering. He hated this confusion. Uncertainty about hidden significances always unsettled him. Experience had taught him that God had plans for everyone, but Joe'd be the first to admit he hadn't always followed them.

"Well, what's so confusing to you?" she asked as she came outside and sat herself down on the other side of the end table.

"I can't shake the idea that this Redone fellow in Tokyo, the one Kawaguchi wrote about, is going to affect my life — our lives. You remember Eric Gunderson? He's coming to Tokyo the same time Redone is here."

"What's the problem? Do you think their arrivals aren't an accident?" Joe didn't answer.

"You're having another of your hunches, aren't you?"

"Remember that time I called you from the hotel in Taiwan? I had the nagging certainty that you had to go home to Minnesota to see your folks. It was perfect timing. Your Mom was critically ill."

"Are you saying you sense something special about the two notes?"

"Yeah, can't get them out of my mind. I'm like Simon of Cyrene that Passover day when he came upon the procession going to Golgotha. Without warning a Roman soldier grabbed him out of the crowd and made him carry Jesus' cross. Here at the lake I'm like a bystander to the world but someone or something is grabbing me."

"Don't compare yourself to Simon," she warned. "Stick to what you know. If God is involved, he won't wait long to tell you. He might surprise you — speak to you through anything."

Reacting to that, Joe said, "Become enfleshed in some part of our lives? I'm trying to listen, be alert like the boy Samuel in the temple at Shiloh."

Anita turned toward the shrubbery. Footsteps approached and branches were shoved aside. *The Japan Times* plopped onto the far end of the porch.

Anita looked at Joe. He looked at her. Looking upward, Joe said, "God, that was quick."

"Aren't you going to pick it up?" she asked.

"Thanks!" Joe yelled to the retreating paperboy, then barefooted across the floor to fetch the paper. No checking baseball scores. Today he looked for special news — news just for him and Anita.

The headlines screamed for attention. His heart skipped as he read:

"Thousands to Commemorate Hiroshima A-bomb Victims"

"Had you remembered that today was A-bomb Day?" he asked.
"Not really. I haven't been reading the news much."
As long as he could recall, the Japanese press had run this same news year after year, almost word for word. Yet, today even his bones signaled something would be special.

Scanning to the lower left corner, he read:

"Hong Kong Governor Admonishes Beijing

"Chris Patten warned Chinese leaders. 'You must,' he said 'honour Deng Xiaoping's promise not to change Hong Kong's political system for 50 years.' In response to a reporter's question, Patten elaborated: 'If Beijing's leaders go back on Deng's commitment, China might as well kiss goodbye to any hope for joining the World Trade Organization. If Hong Kong remains as it is — a free crossroad between East and West — China will benefit the most. Hong Kong is her golden goose.'

"Many Hong Kong residents have transferred assets to Canada, Australia and the United States. Corporations skeptical of Communist promises have set up alternative headquarters in tax-friendly havens of the Carribean and Pacific. Locals joke about these moves, quoting the ancient proverb: 'A smart robber has 3 caves.'"

Anita took the paper from Joe and read it for herself. "This Chinese proverb — I don't get it."
"David Chiang used it once on me. It's like a similar saying in *Proverbs*. Means 'Don't put all your eggs in one basket.'"
"There's more here,"she said. "Listen to this:

"'Anthony Loh, prominent politician with alleged ties to the Peoples' Republic of China was attacked Sunday night at a restaurant in Shatin. Police suspect the attacker has ties to a separtist party inTaiwan or one of several secret societies opposed to Hong Kong's transfer to China.'"

"It had to happen!" Joe exclaimed. "Trouble's already brewing, and there's still another year to go."

"Shatin? That's where we stayed in 1960," Anita said.

"Two years ago David and Annie Chiang treated Arnie Kromphardt and me to a seafood dinner in Shatin, at a fancy waterfront restaurant in a new high-rise development. Lots of changes since '60."

"Have the Chiangs left Hong Kong for New Zealand?" she asked.

"Don't know. With David's father's high position in the old Kuomintang army, he should have sense to get out before the takeover."

"What will happen to the media centre then?"

"Most of the staff were born in Hong Kong, Cantonese speakers mostly. They'll be safe for a while. I've told you about the thugs who tried to mug David in a subway station haven't I?"

"You never told me about that."

"Thought I had. Sorry. His old SIU professor told me."

"I'm sure you never told me."

"Well, this is vintage David. He warned these four guys, 'I'm a Kung Fu black-belt.' But they thought he was bluffing, so they went after him. Must have been quite a fight. David killed one of them. The court acquitted him on grounds of self-defense. People in the station witnessed it all."

"Better not let him pastor a church. Nobody would dare cross him. Let's see, where were we? We've established the fact that Hong Kong can be a dangerous place."

"Many factions," Joe added. "Turnover will exacerbate tensions. We know someone has attacked this Anthony Loh, a pro-Beijing legislator. China won't let that pass."

"I thought the papers said the June 4th Tiananmen Memorial Candlelight Parade went off well."

"Yes, but the police were photographing everyone. Give them time. Storm clouds are bound to roll in eventually. They have good memories. People say five to seven years at the most. Even in California, infiltrators are disrupting Chinese churches."

"Where'd you hear that?"

"Can't say. Sworn to secrecy. Had a letter the other day saying a former student at a Chinese seminary had been shipped off to labor camp, but I'm not supposed to tell anyone.

"What can *we* do?" he thought outloud. "We're only ordinary citizens, retired at that."

"You're making excuses. Suppose everyone refused to take risks. You aren't going to act like a nail afraid to get pounded in are you?"

"But…"

19

"Are you coming down with Alzheimers? Think, Joe! What had Watanabe done? A small man from the tiny village of Nanataki. Didn't he make a difference?"

Joe scrunched down in his chair, ashamed he'd spoken so cowardly. *What's wrong with me? I hadn't always kept my mouth shut. Hadn't I taken on the whole church leadership to found a China broadcast ministry?*

Not being able to read Joe's thoughts, Anita continued to attack. "Why did you bring those three notebooks to Nojiri? If you didn't think your life, our lives, significant, why write memoirs? I don't understand you, Joseph."

Whenever she called him "Joseph," he knew he'd better shape up. He had been all set to begin writing memoir notes today, but the two letters had put everything on hold. God wouldn't interrupt his good plans for nothing. His guts told him an important detour lay ahead.

At that moment a motion above the lake caused Joe to look up. A sea gull resembling a white dove was gliding in on the breeze from the Japan Sea. It wasn't hard for him to recognize the bird as a propitious omen for the day, more so than the black crows that had flown over at 6:30 on their commute to the garbage dumps of Nagano City.

After Anita had gone inside, Joe sat upright, then inhaled a big dose of fresh morning air. He reached for his prayerbook under the table and turned to the final words of the last Confession of the week. He read in the margin, "April 30, 1988 Film." Taking a red permanent marker from the table, he wrote under it, "Watanabe Aug. 6, 1996." Then he prayed, "Lord, I believe. Help my unbelief. Amen."

5

Hong Kong Records

Joe opened the screen door to look at the old 19th century regulator clock hanging on the wall. It said, "7:00." He hadn't even read the biblical lessons for the day nor prayed for the persons listed on Tuesday. Brother Lawrence's counsel eased his conscience at times like this. He taught that necessity rightly should take precedemce over prayer time. This was one of those times. His first priority had to be calling Kawaguchi about the Ping woman. If Joe telephoned early enough, he might catch him before he left for the office.

Anita had gone back to bed with a book. She lay on her side with the book propped up on Joe's two pillows. Diffused morning light softened her face, tempting him to kiss her on the cheek, but her eyes were closed in sleep. The two letters troubled Joe. Anita, on the other hand, could shake off worries quickly. He recalled late night calls when one of her volunteer telephone counselors at Tokyo English Lifeline would call about a suicide threat or domestic violence. She'd make some suggestions, then commit the problem to God and let Him worry about it. In a couple of minutes she'd be back sound asleep.

Joe sneaked past the bed to the closet and ran his fingers along the row of hangers until his fingers touched his familiar khaki safari shirt, the sporty one he used to wear on trips to Southeast Asia. It looked dressy enough for a tropical climate, and it was practical with many buttoned pockets. Wearing it made him feel thirty years younger.

He exited the back door by the shoe shelves, and sat on a chair to squeeze into his walking shoes. Trying to catch his breath he once again vowed to take ten pounds off his strangled belly. He strode rapidly from the cabin through the wet grass. On the downhill road he slowed his pace because of the gravel. He'd sprained his ankles enough for one lifetime. To his right no one was playing at the practice tennis court. When he reached the corner where two dirt paths intersected the road, he turned right and passed the bulletin board and red mail box on the left and the tin garbage hut and tennis stands on the right. Hiratsuka's Vegetable Shop and Mrs. Nakamura's Summer Store were not yet open. Next came the old unused bathhouse. Its eaves provided cover for the public telephone booth.

Hearing a Norwegian woman using the phone, Joe seated himself next to the vending machine. Since he couldn't understand her, the chatter didn't bother him. The dilapidated buildings reminded him of his own visit in '88 to the dingy barracks of the former Shamshuipo Prison Camp in Hong Kong. *How out of place Watanabe must have felt when he first entered those ghoulish grounds.* Joe recalled Watanabe's description of it.

> "A nauseating cloud of miasma hung over the dismal prison. The Japanese Army had posted me there because I was fluent in English. How ironic that my two years of post-graduate theological studies at Gettysburg prepared me to be a gatekeeper at the entrance to hell, waiting until the condemned hear their fateful number called. I wonder if the Emperor knows what his loyal servants are doing throughout Asia?
>
> "If we could have headed off the attack on Pearl Harbor, all this suffering could have been avoided. How could we have protested more effectively? More posters? Bigger peace delegation to America? God, what should we have done to head off the War?
>
> "After the attack on Hawaii crippled the American Pacific fleet, our forces ran roughshod over all opposition. The U.S. and other Western powers proved to be paper tigers. Nothing could stop our crusade to throw the White imperialists out of Asia. The Empire's euphoria even began to entice me. I secretly basked in nationalistic glory."

When Watanabe's troopship steamed into Hong Kong Harbour in 1942, he exalted over the rising-sun flags waving high atop buildings everywhere. Japan had become invincible. Tiny Japan had thrown over the great powers. He thought he might have been wrong to oppose this. Japan actually was liberating Asia from oppression.

At Hong Kong Watanabe disembarked and rode in an uncamouflaged military limousine through the narrow shop-lined streets of Kowloon. To his shock no Chinese smiled or cheered at him. Nobody waved a Japanese flag. The driver kept his hand pressed against the horn, daring any Chinese to get in the way.

"Damned Chinks!" the driver yelled at peddlers in the way. "Dirty coolies! Don't they know we've won the war."

After shuddering for twenty minutes over the driver's callous disregard for Chinese, Watanabe couldn't hold in his anger any longer. "Would you mind not treating people like pigs," he said as gently as his revulsion allowed. When the driver pretended not to hear, Watanabe resorted to the ultimate put-down. "You aren't Japanese are you. Back home Japanese don't act like you."

Suddenly Joe remembered a proverbial saying that described how people cut loose from their moral principles when away from home. He only remembered, *haji mo* and *kakisute*. He couldn't recall the rest of the saying. *Must ask Takeshi about that.*

The Norwegian woman on the phone hung up. Joe pulled his thoughts back to the here and now of Japan, 1996. Pushing his telephone card into the slot, he punched in Kawaguchi's home number. The youngest son answered.

"*Otosan ga oraremasu ka?*" Joe asked. The boy ran to call his father.

"*Moshi-moshi,*" they greeted each other...

Thanking for the mail and note, Joe asked about the Chinese woman who had called the office.

"You'd better call her yourself. They don't open till 10:00. I didn't quite understand what she wanted. Something about a television producer by the name of Redone. He wants to see you about Pastor Watanabe and that film idea we were working on. He seems to know quite a bit about him."

After some idle banter Kawaguchi announced he was taking his wife and three boys for a week at the Bach Inn near Mt. Fuji.

"Good. You can use a vacation..." *Glad he's not feeling guilty for taking time off. In America we feel guilty if we don't take time off.* "See you when I see you. *Sayonara.*"

Mrs. Nakamura was sliding her front doors open at the Summer Store, and the tennis courts were filling up. Two birdwatchers crept out of the bushes. Since they were stalking some find high up in an oak tree, Joe merely gave them a little wave as he hurried toward the hill. He hoped Ani was ready for breakfast. He'd have to return later to telephone the Chinese woman. Since no golf tournament was scheduled today, he wouldn't need to gulp down breakfast in a hurry.

As Joe entered the cabin, he called out, "Ani, we've got to talk." He quickly set her sugarless granola and a giant box of Grape Nuts on the table. "This morning I told you a TV producer from England has come looking for me."

"Oh, no, not again? You've gone up that dead-end before."

"But," he tried to interrupt her.

"I've been thinking," she began pensively. "Why would anyone want to revive that story? Fifty years have passed. No one much cares about World War II. Vietnam eclipsed it. No one makes movies anymore about our generation."

"Yeah, but Redone is talking about Hong Kong."

"Have you forgotten? The Communists are taking over Hong Kong."

"Don't you see?" Joe shot back. "That could be the very reason for reviving the Watanabe story. His bravery could speak to the people of Hong Kong today."

"Act your age, Joseph. You're seventy-two years old, just finished with radiation. Good heavens, do you want to widow me?"

"Don't talk like that. We can do what needs to be done. Even if I die," he said slowly with funerary solemnity, "all my millions go to you."

"Millions?" she snickered. "You do dollar math in yen. One million is only $10,000."

"We'll see," he said, stalling for time. "The peace vase."

23

"Bowl," she corrected him.

"I made a vow never to let Watanabe down again. I've never fulfilled that promise. I almost want to pray in his name. I told you didn't I what that Pastor Fong from Hong Kong told me? The honeymoon with China won't last more than five years."

"No, you didn't tell me. Was Fong predicting that the Chinese Army would turn into an army of occupation?"

"That's what Fong and his friends are saying. Old-timers think it could be a repeat of Japan's occupation of 1941-45."

"That's farfetched isn't it? Well, you do what you have to. I couldn't stop you anyway."

"I'm going to dig out the first filmscript Chiang and his staff developed."

Forgetting about the coffee he'd brewed, Joe went into the study. Pulling back the chair and going down on his knees, he reached under the desk and dragged out a big, dusty "Black Cat UPS" box marked "Watanabe Film." Setting it on the daybed next to the filing case, he bent back the four flaps on top and reached in to lift out a three-inch-deep glossy dark brown cardboard box made for storing papers. He wiggled off the lid, then reached up to turn on the light hanging by a cord from the ceiling. On top lay Joe's handwritten notes of how he would have described Watanabe's arrival at the Shamshuipo P.O.W. Camp in 1942.

"As a typhoon was bearing down on Hong Kong the perimeter of the whirling storm had begun to agitate the rising-sun flags, rattling signboards and scattering loose papers about the streets.

"After a reckless, harrowing drive from the navy pier, they hit a dead-end intersection. Turning left the driver blared his horn to force an opening through the crowd of women waiting outside the prison's barbed-wire fence. They milled around every day in hopes of catching a glimpse of a husband or boyfriend. Stopping about fifty yards this side of the main entrance, a gust of wind almost blew Watanabe's hat off, causing him to look up where the camp's giant military flag flapped wildly. It had slipped down a good three feet from the top of the pole and become hopelessly tangled. For a moment the flag twisted into the shape of a cross' horizontal beam.

"God!" he gasped. Without thinking he started chanting the Kyrie from the liturgy: *'Kirisuto yo, awaremi tamae.* O Christ, have mercy on me.' Without your grace I'll never survive this hell. Don't let me be put to shame."

On the cover of Watanabe's autograph book, were two of his favorite excerpts from what prisoners had written.:

"God gives men all earth to love
But since man's heart is small
Ordains for each one spot shall prove
Beloved over all."

Did this show that Watanabe had seen Hong Kong as a microcosm of the world?

"As though to confirm his thoughts, below it were these words written after the War by Clifford H.R. Fowler, H.M.S. Bermuda:

"'Hong Kong though maybe far from me will ever be fresh in my memory.'"

Even in 1996, Joe had read reports from Hong Kong newspapers that former British Commonwealth prisoners-of-war still decried the way the Japanese guards had harassed them. They felt they'd been treated like pigs.

"That first day of his arrival at Shamshuipo, Watanabe learned that good had become evil and evil good. His whole world had been turned upside down. *Good God, how can I survive in this hell?* he prayed."

6

Too Much Happening

Hoping to clear his head, Joe decided to walk down to the store for groceries. Before leaving, he scribbled a quick note on an air letter to Eric Gunderson, saying he wished Eric could visit Nojiri. He recalled Eric's saying that he'd spent a couple weeks here at a classmate's cabin. The letter might miss him, but at least Joe would have tried to reach him before he left D.C.

Heading by neighbor Dr. Matsumoto's house, Joe recalled how Matsumoto's father had died in Manchuria during the last week of the war. Across the road the bounding of a tennis ball off the practice wall caught Joe's ear. A lanky teenage girl attired in a white tennis outfit was working on her serves.

He quickened his pace on the steep slope, but a hundred yards ahead near the oak tree which overhung the bulletin board, he spotted a little dishwater-blonde toddler standing by himself. The boy looked up toward Joe, then down the hill, and next sideways at the crossroads. He reminded Joe of his four-year old grandson in Alaska.

As Joe approached him, the boy's upper lip quivered, and he looked about to cry.

"Hi!" Joe greeted him. "You aren't lost are you?"

Stiffening up as though the question had insulted him, the boy blurted out, "No! I'm not lost. I just don't know where I am."

"Isn't that your big sister practicing at the top of the hill?"

As the boy started running toward her, Joe shouted after him, "See you later." Joe thought to himself that there's a young man of faith. He isn't lost; he just doesn't know where he is. As Joe walked on by the lower tennis court, he promised himself not to forget the boy's words.

Before dropping the air letter into the weather-beaten mailbox next to Hiratsuka's fruit and vegetable shop, he heard a racing engine coming up from the main road. The postman rounded the bend on a red motorbike and sped up the steep gravel road.

That's odd. He didn't stop at the mailbox. He must be delivering a telegram.

Mrs. Nakamura of the Summer Store greeted Joe. Eyeing his bulging stomach, she smiled impishly and asked solicitously, "How's your baby today? You're sure it's not four months along?"

"Three and a half months," Joe teased back, then pulled out his shopping list. First he picked out two loaves of whole wheat bread, then two ears of morning-picked sweet corn, a couple of huge dark-red tomatoes, Japanese cucumbers, a package of peanuts and two litres of low-fat milk and set them on the glass counter. Nakamura-san punched in the amounts on her calculator. Everything came to 1,815 yen, or about $18. *I know it's expensive, but oh so good... No one wants to lose this store; it's a life line for people who no longer own cars in Japan.* Thirty-five years ago a missionary family from Shikoku Island brought Nakamura-san here as a helper. That summer she fell in love with a local appliance dealer and never went home.

She manuevered all of Joe's groceries, except the corn, into his faded brown totebag, a souvenir from a long forgotten conference. She squeezed the corn into a plastic bag, then laughingly assuring Joe his baby would relish the sweet corn, she bid him goodbye. He promised to come see her again later.

Returning home Joe took the longer, more gentle path rather than the steep rocky road, not realizing that the rainstorm during the night had soaked the volcanic mud into a slimy slide. Stepping quickly, but cautiously, he tried to touch down only on grass or stones. In less than five minutes he reached their lot #56 from below.

After pulling himself up the oozy embankment by holding onto some branches, he cut through their yard of untamed pampas and bamboo grass. He brushed by the wet hammock stretched out between two thick red pine trees, then walked alongside the back of the house and the faded blue plastic water tank. He wiggled out of his muddy shoes, then barefooted it into the cabin. He carried the groceries over to the table kitty-cornered from a noisy, old refrigerator, unaware of the surprise awaiting him.

While mindlessly emptying out the groceries, he saw a blue envelope. On its front, large lettering demanded attention: *"Dempo,"* telegram, it read.

No, not another intrusion. How many more surprises can there be?

Tearing open the envelope, he was relieved to see it was from Kawaguchi. The phonetic characters spelled out "Ping called me at home. You must telephone her immediately at the British TV office. It is urgent."

But no number given. That's smart! I'll have to call him again for the number.

Once more, down the hill he went, running this time. Kawaguchi himself answered the phone.

"A TV producer is here from London, name is Redone I think. He insists on seeing you right away."

"What for?"

"It has to do with China's takeover of Hong Kong next year."

"So?"

"Someone who had been a prisoner-of-war at Shamshuipo had reminded him about Watanabe and what he had done for the war prisoners. He's wondering if Watanabe's still relevant for today."

Joe plopped down on the chair beside the phone, dazed. Eight years already had elapsed since he gave up trying to promote a movie about Watanabe.

Or, had I given up? I'd never thrown away the resource materials, tapes and filmscripts. I stored them in my safest place, under the heavy wooden desk at the cottage.

"Are you still on the line?" Kawaguchi asked.

"Sorry, but I'm a little shocked by what you told me."

"He's here only a few weeks and sounds in a big hurry. His sponsor is pressing him to make a decision. If you call him before noon, you can catch him at BritishTV. His name is Redone."

After giving the telephone number, a sensation of weary resignation swept over Joe. Kawaguchi then said, "It's muggy hot in Tokyo. We're getting away for a few days before some American VIPs come through on their way home from China. Is it still okay to use your membership for putting them up at International House?"

"No problem. I'll call this Redone fellow right away. Say 'Hello' to the staff. Ask Muraoka-san if she wants one of those Nojiri blueberry pies next time I come. *De wa, sayonara!*"

Lifting the folding chair out far enough to catch some breeze, he sat down for a few minutes to collect his thoughts before calling BTV. A woman answered the phone. Joe asked if a Mr. Redone was there. She replied with an English-style accent, but her *r*s were typical of a Chinese, not a Japanese. "Oh, you mean Mr. Reardon. He's stepped out for a moment."

Joe heard a man's voice in the background and footsteps coming closer. "Hello, Mr Weaver, my name's Bill Knight. Reardon will be back soon. Didn't you interpret that speech at the press club about the Emperor's Funeral Rites?"

"Pretty bad wasn't it? That was tough to put into understandable English."

"Reardon thinks he met with you and some Japanese friends in the coffee shop afterward."

"Oh, I remember him. He'd come from England special. He asked questions other reporters didn't dare ask. Short squatty fellow I recall."

"Hey, Stubby, Mr. Weaver is on the line. Says he remembers you. Use the back phone in the corner."

Joe heard Reardon running to the phone. "Hello, Mr. Weaver, my name is Jack Reardon. Your friend Kawaguchi-san told you why I wanted to meet you didn't he?"

"I'm not quite sure I understood. Could you explain it to me?"

"Okay. Several months ago a former colleague at the BBC reminded me of Watanabe, a fantastic little man from Hiroshima. You knew, of course, that the BBC brought him to London for a "This Is Your Life" show in 1969? The man who organized that episode was Liam Nolan, an Irish Catholic. Remember this was back in '69, but Watanabe impressed Nolan so much he ended up writing a book about him, even though he was Lutheran. It's out of print now."

Giving Reardon more time to catch his breath, Joe delayed, then asked, "What do you have in mind?"

"To be up front with you, I'm a delinquent churchman, but this Watanabe intrigues me. The more I ask around, the more people tell me they remember the show he was on."

"That's thirty years ago."

"You know that doesn't happen very often with television."

"I've got a photo of that program here at our cottage."

"When I was a boy," Reardon said, "I had indirect connections with Watanabe. So, I jumped at the chance to do a TV special about him."

"Connections?"

"Want to air it before the Hong Kong turnover."

"How did you find me?" Joe asked.

"We tracked you down through your pastor friend in London."

"That would have to be Ron Englund."

"He looked up the Lutheran Hour phone number in Tokyo. We really lucked out. Kawaguchi-san said you were back in Japan for the summer. I know it's a big imposition, but do you think you could come down to Tokyo? I've got to talk with you. We'll cover your expenses."

Joe started to grab the chair to sit on, but thought better of it. "This is awfully sudden," he replied, trying to delay his answer. "How long will you be staying in Tokyo? Next week we run into *Obon*. Trains will be packed. That's when most Japanese travel back to their hometowns. It's the Buddhist All Saints Festival. Departed souls are believed to return home to visit the living."

"Like your American Memorial Day?" Reardon asked.

"But much different." Joe knew it was hopeless to try to explain what no foreigner could quickly understand. Never having learned the art of saying "No," Joe asked, "What does Friday, the 9th, look like to you? If I go then, I can make it back here before the trains get overbooked. On the 8th I'm signed up to play in the Nojiri Open Golf Tournament. Must keep my priorities straight. Wait a minute. Let me check the train schedule here on the wall. I should have worn my glasses. This print is terribly small. If I take the 6:42, I can arrive at Ueno Station at11:06. How about meeting by the front desk of the Foreign Correspondents'Club around 11:30? Would that be okay?" Your friend there at BTV no doubt is a member."

"Good, 11:30 on the 9th."

"Do you mind if I bring Kawaguchi along?"

"That's fine. Hey, Red, how's the 9th for lunch at the press club?"

After a brief pause, Knight shouted back loud enough for Joe to overhear. "No good! That's the day a Hong Kong VIP, Anthony Loh, comes. He's on the Legislative Council and will be the speaker. Our Hong Kong bureau chief tipped us off that Beijing has handpicked Loh to see to it that Hong Kong toes China's line. I have to sit at the speaker's table, but there's no reason you can't attend. Could be worth your while."

"Sounds good," Reardon answered. Speaking again into the phone, he informed Joe, "This Loh will speak about Hong Kong's future. It's a hot topic these days. Bring Kawaguchi along. We could use some Japanese input."

"Meet you then under the time-zone clocks by the front desk," Joe replied as he placed the receiver back on the cradle. *Good God, could our past labors finally be bearing fruit?* Unthinkingly, he slapped the wall in elation...

Normally the trek up the hill from the Summer Store would feel wearisome, but the phone conversation with Reardon had exhilarated Joe. Before he shook out of his daze, he had turned into the grassy driveway at #56, not even bothering to say, "Hi!" to his new little friend who stood watching him from across the road.

Joe headed straight toward the back porch. As he passed to the left of the red lantern hanging outside the kitchen door, he noticed an air letter stuck in the crack by the screen door. He held it up to see who had sent it. *Good grief! It's from Eric, and I just mailed my letter to him. How did he get hold of our Nojiri address?*

Rather than going inside, Joe walked around to the front porch where he could read the letter without interruptions. He scanned it quickly, looking for an arrival date. "August 7!" *That's tomorrow. He and his stepfather are to stay at the Fairmont. Good, there's the phone number. He wants me to call him.*

Lifting his eyes from the page, Joe gazed out as though he was searching for something, he knew not what. Mt. Madarao, or was it Victoria Peak in Hong Kong?

Too much is happening, Lord. I can't process it.

Not knowing what move he should take next, Joe picked up the filmscript and read from where he had left off, the scene where Watanabe first delivered smuggled medical and food supplements to the "enemy" prisoners at Shamshuipo. Joe tried to visualize how shocked and suspicious they must have felt when out of the dark shadows this Japanese in military uniform appeared in their barracks. Watanabe was lugging a briefcase stuffed with the life-saving supplies they so desperately needed. It defied Joe's imagination to feel what those dying men must have felt when they saw what the case contained.

It took an aimless black-and-white butterfly flitting across the yard to rescue Joe from his speculation... The butterfly flew first one direction and then another. *Where could she be going?*

For a moment Joe seemed back in Hiroshima the day the A-bomb incinerated Watanabe's wife and daughter Miwa. Masses of bleeding people, skin hanging shapeless and eyes melted, roaming blindly through clouds of radioactive dust in search of relief, longing for the cool channels of the Ota River. *Why did we have to obliterate 200,000 people in Hiroshima? Weren't there rules about bombing civilians? What made the generals decide to bomb Coventry, Dresden, Wurzburg, Hiroshima and then even Nagasaki, when surrender was inevitable?*

Glancing skyward Joe saw a black hawk glide in from the west and circle around and around, surveying the earth to spot some careless creature on which to swoop down. Joe could empathize with all the little mice and animals who were defenseless. One thoughtless move, and Joe too might be snatched away by a similar unseen, malevolent marauder.

7

Dr. Aske Counsels

Going inside to break away from foreboding thoughts, Joe poured a cup of coffee and grabbed a graham cracker. He went in to Anita, who was lost again reading one of the Cadfael mysteries.

"You haven't had your morning kiss." Joe stooped over and pecked her on the cheek.

"Yuk, your mouth is all wet."

He massaged her shoulders to grab her attention. "When you come to a break, can I ask you something?"

Anita set the book down right away because Joe sounded genuinely serious. Like a trained counselor she steeled herself against becoming overly caught up in her husband's emotions.

"I'm torn up over this Brit," Joe said. "He wants me to go meet him in Tokyo, but I don't know if I should."

Anita quietly repeated in her own words the ideas Joe was conveying. Weighing her words carefully, she floated a tentative response: "I can't tell you what to do, but you'll have to meet this man from London. You've probably already promised to see him haven't you?"

"How'd you know that?"

"It was written on your face," she smiled back at him. "There's one idea you could consider. Imagine yourself talking with someone you completely trust."

"I trust you." Then as usual he had to make a joke of it by adding, "almost always."

"I'm your wife.You need someone outside family, someone neutral on whom you can rely, a man who has been there before. Fought a similar fight."

They sat in silence as Joe conjured up names of persons who might qualify. "I guess that would have to be my old boss in Geneva, Sig Aske, but he's been dead four years."

Not letting Joe off, she pressed further. "Imagine you're talking with him, nothing wrong with that. Try it. It's a proven psychological technique, different from a seance. I think I know what he'd tell you, but you ask him. Take your time. Don't be impestuous. Really listen."

Giving her advice time to sink in, she then asked, "Remember that sermon Sig preached in Tokyo when you interpreted for him?"

"He told about meeting an old Chinese colleague when he visited China in early 1980. Sig wished he'd been able to tell his friend that he'd been praying for him, but he couldn't. Then and there he resolved to reactivate broadcasts to China. It took him and some of us four years before we could launch Kairos in '84."

Anita had drawn that success story out of Joe to confront him. "You did it, didn't you? Talk with Sig. See what he tells you now."

"This is crazy." But he shut his eyes anyway and surprised himself by imagining Dr. Aske sitting in front of him, real as life, dark gray suit, blue tie and all. Joe sat motionless. As though hypnotized, he began describing a conversation with Aske a decade earlier.

"We were in the coffee shop atop the Transportation Building in Tokyo. Sig shared his own indecision about his next step in life. He honored me by asking my advice.

"I've been offered the directorship of *Lutherhjalpen*, the Norwegian relief agency," he confided.

"How do you feel about the offer?"

"People say my experience in managing the RVOG radio station in Ethiopia fits me for the relief job. They think I'd be good at raising money for Third World people."

"Sig wasn't relishing his coffee. He used it more as a crutch to make it easier for us to talk.

"I remember telling him, 'I can't be impartial on this. You saved my neck with the Japanese churches. I need you, Sig.'

"But you forget," he stopped me, "John Bachman is still Chairman of the Commission, and he's 100 percent behind your multimedia campaign."

"I know, but…" and I turned speechless. The Apostles came to mind. When Jesus no longer was with them in the flesh, they had to rely solely on his Spirit.

Anita, who had been listening patiently to this imaginary conversation, asked, "Is that all?"

"I admired Sig. I'd seen how his simple trust in Jesus had shamed doubters. His humble intellect disarmed opponents and unraveled their sophistry. From then on, he would no longer be my boss. Nevertheless, he continued to visit us in Japan."

Anita verbalized her own memories. "I've always cherished the Ethiopian cross he gave me."

Joe continued. "Sig always brought encouragement. By the time he'd leave Japan, we'd be convinced everything would work out okay, no matter how tough our problems.

"I'm imagining him again. He's sitting there on the rocking chair in front of the radio. He's taking off his glasses, wiping them with his handkerchief, then slipping them back on.

"Reminding me of a blacksmith like his father, Sig leans over toward me. Grasping my hands in his huge ones, he peers into my eyes, his smiling cheek muscles more noticeable because of his wide, slightly protruding jaw. I've always thought he would have made a great family doctor."

"Joe," Aske asked, "what do you think Watanabe would have you do? Sit here and stare at your navel, or take the TV project as God's call to you? Wouldn't he want you to help the people in Hong Kong? That will help China, too, and people everywhere who must pay a price for faith and freedom?"

Then Joe repeated it aloud, "Pay the price! He'd want me to pay the price. I can't fail Watanabe again."

Burying his head in his hands, Joe blurted out in Anita's direction, "I don't want to go down to Tokyo. We've signed up for that tour on Friday and Saturday — to visit the Winter Olympic sites. They won't refund our tickets. They say the inn at Hakuba is fabulous. Aren't we supposed to be retired and enjoying life? I don't know if I have the guts to fight for another Watanabe project. Besides, Tokyo is like a sauna these days."

"You wouldn't gripe if it were a golf match. You've admitted as much. What was that *haiku* you composed on a hot summer day when you had to carry your heavy briefcase up the hill to the Tokyo Center?"

She had him. His own words convicted him, and he'd been so proud of that *haiku*.

Ase mizuku	Wet with sweat
Saka mo mata yoshi	Climbing the hill
Gorufu tote	If it were only golf

"What shall I do?"

From somewhere deep within his sub-consciousness a cloud of apprehension enveloped him.

Intellectually assenting to Aske's exhortation to move forward with the project, his emotions cried out, "Hold on! What are you trying to do? Who do you think you are?"

"Am I rushing into this too fast? Can this imaginary conversation be trusted, or is it only a clever way to suppress guilt? Maybe I'm finding a way to blame Aske if I fail again. O God, help me. Give me a discerning heart — and a discerning mind.

"But oh, the price! If I only could be sure..."

Anita, who had been sitting on the sofa listening and watching Joe, had been trying to decipher what Joe was experiencing. Failing in that, she probed him in a new direction.

"What are you going to do about Eric? You'll have both Reardon and Eric in Tokyo at the same time."

"That will be tricky," Joe acknowledged, "managing an English television director and a young American in search of a media career — his father with him.

"At least I can start by doing what I can — find out if I can reserve a seat on the 6:42 train Friday. I must call Kawaguchi again anyway. Wish we had a phone here at the cabin." Joe quickly squelched that idea. "One reason we come here is to escape the phone."

So, again Joe headed down the hill, resigned to whatever waited him, believing all things would work together for good. Joe's little four-year old surrogate grandson was playing with his sister now. She was lobbing balls over the net for him to hit back. *No wonder he likes her.* The picture of their tenderness gifted Joe with a serendipitous feeling of peace and confidence.

Passing in front of the Summer Store, he waved at Nakamura-san, who was standing next to the old-fashioned ice cream freezer. She greeted him with, *"Orimura-san, dou shitan desu ka? Mou sankai me desu.* (Mr. Orimura, what's wrong? This is the third time you've come down today.)

"I'll tell you on the fourth time," he kidded back.

After calling the Kurohime Station for a reservation, Joe telephoned Kawaguchi to ask him to join them at the press club on the 9th for lunch with Reardon.

"I've got to beg off. That's the day our family is going to the lake by Mt. Fuji. I can't break my family promise again." To needle Joe, he added, "I'm becoming a *kyousaika* (wife-fearer) like you."

"That's too bad. I'd feel much better about this meeting if I knew you'd be there. We need Japanese input. Reardon knows only the British bias about Hong Kong and the War." *But was it really fair to say former prisoners were biased? After all, they'd been beaten for even the slightest reasons.*

While trudging home, Joe caught himself thinking that more than the forty-two year old Kawaguchi's opinion, they'd need to consider the world-wide TV audience's viewpoints, especially children like his grandchildren who knew nothing about the war with Japan.

After turning left at the corner, the same little boy and his sister came sauntering down the road. The boy gripped his green-stringed racket with the right hand and had it resting on his shoulder. When they'd come about twenty feet from Joe, he dropped the racket down to his side and swung sidearm at an imaginary ball. Responding, Joe ran forward to smash his return, but pretended his volley went into the net. "Your point," he yelled.

"And a little child shall lead them." Of course, that's it! We need youth's views for the sake of kids like this boy. Many of those British Commonwealth

35

prisoners-of-war hadn't seen their 20th birthdays — especially those pitiful new recruits from Canada. They hardly knew how to button on their uniforms — let alone shoot, before they landed in Hong Kong just in time to be captured before Christmas.

The boy's sister said, "You've played a lot of tennis, haven't you?"

"Not reallly, but I fake it pretty well don't I?"

Shamshuipo must have felt like the end of the world to those young prisoners. Somehow we must understand what it was like to be so young, so far from home and so in need of someone to rely on. Like that little boy?

Two of Joe's friends came along, but he didn't answer their "Hellos." Joe was re-living the prisoners' hopelessness, trying to recall the details he had heard. *The prison guards despised the captives. They called them "white cowards" who surrendered rather than fight. Malnourished and with little or no medical supplies, they'd abandoned all hope. To them Hong Kong was not the renowned "fragrant harbour;" it was a cesspit steaming in the stench of death.*

Joe stopped at the water faucet across from their cabin. He stooped low and put his mouth below the spigot to get a drink of water. A yellow wasp wanted to drink, too, so Joe took only one sip and retreated to the road.

While the wasp buzzed around threateningly, Joe waved him away, then stood still long enough to find his train of thought and empathize again with the young prisoners. *How comforted they must have felt when one night a glimmer of light shone into their black hell? A friendly hand reached into their darkness and touched them, grasping their hands and assuring them,"We haven't forgotten you. There will be a tomorrow."*

If we can only get that message across in 1997 to the new potential prisoners in Hong Kong.

By the time Joe turned into the cabin, he'd talked himself into telling Reardon that he would bring an unexpected guest, a young man who fifty-five years ago might have been exactly like one of those teenage Canadian kids in the camp.

How better could Eric learn about the real Asia, with its lingering wounds and unabsolved guilt? I'll have to tell him that the International War Crimes Tribunal never did charge Emperor Hirohito with guilt over the war, but older Asians have never forgotten nor forgiven him.

After lunch with Anita, he moved to the back living room and aimed the fan at the long couch where he took his daily nap. The steady buzz of the fan anesthetized him quickly. It wasn't until three o'clock that a voice from the road woke him.

"Joe, hey, Joe! Do you want to join David and me for golf? We need practice for the Open tomorrow." He recognized Ray Boone's voice. He and David, his colleague at the American School, were good friends of his. As a Brit,

David probably had a wealth of wartime memories from England but never wanted to talk about them. *Maybe I can get him to talk, if he knows what I'm into.* Hurrying out to the back porch, a sleepy-eyed Joe yelled back, "Join you up at No. 1. Go on ahead. I'll catch up."

For the next hour and a half Joe made all the usual golf motions, including transposed expletives after missed shots. He tried to act sociable, but his thoughts were flying as randomly as his shots. He didn't have much hope for the Open. When on No. 8 Ray and David decided to play a second round, Joe called it quits and crossed the road to home.

"Tadaima!" he announced so that Ani would know he was back. After re-heating the morning brew of coffee and tearing off a piece of diet-breaking pecan bread, he grabbed pen and paper along with his red datebook and moved out front to sort out what looked to be a momentous week ahead.

I wonder if Eric made it safely to Japan. He should have reached the hotel by now. Better wait until after supper to call him. Need to catch him before he makes plans for the 9th.

Sitting on the porch with grass and flowers, lake and mountains framed by pine and cedar trees, time coasted by as effortlessly as a car in neutral wending its way down a gently sloping mountain road. Before he realized how late it had become, the yard and trees below had darkened in shade, and a fine mist was rising from the lake.

It must have been about 6:15 when he heard the crows returning from their scavenging. They headed straight into the westerly breeze blowing in from the Japan Sea. Soon they would reach their bedtown at the foot of Mt. Myoko.

8

Graced by a Typhoon

That night about three o'clock, the wind began shaking the curtains against the screens, and a door banged shut. The red lantern by the kitchen door was swinging much too hard for the wire to hold it, so Joe took it down and set it inside.

He faulted himself for not listening to last night's weather report. He wondered if this wind might be the outer effects of the typhoon heading for Korea.

The night wind was chilly enough so that he put on his padded *tanzen* jacket and crawled back into bed. Then it hit him. *I forgot to call Eric.* Anita pulled back from him and asked, "What's wrong?"

"I forgot to call Eric."

"Let me sleep," she grumbled.

Talking more to himself than to Anita, he poked his head under the sheet and said, "Oh, well, Eric and his Dad will wake up early. I'll call before breakfast. They'll be more alert then anyway."

"Unless they've taken melatonin or sleeping pills,"she quipped from under the covers.

The wind and occasional falling branches accompanied by the squeaky flapping of the veranda's plastic roof kept Joe on edge till morning. He kept waking every few minutes until eventually light through the front windows heralded that the mountain and lake were about to move on stage again. It was time for Joe to rise and move outside to his customary seat on the porch. The curtain of fog was drifting away.

With a mixture of trepidation and expectation, Joe opened his prayerbook to Thursday and began reading. The words sped by until he reached the close of The Confession: "Make haste to help me, O Lord (Psalm 70:1). Amen." Thereupon, in the Augustinian tradition he took those words as God's message for him today. "Make haste to help me. Please don't delay."

About 7:00 Joe hustled down to call the Fairmont Hotel. He caught Eric as he and his father were leaving to go for breakfast. After briefing him about what had been happening and that he hoped to meet him at the Press Club, Eric asked, "You don't mean the Foreign Correspondents' Club at Yuraku-cho, do you?"

"That's right. You know where it is?"

"Yeah, Dad used to be an associate member."

"Well, there's not time to explain everything on the phone. My card is about used up. Your timing for coming to Japan was perfect. I have to meet some Brit there under the time-zone clocks at 11:30. The conversation may clue you in on what's going on in this part of the world. At 12:30 we'll eat lunch and hear a speech by a Hong Kong VIP. He's supposed to explain what will happen when China takes over next July. Should be great background for us. Okay?"

"I bet my Dad would like to hear him, but I know he's tied up all morning with his company. In the afternoon he's seeing people at the Defense Agency."

"Japanese Defense Agency?"

"Yeah. Don't worry. I'm sure he'll be happy I'm staying out of trouble. Eleven-thirty did you say?"

"That's right."

"Meet you then tomorrow, 11:30 by the front desk on the 20th floor."

As Joe turned to walk home, no one was on the road, but tennis addicts were already up on the courts getting their exercise fix for the day. On the upward climb, he heard golfers on the course, hitting warm-up shots. Joe was tempted to stay home, but he knew golf could relieve his anxiety over meeting Jack Reardon.

Defying Anita's frowns, Joe fried an egg and two fatty strips of bacon to go with his toast and bowl of Grape Nuts. After breakfast he bolted out the door and up to the clubhouse just in time to hear Tournament Chairman Kazuo Takahashi's review of the unique ground rules for Nojiri golf. "You can move your ball only one club length, not nearer the hole and one-and-a-half club lengths away from a fence. On the greens you can drag the sand only once. No second drags."

"What if it rains?" someone asked.

"Get out of the rain," a wisecracker in back joked.

"Try to finish," Kazuo replied. "In case this wind blows up a storm tomorrow, we'll play the last eighteen on Monday. Friday and Saturday are out. Four people are signed up for the tour of the Olympic sites. That's why we'll have to play the last round on Monday if it rains Thursday. Men and senior men play together, but there are separate prizes for anyone fifty-five or older. Women start at 9:00, teens at 2:00 and juniors 3:00. Who's ready to tee off?"

By the end of the second nine holes, Joe's knees were buckling. It felt as though he had lead weights in his shoes. The humid tropical heat blown up after sunrise had sapped the energy out of all the seniors, except for one skinny Finn who thrived on sauna heat. He led Takahashi and Joe by six strokes.

Takahashi had finished ahead of Joe and was watching him struggle up the steep slope of the last hole. After Joe holed out, Kazuo called to him. "Come over here in the shade. I'll treat you to a coke."

"Diet, if they have it."

"Never give up," Kazuo counseled. "The narrow fairways and trees can raise havoc for any golfer, especially if a gale blows in. We don't need to give up."

"Even for an old cancer survivor like me? We'd have a better chance if rain postpones the final round till next week. I'm wiped out."

In the evening, by the time Joe had stacked the last pan atop the drying dishes, he heard rumbling in the mountains. The lanterns in front and in back began to sway wildly. A storm was rushing in fast. By eight o'clock the rain swept in from across the golf course. Anita and Joe scurried to slide windows shut and pull outdoor chairs and golf clubs in under the eaves. Within an hour, the storm settled into a rainy-season type of steady patter, peppering the metal roof, drowning out all other sounds. That night, even though Joe crawled into bed anxious about the next day, the relentless metallic pounding soon put him into a deep, restful sleep.

He recalled only one dream of vaguely being flown along on a thin vaporous stream. He didn't fly like a butterfly this way and that, but on a straight course over many jagged mountains — with the uncanny sense he wasn't flying alone. Yet, he never recognized the person who rode atop the cloud with him.

At 5:00 a.m. when normally the sun brightens the view from the windows, clouds still banked the hillside. The low humming clatter of rain gradually turned into a crescendo of banging noise not unlike the racket from the student drum corps practicing at the music camp by the beach. It would let up for a while, only to be followed by more rattling which sounded like racoons throwing buckets of gravel across the roof.

This rain is not going to stop. At 6:55 I'll turn on the radio for the weather forecast, even though it rarely changed. But today was different. The weather lady voiced alarm: "Rain, sometimes heavy in the mountains and continuing through tonight. Typhoon No. 6 is heading west along the Japan Sea and will run ashore into Korea. Rain is expected until late afternoon for Nagano Prefecture. Trains are on schedule, except for the north coastline in Western Japan."

"Rain today is a blessing in disguise," Joe said to his wife, who was beginning to stir out of sleep. "It will give me a quiet day at home to think about who could help on the TV project. I should listen again to the tape interviews with Watanabe and Nolan. Who's left in Hong Kong?"

"Can't David and Annie Chiang help?" a sleepy Anita asked from beneath the covers.

"Problem is they're emigrating to New Zealand — maybe there now. No one I know is left at the Hong Kong Christian Council. Oh, Annie Wong, I forgot about her."

"Anyone in the broadcast or advertising industry? Is Bill Dingler's daughter still there? Her husband is high up in an ad agency isn't he?"

"My pile of business cards is dated, but at least I ought to cull through them. It shouldn't be difficult to pick out possibilities, but who'd be willing to help us? Most media people are running scared, like rats jumping off a sinking ship. But there has to be someone."

The day went by uneventfully but for a walk in the rain to the vegetable stand on Friendship Highway beyond the golf course. On the way home, Joe circled by way of the Summer Store for a can of Campbell's mushroom soup. Anita needed it for her tuna casserole. He then called to reserve a taxi for 6:20 the next day.

That night before turning in, Joe packed his overnight bag, but didn't make up his sack lunch until morning. The taxi arrived shortly after he'd downed cereal and the usual cholesterol-loaded eggs and bacon.

The driver turned out to be Ikeda-san, the same roly-poly woman in navy-blue slacks he had last time. Her cheery smile and manly gestures witnessed to her own self-esteem in doing a man's work. Her gracious handling of Joe's bag, plus the clearing sky boded well for the four-hour trip. Before he stooped to slide into the taxi, Anita ran out in her bathrobe to wish him well, "*Gambare!* (Give it your all.) I'll be praying for you."

Stepping back to her, Joe paused a moment, his eyes moist. Even though Ikeda-san stood waiting, he clutched Anita's arm, and embraced her as he pressed her lips hard and slid his right hand down her back, ending with a gentle pat which he didn't mind Ikeda-san noticing. Instead of "Goodbye," he said, "Pray for me. Pray for every one of us."

"You all right?"

Joe hesitated, groping for what to say. "I feel over my head, in a stream I've never been able to cross before."

Upon reaching the pavement, the black Nissan sedan took off down the narrow paddy-lined road, but rather than heading straight, Ikeda-san turned right to cut across Highway 18 at the stoplight so as not to be blocked by trucks and commuters heading for Nagano City.

At the station, Joe zigzagged through the crowd of vacationers and commuters like a running back in a football game. Ikeda-san trotted at his heels up to the wicket. After Joe entered, she waited there, waving farewell. People around her must have guessed that Joe was taking no ordinary pleasure trip. She continued to wave until he walked the full one hundred yards to board the no-smoking coach. Thus, Joe Orimura set out on a long journey. He had no idea how it would end.

9

Encounters at the Press Club

The express train soon sped along through the mountain pass until it reached Nagano City. From there farms, forests and mountain streams passed quickly. From the highest elevation at Karuizawa down the steep mountain pass, Joe counted twenty-eight tunnels and thanked God for electric engines and air-conditioned coaches. At Yokokawa most of the student passengers leaped off the train to run back to the kiosk for steaming bowls of rice smothered with vegetables soaked in the famousYokokawa sauce. Joe stayed put, pretending to be content with his gouda-cheese sandwiches and Coke.

From Yokokawa the train picked up speed as it raced through the Kanto Plain, passing autos on the parallel highway. Now instead of terraced rice paddies dominating the view, all he could see were long strings of villages and towns separated by truck farms which supplied the Tokyo metropolis with fresh vegetables. After leaving Takasaki City, Joe dozed off, awaking only when the conductor called, "Ueno, five minutes to Ueno at the end of the line."

Since he'd taken the trip from there to central Tokyo many times, he shifted his mind into auto-pilot when he boarded the Yamate-Line commuter train. Ten minutes later he got off at his old home neighborhood of Yuraku-cho, Tokyo's Time Square. Here was where his communication office used to be located in the '60s and '70s. It felt like a homecoming to walk through his own Yurakucho Building and over to the New Yurakucho Building next door, wondering if someone still might recognize him. No one did. He felt that they took him for just another tourist.

Jumping into one of the six elevators as the doors were closing, he recalled that this was the very one where he'd shaken hands with Kim Young Sam the day he spoke so hopefully about reforming South Korea. Now he had become President. A flood of other memories began streaming through Joe's mind.

As the elevator launched upward toward the top floor, his stomach stayed at ground level. He had forgotten how fast that lift could rocket up to the 20th floor. That's where there was a windowless bar reputed to be the safest earthquake haven in Tokyo. Supposedly the Big One couldn't topple this building because of its *Daruma*-like wide-at-the- bottom structure, the underground sections occupying a wider space than the above-ground ones. Contrary to Jesus' admonition to build on rock, the whole building rested on sand so that it can float in time of an earthquake. At least that's what they say. He wished he could marshal up that kind of confidence today for his Big One.

The elevator slowed to a gentle stop. He took a deep breath and prepared to step out. The door opened. At that moment Eric exited from the men's room down the hall to the right.

"Hey, Eric, good timing. It's not 11:30 yet, but let's see if Reardon has arrived." They looked in the lobby and also checked the coffee shop, but Reardon didn't seem to be there, so, Joe suggested they go over to the dining room for a birdseye view of Tokyo.

An aroma of Chinese food filled the room. Waiters and waitresses were setting tables. He knew several of them from before. Television crews were busily setting up cameras and testing sound levels. He spied headwaiter Hirabayashi-san over by the entrance to the kitchen. Joe walked over and greeted him warmly.

"Hirabayashi-san, *ohisashiburi desu* (It's been a long time).

"Orimura-san, isn't it? Or, do you use only 'Weaver' now?"

"Good memory. Orimura to you. I'd like to show my friend the view from here. Much has changed since five years ago." Turning to Eric, he asked, "Do you remember Tokyo Station over there in the distance?"

Pointing to the right, Eric said, "that's a bullet train pulling out on the far track? How fast do they go?"

"About 140 miles an hour, I think. I get miles mixed up with kilometers."

"Isn't that a new building in front?" Eric asked.

"Must be the new International Conference Center. From the windows on the left you can get a magnificent view of the Emperor's palace and moat. Farther to the west is Kasumigaseki, where the main government offices are located."

"Dad's going there this afternoon."

"He must have important business. This view is even more beautiful at night."

Returning to the front reception area, a broadish, short man with a bald spot on the back of his head was standing in front of the news bulletins tacked on the wall to the left of the library entrance. "If he'd only turn around," Joe said, "I think I'd recognize him. Over the phone I heard Bill Knight call him 'Stubby,' and that fellow certainly looks stubby."

Down the long hallway elevator doors opened. Out stepped several dark-suited no-smile types who came toward Eric and Joe, escorting an elegantly mustached Westerner in an executive-gray suit. Alongside him marched two others, a smallish oriental in seersucker and a man whom Joe recognized as the long-term Japan correspondent for the *Los Angeles Times.* They walked by briskly and headed back to the reception room reserved for pre-luncheon cocktails and get-acquainted time with press club officers.

The short man by the wall turned around to appraise the group walking by and noticed Joe and Eric also. From the front he looked to be in his early fifties, but maybe that was because of his baldness and no-nonsense scowl. His blue serge suit gripped him tightly. He hesitated to speak, so Joe took the initiative.

"You aren't Mr. Reardon are you?"

"Yes, you must be Weaver." Studying Eric he added, "I expected Kawaguchi to be older and Japanese."

"I'm sorry, I should have called you again. Kawaguchi left town this morning with his family."

"So, who is this young man?"

"Right after I'd spoken with you on the phone, I received a letter from — excuse me, this is Eric Gunderson. He returned to Tokyo several days ago and wanted to see me about exploring journalism opportunities in Asia. I thought he'd benefit from joining us. Hope that's all right?"

Reardon cocked his head to the side and scratched his cheek. He hesitated as though weighing the pros and cons. Nodding consent, he said to Eric, "Journalism eh? A noble profession! Hope I don't disillusion you."

"I'm sure you won't. I'll try not to be a bother."

"Bill Knight is holding a table for us in the coffee shop. We can talk there a while before the luncheon gets under way. Knight's assistant, Mei Li Ping, will join us later at lunch. She's anxious to meet you. Says she'd heard about you and Watanabe in Taiwan."

"In Taiwan? Who in the world is she? How did she learn about me? Any idea why she wants to see me?" But Reardon acted as if he hadn't heard the question. Then Reardon led them to a corner table where a tall red-haired man stood up to welcome them. "Bill Knight, this is Joe Weaver, but to some Japanese he's known as Joe Orimura — or should I say Reverend?"

"Around here I went by Mr., but some members knew I was clergy."

"This is Earl?" Reardon asked, but he read Joe's lips and corrected himself. "Eric Gunderson is Joe's friend and will be joining us in place of Kawaguchi. Okay?" Putting a favorable spin on this, he added, "Joe thinks he can help us."

After Knight ordered the coffee, Reardon motioned slightly with his head toward the door. Knight took the hint, excusing himself by saying he had to go meet the speaker for the day.

As he walked by, Joe caught sight of a thinnish Asian staring at him from the next table. He looked familiar, but here in this setting he couldn't recollect who he was or where he had met him. Joe's hunch was that he was either Chinese or Korean.

That's awful! Is my memory failing?

When their eyes met, Joe decided to nod to him, but he didn't return the nod. He knew a Korean or a Japanese would have nodded back. Instead the man tilted his head and waved his right hand, then came over to greet Joe.

"Joseph Weaver, remember me? PeterYu from Hong Kong."

"Peter Yu, of course, what are you doing here?" Joe exclaimed as his mind telegraphed memories of him from the past. As soon as Joe recognized Yu, an old Japanese phrase came to mind: *Hito o mireba, dorobo to omou.* (When you first see a man, you suspect he's a thief.) *That's awful! I should know better, but why this ghost from the past?*

Reardon, and even Eric, noticed how Joe suddenly looked discomforted.

Joe couldn't forget what other Chinese had said about Peter. For the meetings Joe attended with Yu, the secretaries never listed his first name. They always wrote, "P.Yu." People relished calling him "P.Yu" behind his back, not meaning that he smelled, but that they couldn't trust him. Yu's nervous eyes and calculating ways made colleagues suspicious of him even though he could mouth pious phrases as well as any Bible-thumping Fundamentalist. In Hong Kong's Chinese circles, rightly or wrongly, Yu had gained the reputation of a schemer. One British missionary compared him to Iago. All his good deeds smelled of self-promotion.

Reardon pulled out a little notebook and wrote himself a memo.

Joe hated himself for thinking ill of others, but he couldn't forget how suspicions about Yu mounted in the early 1980s when Yu showed up at a meeting of the Hong Kong Christian Council accompanied by a representative of the China Religious Affairs Bureau. He turned out to be the same man who blocked the production of a movie about the Boxer Rebellion. He accused the missionaries of being puppets of the West, "criminals against the Chinese people."

Joe avoided identifying Jack Reardon when he introduced Peter to the others. *Who knows what he might be up to? His clothes reeked of beer and cigarette smoke.*

Joe peeked past Yu at his table companions. By the accent of the loud Anglo, Joe guessed he was Australian. The Korean to his left Joe knew to be a free lancer known to have connections with both North and South Korea. The expressionless Oriental on the right with a loose-fitting gray suit looked like what a Chinese cadre might wear.

Peter Yu started the conversation. "I'm here from Hong Kong to cover Loh's trip for *Xinhua.* That's the New China News Agency."

"Xinhua? Don't tell me! Wow! You've really come up in the world."

"I'm also going to Nagano to do background stories on the Olympics."

Not thinking of what he was saying, Joe told him, "Maybe I'll run into you up there. We're staying at Lake Nojiri, only twenty miles north of Nagano City. Please excuse me now. Maybe I'll see you after Loh's talk."

"Sorry, but I have to go with Loh to the British Embassy. We're still a colony you know. You and I better talk sometime."

"We certainly should."

10

Confidential Talk

As soon as Peter Yu was out of earshot, Reardon moved his chair closer and leaned halfway across the table. His puffy eyes tightened into wrinkles as he whispered, "What we talk about has to be kept confidential." Turning to Eric, he asked, "You hear that, Eric? How good are you at keeping secrets?"

"Okay, I guess." Showing puzzlement, Eric muttered slowly, "Unless..."

"Unless what?" Reardon shot back.

"Unless you're doing something wrong."

"Good boy! Don't worry about that. I wouldn't ask you to do anything wrong. If you ever doubt, speak up."

"Yes, sir."

"At this stage of planning we can't allow any leaks. We don't want roadblocks thrown in our way.

"We can expect the Chinese to be very uptight about this turnover business. The Tiananmen Square killings burned them badly. Now they've got all the dislocations caused by privatization of government-owned businesses. The gap in income between the new rich in the coastal provinces and the neglected interior provinces is provoking discontent — especially amongst Tibetans, Muslims and rural poor. Peasants make up two-thirds of the population."

"That jibes with what I hear," Joe affirmed while nodding his head.

Reardon continued, "Ever since Ayatollah Khoumeni overthrew the Shah of Iran and the Eastern Europeans overturned the Communists, they've been frightened. You remember Khoumeni's revolution grew at the grassroots by the underground dissemination of audio cassettes. That undermined the Shah's people with all their ostentatious opulence.":

"I've heard that, too," Joe said.

The tuxedoed waiter came back to re-fill their coffee cups. Reardon paused a moment and then sipped some coffee before continuing. "Some believe Radio Free Europe was what did in Communist control. If the Chinese think we're fomenting rebellion, we're dead in the water."

"I can imagine that," Joe agreed. "We have to stay apolitical."

"On top of that," Reardon said softly with his hand over his mouth, "one reliable source reports that Japanese right-wingers are mixed up in things. They're leftover from the days when Japan occupied northeast China. They've tied in with some powerful Hong Kong industrialists to push Hong Kong toward a Stalinist or Fascist economy."

46

Eric looked on in disbelief. "Good God!" Joe exclaimed. "I've never heard that. Are you sure?"

Again whispering, Reardon said, "I haven't even told Knight what I'm doing. I think the Chinese woman suspects something. We can't let our plans get leaked to a competitor or to some stool pigeon in Hong Kong, and especially not to the mainlanders."

"You mean," Joe interrupted "this TV program could end up a political issue?"

"It shouldn't, but you never can be 100 percen sure. Strange things are going on in Hong Kong, things the press doesn't dare report. The PRC has placed 5,000 agents there already."

"You must be kidding."

"It's hard to put into words, but it shouldn't be seen as political, but at a very profound — almost unconscious level, some people might get frightened. I don't know what to believe."

"Any way to test the winds?"

"One political analyst, can't mention his name, claims Anson Chan will be the assistant to whomever Beijing picks to head the Hong Kong government. He said she'll act like a canary in a mineshaft. Her pulling out of the new Hong Kong government would signal poisonous winds for democracy."

"Not very assuring," Eric dared to say.

"But we'll never accomplish anything gazing up at the black clouds."

"I follow you," Joe agreed.

"I'm hoping you can help us," Reardon said in a commandeering voice. "We must have your materials."

Joe waved his coffee cup and clanged it down on the saucer, not knowing what to say.

"When you were hashing out the Watanabe story, I understand you were working with Japanese, Chinese and Hong Kong people. Didn't you run head on into conflicting views of history?"

"Oh, did we!"

"These days," Reardon explained, "on top of everything we've got tension caused by the reversion. Many Hong Kong residents are running scared. It will take a lot of skill to sort out all this. Your President Clinton isn't making it any easier. China fears America is trying to contain China. They claim what you call 'engagement' is raw American hegemony. They're paranoid about your rearming Japan and stockpiling nuclear weapons on Okinawa."

"I've heard that, too. But don't you think it's exaggerated?"

Reardon began tapping the table with his fingertips and his leg began to shake the table. "You must understand that for Chinese leaders nothing outranks

47

stability in importance. They feel that feeding their 1.3 billion mouths is top priority. The very idea of freedom scares them to death."

"Understandable, but not nice. Somewhere I read an interview with one of their leaders. He excused the lack of democracy because of the 5-700 million functional illiterates. Demagogues, he claimed, could easily stir them up if they had our kind of democracy."

Covering up his sarcastic chuckles, Reardon finished his point."It's not hard to understand. From their perspective, pro-democratic, capitalistic elements could overthrow the government. That's what happened in the old Soviet Bloc. As with Mao Zedong, the disgruntled peasants could revolt and push China back into an era of regional warlords. Not too farfetched. We must be careful."

Joe turned to Eric and said, "I think Mr. Reardon wants us to 'be wise as serpents and harmless as doves.'"

"Quoting Shakespeare eh?" Reardon smiled.

"Could be, but I think Jesus said it long before Shakespeare, but, of course, he wasn't English."

Speechless for a second, Reardon exploded with a guffaw. "Your point, preacher.You've got a sense of humor. That will make our job easier. We English love to poke fun at ourselves, but not too good at accepting others who do it to us. So, don't push it."

"I'll remember that — maybe. Since you're throwing out compliments, let me give one to you. Frankly I dreaded meeting you. Don't look so surprised."

Reardon squirmed, but kept as straight a face as he could.

"Film directors often act like dictators, especially the Westerners," Joe explained. "Our stress on individualism corrupts them. They're all trying to become the heroes of their own productions, but what comes out rings false, at least it does to Japanese."

"What are you trying to say?"

"In Japan you see much teamwork in really good, true-to-life productions. For any believable presentation about Watanabe, you'll need various viewpoints. I'm relieved you're aware of this."

Reardon looked flabbergasted. Joe had verbalized what Reardon intuitively had grasped already. After this had soaked in, he shifted to a hardly perceptable frown and confronted Joe with a question he obviously had been waiting to ask for a long time.

"Why weren't you able to complete the movie about Watanabe?"

"I figured you'd ask that. It's puzzled me, too. Even now I'm not 100 percent sure of the answer. It would have been a winner, especially if it had hit the theaters at Christmas 1991. That would have coincided with the 50th anniversary of Hong Kong's surrender to the Japanese.

"To answer your question, I think the immediate reason was financial. The Geneva staff were worried because of the decline of the dollar. They couldn't risk lending us more money for script development."

As though he had experienced that predicament before, Reardon nodded sympathetically, "That must have been a letdown."

"We struggled over it, but the committee wouldn't give up, so we invited Liam Nolan, Watanabe's biographer to visit us."

Leaning back and looking at the floor, Reardon asked himself outloud, "I think I've met Nolan around the BBC. I'm sure I have — skilled producer of documentaries."

"We believed he was on board with us, so I cabled Geneva and sent a strong letter appealing for them to re-activate the $50,000 loan they had approved earlier."

"That wouldn't go very far."

"It was for script development and fund raising. We asked them to call Nolan in Dublin and set up a meeting with potential ecumenical sponsors, not just the Lutherans."

"Catholics, too?"

"Nolan himself was Catholic. We thought he might have some clout there. He said he had contacts with suitable film directors like John Boorman and David Puttman. The meeting in Geneva never came off. I suspect Nolan gave up on us. I lost contact with him, a complete breakdown in communication. Made me feel lousy. I felt I must have failed him."

Neither Joe nor Reardon knew what to say. They just stared at their coffee cups.

Reardon broke the silence. "Once a director gets going on a film, he can't put up with indecision by sponsors."

"We all liked Nolan and can't fault him. He was a great stickler for the facts. He adamantly insisted that we control the film's content."

"A man after my own heart."

"Once before," Joe continued, "he had given film rights to a Hollywood writer, but withdrew it when she jazzed up the story with fiction. He was a purist. He hated distorting truth for effects."

Reardon turned his eyes away from Joe and Eric to gaze out the window — trying to sort out Joe's reply.

Then Joe said, "There's enough material to work around the original author. Some of those prisoners-of-war must still be living. I have quite a few addresses."

"Tell me, Weaver, did Watanabe become humanitarian only after the military assigned him to Shamshuipo?"

49

"I'd wondered about that, too, but I learned for a fact that he was putting up peace posters in Hiroshima right up to Pearl Harbor. He was genuine through and through. His story possesses staying power. He was the real thing — a man for all seasons."

Reardon nodded. "That corroborates what I've heard, too."

Joe sensed they were in basic agreement, so he pushed the conversation one step further. "Even if the new arrangement in Hong Kong succeeds initially, it can't last too long. Watanabe's story can help ward off future corrosion of people's rights. Once Beijing puts the screws on, rust will make it impossible to loosen them."

"I agree, though I'd say it differently," Reardon said.

He pinched his eyebrows down over his squinting eyes. "I'm always skeptical about reputed noble characters. Fishermen have a saying I think applies here: 'Great figures often are like mackeral, beautiful from a distance, but stink up close; they're phoney.' Are we absolutely certain Watanabe had no skeletons hiding in his closet? What about that Irish woman who worked with him in the smuggling operation? No affair with her?"

"No one has ever charged that. It would have been completely out of character." Pausing to reflect further on Reardon's question, Joe added, "Watanabe loved children. He must have loved playing with the woman's three little girls. That's all it was. They reminded him of his own family in Hiroshima."

"Excuse me. May I ask a question?" Eric said.

"Go on, what's your question?" Reardon replied.

"See if I understand this right. You Weavers worked with Watanabe. Did he talk to you about his experiences in Hong Kong? Silly question, I know."

"No not at all," Reardon answered. Turning to Joe, "Well did he?"

"On his off days, he'd excuse himself because of malaria aftereffects. He never talked about what he'd gone through in Hong Kong."

"Strange," Reardon mumbled.

"I thought so, too. I never understood why until I heard of a holocaust victim who never told his children what he'd experienced. He didn't want to scar their souls indelibly with those horrors. I think that's why his children never talked about it. He had never told them. We had to pry the story out of him."

"What horrors?" Eric asked.

Joe had some words on the tip of his tongue, but stopped abruptly. "Not before we eat. Let's wait for that part of the story."

11

Views from the Top

Jack Reardon saw that the other tables in the coffee shop were emptying. "Let's go try for decent seats. Knight will be at the speakers' table. He's worried about what kind of clever question he can ask. We mustn't forget to save a seat for Mei Li Ping."

Reardon hurried ahead and picked out four seats on the left of the two long tables reserved for the working press, two seats facing the podium and two with their backs to it.

"Jack, — may I call you 'Jack'?"

"Fine. I've already called you 'Joe.'"

"Joe's okay, unless you're writing me a check. Bank prefers Joseph Weaver."

Two Japanese in black suits swaggered down the aisle. By their demeanor, Joe guessed they weren't club members, long black sideburns ruled out their being business men. After they took their seats, a young woman with smartly coiffered black hair approached.

"Here's Miss Mei Li Ping," Reardon announced as though introducing a contestant in a beauty contest. Eric's mouth dropped. Joe could only think, *The Dragon Lady has returned.* He guessed Miss Ping to be in her late twenties, although she oozed a sensuous warmth more typical of an older woman. *If only I were single and twenty-five again.*

Exchanging pleasantries, Joe tried to impress her. "Don't expect too much of today's speech. No politician ever says anything the journalists don't already know."

She giggled, revealing actress-perfect teeth, and seemed to appreciate Joe's advice.

Encouraged by her attention, Joe elaborated. "The fun comes when the journalists try to trap the speaker. They'll tempt him to say more than he wants to. You know, of course, this was the club where the press cornered Prime Minister Tanaka twenty years ago."

Eric still hadn't closed his mouth.

I bet Eric's worried she might learn he's only seventeen.

Glancing at the two sober-faced Japanese next to Joe, Jack leaned closer and whispered, "We can finish talking afterward. Let's enjoy ourselves for now."

"As they say," Miss Ping inserted, "all work and no play makes Jack a dull boy." She put her hand to her lips. "Oh, sorry, your name is Jack." She laughed at herself, then said, "Mr. Knight says we can order drinks, and he'll sign the chit. What would you like?"

"Tomato juice for me," Joe said. "Eric, what do you want?"

He studied the menu. "I guess, Ginger Ale."

"Ditto for me," Jack said. "Ginger Ale at least looks like beer."

Ping gave the order to the waitress. Judging by the stream of people coming in, it would be a full house. Both journalists' tables had filled up. Some regulars were upset because they'd been downgraded to sit with associate members. In back, NHK, Fuji, and CNN camera crews were standing at their posts.

The drinks arrived: two Ginger Ales, a tomato juice, and a glass of sherry for Ping.

Miss Ping, who sat opposite Eric, asked him, "What brought you to Tokyo?"

"My father brought me," careful not to tell it was his high school graduation present.

She sensed Eric was holding back, maybe something with news value.

"What business is he in?"

"I dunno. He doesn't talk about it, even with me."

"We all hide our secrets, don't we?" Reardon chimed in.

"Where are you staying?"

Eric paused a bit and hedged with a vague reply, "Near the Indian Embassy."

Joe was relieved when their bowls of ice-cold vichyssoise arrived before Ping could pump him about his connection to Reardon. Over the lunch of Chinese-style chicken salad, roast duck with stir-fried vegetables, egg roll and a huge bun, they sparred back and forth trying to extract information from each other. For Joe's part, this worldly-wise woman intrigued him. He wanted to learn who she was and why British TV had hired her.

Behind the speaker's podium hung a huge banner which read: "Foreign Correspondents Club of Japan." Its immensity accentuated Anthony Loh's diminutive stature as he stood up and began plodding through his written text. He blundered badly at the beginning when he told the journalists they could pick up copies of the speech afterward. That gave them license to doze off as he droned on and on in his Chinese-English monotone. As Joe predicted, Loh dealt only with points the journalists would have known already, not a word about such matters as:

How much real authority will Beijing allow the Hong Kong Legislative Council?

Will there be a litmus test for candidates?

Will the judiciary be free from Beijing's interference?

Joe looked up and down the two long press tables and spotted several veteran correspondents shrugging their shoulders and sucking breath. They could smell a cop-out a mile away. *If Loh carries on like this with mere generalities, one of*

*those journalists, or maybe that pesky young reporter from the GUARDIAN will
surely pin him down, make him sweat blood.*

Eventually the tedious recitation ground to a halt, and the MC opened up the
floor for questions from the press. One of the older male journalists tilted his
head to the woman from the *Guardian* and motioned for her to go first.

Imitating a self-effacing Japanese woman, she shuffled to the standing
microphone.

"Thank you very much for enlightening us so thoroughly today."

Joe was right about her. Slowly, but surely she set about to light a fuse under
the honorable Mr. Anthony Loh. She intoned her words, though in crisp
university English, exactly as a Japanese does before coming to the *ga,* or *but* of
the sentence. *Ga* alerts an audience that the questioner is about to blow the
speaker's cover. The politeness is all show. After the *but,* though still in the
methodic rhythm of politeness, the questioner draws out a dagger of a question,
then thrusts it into the unsuspecting speaker's chest. Everything goes downhill
from there.

"But, Mr. Loh," she queried, "are we to believe the hard-core pro-democracy
forces and those Tiananmen Square demonstraters who fled to Hong Kong will
sit idly by and watch China subject them to Beijing-style democracy?"

Eyeing Loh's twitching cheek, she knew she'd trapped him. She waited
politely to see how he'd try to wiggle out of a direct answer.

Again she thrust at him, though veiled in traditional feminine softness. "What
about the remaining pockets of Kuomintang Nationalist diehards who back
Taiwan?"

Loh lowered his head and glanced furtively at the British ambassador to his
left. Hiding his mouth, Loh asked him something.

Pretending to cough, the ambassador covered his mouth with his
handkerchief, but must have urged the speaker to be more forceful, because Loh
immediately raised his voice several decibels when he replied: "You are overly
skeptical. I am sure the Peoples' Republic of China's leaders will honor
paramount leader Deng Xiaoping's promise of no changes for fifty years. They
will do their utmost to satisfy the interests of all people in Hong Kong. At heart
the Chinese are pragmatists, not doctrinaire ideologues. They desire a united
Hong Kong. The Chinese will hold to their promise of 'one country, two
systems.'"

An old-timer, whom Joe knew had covered China and Hong Kong in the
past, jumped out of his seat and ran to the microphone.

"Pierson of *Far East Media Alert.* Are you suggesting, sir, that Beijing will
set up a United Front separate from the Legislative Assembly?"

Loh's face flushed crimson, and again he turned to the ambassador, who
looked embarrassed by thiis deference to the old colonial power.

Joe thought the audience must be thinking that if all Hong Kong's leaders kowtow like this to the British, why should they expect them to stand up to Beijing after turnover?

Loh replied very slowly. "That could happen. We can only wait and see."

Joe was glad to see the youngish Japanese-American female correspondent from California move up to the mike. "Maria Kobayashi, *Los Angeles Chronicle.* On the US West coast we have a great number of Chinese, many originally from the mainland. A major concern for them is freedom, freedom of expression and freedom of religion. What can you say to them and their families left in Hong Kong to alleviate their fears? Also Catholics in Hong Kong worry that Beijing will force them to cut ties with the Vatican. Do you foresee such a danger?"

Trying to stand more erect and pushing his shoulders straight back, Loh asserted almost too loudly and with seeming over-confidence, "You can see by my printed text that there is nothing to worry about. Absolutely nothing, I promise!"

"But, Mr. Loh," she objected, "Why are so many Hong Kongers leaving, and businesses setting up 'fall-back' headquarters in Taiwan, Vancouver and California?"

The MC stood up, and looking down at his watch, announced, "Time is up. Thank you all. Mr. Loh, we hope you can come back in two or three years to report on how your predictions turned out. Thank you for taking time out of your busy schedule. May I present you with this honorary membership card."

Eric breathed out emphatically, "Holy cow! He sure saved Loh's neck didn't he? You could almost see the noose tightening."

"End of East Asia 101." Joe grinned. "Are you okay on time, Eric?'

"Dad's busy until late afternoon. We're to meet at the hotel by 6 o'clock. Last night we went to bed at 8:00."

Miss Ping moved in closer to Eric and was about to speak, but Joe intercepted her. "Let's hear what Jack has in mind."

Stepping over next to Reardon, Joe asked him discretely, "How well do you know Miss Ping? What's her background? If you want things confidential, we'd better not be blabbing in front of her until we know more about her."

Reardon grasped his lower lip and chin, fishing for a response. "You know, I think I'm going to like you. We might be in their way over at Knight's office. They'll be putting together a soundbite for the morning deadline in London."

"Any idea where we should go now? Some place quiet."

"I know just the place," Joe suggested. "Up on top the Transportation Building. They've got a revolving tea room. What do you think?"

"Sounds good to me."

"I used to go up there to get away from people. There's something about being up high to put problems in perspective. Anyway, we couldn't finish our talks in time for me to catch the 5 o'clock train for Noriri. I'd better try for a room at the Marunouchi. If that's full, I'll call your hotel, Eric."

In a few minutes, Joe joined the others back under the clocks. "Marunouchi is booked solid, but there's a single open at the Fairmont."

Facing around to Miss Ping, Reardon in a regretful-sounding voice told her, "Will you excuse us? Tell Mr. Knight I'll call him tomorrow."

With a look of disappointment, she asked, "Aren't you meeting at our place? We were expecting you."

"Thanks anyway. You'll be busy meeting your story deadline. So, it's better we stay out of your way today."

Jack, Eric and Joe took the elevator down and then walked through Yurakucho Station to the far side where they entered the Transportation Building and headed for the elevator. When the doors opened, they got in, but before the doors began to close, a man impolitely pushed in and rode up with them all the way to the 15th floor tearoom. A waiter pressing an oversized plastic menu against his chest ushered them in.

"Will this table by the window suit you?"

"Fine," Joe replied. The other man said in Japanese, "I'm not with them," and he moved over to a place behind some tall plants several tables away.

From their vantage point next to the window, they could gaze out over central Tokyo as the revolving floor worked its way around inch by inch, completing the circle once every hour.

"Helps you get the big picture when you're up here," Joe philosophized.

"That's what we must get," Reardon agreed. "I loved the way those journalists circled in on Loh like a pride of lions. One more second and they would have clawed him to death." Eyeing Eric, he said, "So, you want to become a journalist, eh?"

"I'm not sure, but I can see it wouldn't be dull."

"Remember this, son," Reardon intoned in fatherly solemnity as though admonishing his own son, "it's the real truth you must go after. There are many blowhards pretending to act like journalists."

"What do you mean?"

"We, and I'm one of them, we think we know everything. We don't wait to hear the answers people give us. We just write whatever we please, or we put our personal slant on their opinions. There are guys who think they know the truth. They sit at a bar and hear what other drunk blokes say but don't check the facts. It takes one to know one. Know what I mean?"

Shifting toward the window, Reardon looked far off in the distance. "Two years ago," he suddenly blurted out, "I hate to admit it, but I was a drunken slob. I couldn't even eat breakfast without first taking a shot. I hated myself. It's a miracle I didn't blow my brains out one night in Sarajevo. God, I felt awful. Hell outside and inside. But I shouldn't load my past onto you."

An awkward silence ensued.

"I've a brother serving in Tuzla," Eric put in, trying to insert some calm after Jack's outburst.

"If my company hadn't fired me, I might have ended up as just one more corpse in a killing field. I'd hit bottom. To make it short, I got help and haven't touched a drop since. It's poison to me." Glancing around, he slapped his hand against the wall paneling. "Knock on wood. I can never be sure of myself."

"Hitting rock bottom could help you get at the truth behind Watanabe."

Reardon looked at Joe quizzically.

Emphasizing each word, Joe said, "Our — chief — aim — should — be — Truth. Truth with a capital "T". Of course, we must not stray from the bedrock facts, but mere facts don't always reveal the main Fact — or Truth."

"If I follow you up on that," Jack asked with sudden warmth, "wouldn't we need to show visually the POWs' despair? There were 9,000 in all I'm told, not just English, but Indians and Canadians, too, from all over the Commonwealth. Also Australians and New Zealanders."

"We can do that," Joe said. "I've been at Shamshuipo."

"Good, then you'll have a feel for it."

"It must have been terrifying." Joe paused. "Looking at Japanese today you'd never believe they'd been so cruel. Our Japanese scriptwriter thought the guards must have been Korean or Taiwanese. He believed they were trying to prove their loyalty by outdoing each other in viciousness. Crazy! The more sadistic they behaved the more Japanese they'd look like."

Reardon lifted his arm. "Wait a minute! You're getting ahead of me. Those details come later. What I need to know now is what kind of materials you have on Watanabe."

"Sorry, I got carried away. We'll need to cull through them thoroughly. I have letters and photos, newspaper clippings, signature book, tape interviews and the like. Plenty of material. I worked with him in Hiroshima, so I have stuff from there and from his acquaintances and his daughter, Kimi. She keeps sending me news clippings, even now. People can't forget him."

12

Dangling Truth

Don't look now," Reardon said. "That fellow who rode up with us. He's sitting behind the plants. He looks too interested in what we're saying."

"I won't talk so loud, but that gives me the creeps."

Eric in a half-whisper asked, "Have you ever played with the idea of portraying Watanabe from the angle of children? I believe that both children and people my age would be fascinated by the story."

"That's good, Eric. Hang onto it," Jack said. "Keep reminding us of that. We always forget the kids."

"The last time I saw Watanabe, his Arao Church operated a kindergarten. You know he lost two daughters five and six years old to dysentery. His first wife, Shigaru, died when Miwa was born. Those deaths deepened his love of children. He kept talking to us about his dream of building a big kindergarten in Hiroshima."

Reardon jotted down the comments in his notebook. "I meant to ask you, Joe, would you take notes of what is happening. You or I may want to write about our Watanabe project in the future."

"He talked the national church into buying an acre of land in the Ujina section of Hiroshima. A year or two later we purchased land for another kindergarten up at a little fishing village in Shimane Prefecture. His sister-in-law, Hamaoka-san, taught music in the local middle school."

"That's a long way from Hiroshima, isn't it?" Jack asked.

"Sure was, nine hours by train, but Hamaoka-san begged us to evangelize the fishermen and their families. You won't believe it, but this city boy from Gary, Indiana, even lectured to the farmers about the cooperative movement. Preached in the village hall, too, but all people remembered was Ani's singing."

"Hard on your ego, eh?"

Joe tried hard to look unplussed, so quickly changed the subject. "Ironically, the A-bomb killed his second wife who was working in a kindergarten near the bomb's epi-center, and daughter Miwa was also killed that day. Thousands of Korean slave laborers in the neighborhood died, too." Joe grabbed onto the side of the table, gripping it tightly, his face flushed crimson.

"I've seen the memorial for the Koreans," Eric said. "Japanese wouldn't allow it inside Peace Park. At least that's what a Korean classmate told me."

"Discriminated against, even in death?"

Nodding, Joe continued to fume. "The Regional Army Headquarters was only half a mile away, but it was no excuse for dropping the bomb on Hiroshima. Why not on some deserted island in the Inland Sea?"

Reardon and Eric held their peace, unwilling to contradict him. When they thought Joe had finished, he took a deep breath and started talking again. "That's not all. Something else troubles me. Eyewitnesses reported the U.S. planes flew over the city at seven, setting off the air- raid alarm."

"I thought they came at eight?" Jack interjected.

"People rushed into air-raid shelters, but when the planes flew past without dropping their payloads, everyone breathed a sigh of relief and returned to what they believed would be a safe, uneventful day. But suddenly without warning the planes circled back and the Enola Gay dropped the atomic bomb. Now get this:That was so the greatest number of civilians would be killed. But to this day, I don't know any American military leader who has admitted it. It tears me up inside to say this."

"God!" Eric groaned.

"Wouldn't surprise me," chimed in Reardon. "But who said that?"

"A Japanese military officer. He caculated that's why so many died, but I hate to believe it."

Eric had been staring out the window as we inched along. "Over there," he pointed. "That's Kasumi…"

"Gaseki," Joe helped him say. "The palace is back to the right." Joe felt glad Eric had diverted their thoughts from the bomb.

"Yesterday while it was raining," Joe said, "I drew up a list of what's stored under my earthquake-proof desk at the cabin. I had no idea what to bring, so I just took the English translations of the scripts."

"I'd like to see them," Reardon said.

"It will be hard to sort out all the different ways we viewed the war. Our viewpoints changed every day."

Eric looked puzzled. "Even if the basic story was the same?"

"Did you ever see *Rashomon*, the famous post-war film by Kurosawa? It was about how one event was viewed from three different angles. Each witness saw it differently."

"I did a film once that worked over at least ten scripts," Reardon said. "We changed things up to the very end. You grow, too, as you struggle through a story. Just when you feel you've finally got it right, someone comes up with an idea no one had thought of before. Filming is a strange process. Actors often even change their lines during the filming."

Joe took a moment to digest Reardon's comments. Then he said, "Back in December, '87 when we discussed making a film with Nolan, he counseled us not to worry about varying national views. He insisted Watanabe's story wasn't about Hong Kong or the Far East, so we should stay clear of factional interests. Otherwise, he said, we'd try to please everybody and end up satisfying nobody."

"I can agree with that," Jack said.

"The story speaks for itself," Joe recalled Nolan saying. "It is its own symbol, but I don't think the Chinese and Japanese on our committee bought that view. I didn't either. We can't disregard culture. Asian leaders are always stressing that."

Nodding consent also to that perspective, Reardon looked intensely straight at Eric. Slowly and with deliberate emphasis on each syllable, Jack asked, "Did you hear that, Eric?"

Jack's bluntness didn't seem to intimidate Eric.

"I've met so many Americans with tunnel vision. They see only Uncle Sam's point of view." Reardon stopped to see how Eric would respond.

Hesitating a moment, then taking a deep, audible breath, Eric managed to squeeze out a defensive reply. "Mr. Reardon, I may be only seventeen, but I'm not that dumb. I'm proud I attended the American School in Japan for five years. We were anything but isolated. No one tried to brainwash us or cloak us in the American flag."

Joe thought back to the Vietnam War years and how independent the thinking of his oldest daughter was. Twenty-five years later, here Joe was hearing a repeat of that older generation's independence.

When Joe again began paying attention to the spoken words, Eric was saying, "We had close to forty nationalities in the school — lots of Japanese and even Chinese and Russians. They'd call us on any onesidedness. I want you to know we had some pretty wild arguments. I'm well aware there are many ways to look at events."

Reardon had listened and smiled as Eric finished. Then Jack added, "We must never forget that the world looks different from Beijing and Taipei, Tokyo and Seoul."

Attempting to add a little extra to this wisdom-teach-in, Joe said, "But don't we run the risk of overlooking some basics that can't be compromised or watered down, truths that apply to all cultures?"

"Thanks, pastor," Jack answered. "You're right, of course, but we can't be preachy or tell the audience what it is. We have to dangle truth out in the air and make them want to leap up for it."

"Are you Chinese or something?" Joe asked. "I once received a carving from friends in Taiwan. It's of an old bearded Chinese fisherman holding his pole so that the bait dangles above the water. It illustrates a famous Chinese saying that exhorts people not to force truth onto people, but entice them to jump up for it."

"Now," sounding like an old fisherman giving his grandson his first fishing lesson, Jack said, "we need to define what the truth is and then lure the audience to leap up and catch it."

Eric and Joe didn't know what to say, but Reardon appeared to expect silence as they waited for his next words of wisdom.

Instead, Eric interrupted the quiet: "I heard a good one the other day. Do you mind? A young Minnesota boy went ice fishing. That's when you saw a hole in the ice and let your line down through it. Well, the boy couldn't catch anything, while only a few feet away an old codger was hauling in a fish every few minutes.

"'Say, mister, how come you catch all the fish, and I haven't snagged a one?'

"'O ya ba mo na shu arm' or some nonsensical words the old man murmured back.

"'I can't understand a thing you're saying,' the boy complained.

"'Oh sorry,' he gestured with his hands. Then the old fisherman stuck his fingers into his mouth and pulled out a big glob of something.

"'Sonny, the secret is to keep the worms warm in your mouth until just before you bait the hook.'"

Jack and Joe laughed hilariously, but Eric felt he had been presumptuous."Sorry for the gross humor." Even so, he went on to moralize from the story. "The old man had a point. The bait had to be kept warm. When you're trying to present truth, for instance, in a story or film, you can't use the word *truth*. By itself it's an icey word — like the cold bait in the story."

"How old did you say you were?" Jack bellowed. "I was supposed to say something like that, minus worms in the mouth. Truth plus warmth. That's what we need. How do we accomplish it?"

For several minutes the conversation went silent. The three of them stared out at the passing buildings and the people working in them. Down at street level commuters were hurrying to catch their trains.

"It's still there. Look over there," Joe said. "See that little stand-up noodle shop on the corner? Blue curtains in front. I used to eat fried noodles there. I'd line my stomach with greasy noodles so I wouldn't get drunk at parties. Good trick to remember, Eric."

"Wouldn't work for me," Jack said. "Can we get back on the subject?"

"Sorry, where were we? We were trying to serve the audience a delicious, irresistable bowl of noodles, right? We want to innoculate people against — can we say the coming powers-to-be? Jack, you're a visual man. Does this make sense to you?"

"Warm worms and greasy noodles! Let me digest that. I need to think a while about it."

The setting sun peeked out from a building one block to the West. For an instant Joe remembered a description of Watanabe standing in the shadows of the prison barracks looking toward a reddened sky. Army Chaplain Davies, his face reflecting the glowing sunset, was praying as several prisoners lowered a crude coffin into the ground. Surrounding the desolate field, the shadows of emaciated prisoners were interspersed with rifle-bearing soldiers.

Just then a sudden jerk in the movement of the revolving tearoom jogged Joe back to the present. Noticing that they were passing the palace for the third time, he looked at his watch.

"Shall we go around a third time? Or, should we let ideas ferment overnight?"

"That guy behind the plants is still there," Jack whispered. "Eric, aren't you supposed to meet your father at six?"

"Why don't we hail a cab and go over to the Fairmont," Joe suggested. "I'll check in, and if your dad is back, we can all go eat together."

"Sounds good to me. Let's get out of here. Give me the check."

"We'll have to convince your father we're not *furyo gaijin.*"

"Gee," Eric said, "I haven't heard that phrase since I left Japan. Doesn't it mean depraved foreigner?"

"That's right."

"Maybe I shouldn't meet him then," Jack said with a grin so wide the ceiling lights reflected off his gold fillings.

They exited the building and approached Yurakucho Station where a line of a dozen or more weary looking salarymen stood waiting for cabs.

"Follow me. This is hopeless," said Joe. "Let's walk a block over to the front of this building. General Douglas MacArthur used it as his headquarters. We can flag down a taxi there." Eric, who was bringing up the rear, glanced back at a honking taxi, and saw that the man from the tearoom was right on their heels.

Joe led the way down the sidewalk until they reached the front of the building. "This is where Emperor Hirohito came to pay his respects to Supreme Commander MacArthur. Across the street was where the trade unionists and Communists rioted in the early 50's. They were protesting the government's collusion with the Occupation."

"That guy is still tailing us," Eric told them.

A medium-sized black Toyota taxi soon stopped and they crunched their way in. Joe sat in front to the left of the driver and told him to take them to the Fairmont. The driver flipped on his righthand signal and gunned the engine, weaving his way into the middle lane, then right at the next corner passing along the moat toward Kasumigaseki. They next went by the Supreme Court Building and the British Embassy.

"Right after the War, Watanabe worked a while there."

At the next stoplight they made another right turn and continued along a line of cherry trees. Sounding like a tour guide, Joe said, "This is one of Tokyo's most picturesque lanes. Many a young couple walk along this meandering stone walkway during blossom time in April.

"On the left is *Chidorigaoka*, the official secular monument which has memorialized all persons who died in The Great East Asia War, even enemy military and civilians.

"Straight ahead at the end of the block is the huge Shinto Yasukuni Shrine. Most pilgrims to Tokyo go there to honor the war dead. The priests claim eight million people visit it every year."

The driver swung in to the left and parked in front of the Fairmont. As they climbed the steps up to the entrance, Joe said to Eric, "Can you check with your father? We'll wait back in that little alcove lounge."

"I'm going to phone Kawaguchi's secretary before she leaves for home."

Jack went over to the newspaper rack by the wall. He picked up the *Asahi Evening News* which headlined the anniversary of the Nagasaki bombing on the 9th.

"Kawaguchi is gone isn't he?" Joe said on the phone. "I thought I should warn you I may bring a few friends over Saturday morning even if no one is there. I have a key. No blueberry pie this time, sorry. Next time, I promise."

As Joe passed the lounge, he said to Jack, "I'm going to check in and leave my bag in the room."

His room faced out toward the parking lot in back. After he washed, he sat and relaxed a few minutes, but too many concerns and nostalgic memories made it impossible to relax. *Somehow I've got to calm down and get my bearings.*

"Lord," he prayed, "stay by my side. Keep us from wandering astray. For your sake, help me succeed. I must not let Watanabe down again."

13

A PRC Connection

The rapid descent of the elevator reminded Joe of the weightless feeling he had when a rung on the ladder at the cottage collapsed under him one time, tumbling him backward onto long bamboo grass. Breathing in deeply, he stepped out and walked toward the lobby. Jack Reardon was standing next to the wall by the coffee shop, talking to Bill Knight on the phone.

"Okay, I'll call you about eleven tomorrow. We can take it from there, maybe lunch together."

Returning to the lounge, Reardon informed Joe that Bill would see them in the morning, but no promises.

Joe turned and saw a tall, prematurely gray gentleman sporting a striped red and blue tie walking toward them.

Looking past Joe, Jack said, "That must be Eric's father."

Assuming the voice to be coming from Reardon, Mr. Eilers said, "Glad to meet you. My son thinks you're onto something good. I'm anxious to hear more."

Out of habit, Joe reached into his pocket for business cards, forgetting that Westerners don't flash out their cards as quickly as Japanese. "I'm Joe Weaver. This card doesn't say much, but when you're retired it's hard to know what to put on it. In Japan, if you don't have a card, you might as well be walking around naked."

Holding the card to the light, Eilers read aloud, "Christian Communication, Asia-Pacific Region, Retired Lutheran Missionary (Japan)."

"It's sort of a generic description," Joe explained.

"I'm Ralph Eilers, Eric's stepfather. My card won't do you much good, but here it is anyway. You have to be Mr. Reardon, then?"

"Sorry, but I'm already out of cards," Reardon said. "I should have known better. I'm a free-lance television producer."

Eiler's card had an elegant sheen, with embellished print, stating he was SeniorVice-president for Development at Airtech Incorporated, Gaithersburg, Maryland, U.S.A.

"Sounds like aerospace work, but let's not stand here. Why don't we try for one of the window seats in the coffee shop. Then we can pretend we're eating under the cherry trees."

Passing by the cake-display counter, Joe recognized the cashier as the same attractive Chinese student who worked there two years ago.The days of straight hair and baggy Mao uniforms are gone forever.

"Great view isn't it? The dining room is nice, too," Joe said, "but they don't serve light meals. I trust Airtech let's you eat well on the road."

"My Japanese hosts take good care of me. At noon they took me to the Imperial Hotel for a lunch of *teppanyaki* Kobe beefsteak. They told me the farmers actually fatten them on beer. Made me feel like a stuffed pig."

When the waitress left with their order, Eilers glanced around and under his seat, then stood up. "Where's my briefcase? Eric, do you have it?"

"No, do you need it now? I can run up and fetch it."

"No, you stay here." Eiler's eyes began twitching, and his temples bulged with reddish wrinkles as he rushed away toward the elevator.

"This must be serious," Joe said.

To cover up their anxiety, they began filling in the time with trivial comments about passersby — white-shirted men scurrying along in pursuit of one more sale for the day and lovers strolling hand in hand oblivious to time. An older man wearing a tam, the artist's trademark, sat on a bench sketching the Martial Arts Building on the other side of the moat.

Eyeing an elderly jogger chugging along, Reardon joked that if it were England the man might be arrested for loitering.

No one laughed. Everyone was too concerned about Eric's stepfather. Reardon, still chuckling over his own humor, attempted some philosophizing. "Jogging is supposed to help you quit smoking, but I believe that's only wishful thinking."

But Joe said, "Jogging can be a good way to case out a new city to find location spots for filming. If we do this Watanabe mini-series, I propose we appoint Reardon to go location hunting on early morning runs. That's a great way to explore Hong Kong — the real Hong Kong of early morning *tai-chi* enthusiasts, vegetable and fish peddlers, homeless refugees and the like." Aware no one was listening, Joe cut himself short. "Sorry, I've been talking too much again. By now I should have ingested Japan's wisdom that 'Silence is golden.' A talkative person is considered a fool."

Eilers soon strode back in, carrying his case, but his flushed face warned that he still was upset. After the waitress brought coffee and Cokes, Eric confronted him, "You okay, Dad?"

Surpressing his agitation, Eilers reassured them, "I'm all right," but unable to hold in his true feelings, he grumbled embarrassingly loud, "It makes me furious." Then he pressed his teeth together onto his right forefinger as though he were tearing off a piece of dried squid.

This explosion left the others puzzled.

"You see," he fumbled, "my business has many competitors. They're all trying by hook or crook to ferret out our new technologies. I don't dare trust anyone. Last time I was in Tokyo I got taken, but not this time. I'm going to catch the crooks."

"Catch them?" Eric asked. "What do you mean? You've never mentioned this before."

"It's nothing to be worried about, but the last time I stayed here, but at a hotel nearby, someone stole a classified document from me. I wouldn't have known it except on the very next day, a Japanese competitor submitted a patent with the very same specifications. Makes you want to cry sometimes, but this time I'm going to catch them. Don't worry about it. I'll get them. I have to." Reading his silent lips, Joe thought he said, "for the sake of peace."

Wishing to calm the atmosphere, Reardon asked, "How long have you been coming to Japan?"

"If you count military service, I've been coming here off and on since the late '60s. First time was on R&R from Vietnam, but the second time on a stretcher. The Army had put me into an intensive Vietnamese language course. I picked up Chinese later at Yale. When I graduated, one of the old-time computer companies hired me for their export division and shipped me to Beijing. That was in the late '70s, just as China was recovering from the Cultural Revolution."

"You were there at the turning point in Chinese Communist history," Reardon interjected.

"I spent time in Hong Kong, too, in the early '70s. Britain was shifting her colonial policies to a more democratic set-up with free elections, but it never panned out.

"What do you mean?" Eric asked.

"The excesses of the Cultural Revolution spilled over into Hong Kong and created havoc. Things were chaotic — lots of unrest and uncertainty about the future."

"You must have been at Beijing in '81 when the court found the Gang of Four guilty," Reardon said.

"What a time to be working in China!"

"Funny, too, sometimes. Even the Communists have a sense of humor. I'd gotten to know a Party member. One day he mouthed the Party line and began denouncing the Gang of Four. Instead of holding up four fingers, he raised his whole hand. That was the people's way of denouncing Mao, too. "He was," he confided, "the biggest scoundrel of all, the thumb."

"So, that's what it meant," Joe said. "I'd always mistaken it for the old Nazi-style salute."

"It was in Beijing," Eilers said as though he'd repeated the story a thousand times and could think about other matters while he talked. "It was there I cut my teeth on Asian bureaucracy and the fight over technology. I had five years in Tokyo, too, up until '93. My bosses, I think, felt I was getting too Asianized, so they called me back to State-side headquarters in Maryland. I was a real misfit there. That straitjacket micromanaged environment strangled the life out of me, so I resigned. They were too big and clumsy to compete in the new world of wiz-kid computer nerds."

"Didn't IBM conclude the same, but too late?" Joe asked.

"I'd thought first of going with Apple," Eilers continued, "but decided Airtech had more of a long-range future. They were light years ahead of the industry, and I liked what they were attempting to create."

Joe interrupted. "Shall we order something to eat?"

Knowing Eiler's information was classified dampened conversation. Everyone stuck to banalities about the past or the weather. When they finished eating, Eilers offered to take the meal check and signed for it. His room key was for 601, which Joe remembered was the deluxe corner suite looking out onto the moat and cherry trees.

"I'll catch up with you in the lobby," Joe said. "We haven't decided on plans for Saturday."

At the counter he asked the cashier if she still felt homesick for China.

"Sometimes, but I've made friends here. There are two Chinese fellows who work upstairs."

"What about students from Taiwan and Hong Kong?"

"Oh, I'd get in trouble going with them."

"Japanese life seems to suit you. Well, see you tomorrow."

When Joe stepped out of the coffee shop, an august party of eight somber-looking business and diplomatic types were entering the main dining room at the far end of the lobby. He recognized PeterYu immediately because he was strutting with arms held out from his body as though they'd been fractured and weren't fully back to normal. The fellow who precededYu and stayed close to Anthony Loh was one of the men seated next to them at the press club.

Joe was perplexed about why at their first meeting Peter had said he wanted to talk to him.

When Joe rejoined the others, Reardon asked, "How are we going to use our time tomorrow?"

At that moment the automatic front door swung open. What Joe had faintly suspected of being the beating of shrine drums suddenly sounded loud and clear.

"Those are festival drums," he said. "Anyone game for going to the shrine tonight? You don't have to pray to the dead soldiers. No one will mind if we just look. It will give you an idea of how patriotism still flows in the veins of the Japanese even after fifty years of peace."

Sensing he had a captive audience, Joe pontificated, "I'd wager that if Watanabe had been killed in Hong Kong, his soul would be enshrined here. They'd worship him along with the others."

"Even if he opposed the War?" Eric asked.

"What shall we do in the morning?" Reardon asked again. "Red Knight wants us over at BTV around 11:00."

"Why don't you join us here for breakfast? Take a Hotel map and show it to the taxi driver. We can be done with breakfast by 9:00 or so, stroll through the shrine grounds while it's cool, then go to the office behind the shrine. It will be quiet and private there. We can take a cab to BTV from there. Lots of places in Roppongi area where we can eat lunch. What do you think?"

"I'm not here to sightsee," Reardon objected.

"Yasukuni," Eric said, "will give you a feel for the Japanese spirit."

"Explain yourself."

Looking toward Joe, Eric reluctantly began. "The Japanese have some weird ideas by Western standards, but..." He couldn't find the right words to explain it.

"See if this says it," Joe asked Eric. "The Japanese have a gut feeling that they're unique. The festivals and the people feed on each other, so the ancient tradition lives on alive and well."

"Would it be fair to say," Reardon posited, "that it's more feeling than reason?"

"I wouldn't want to say Japanese are unreasonable; yet, in a certain sense it's true. Or, said differently, by including passion in their thought, their minds transcend Western-style Greek logic. You've got to feel it. We must remember they are an island people — shut off from the world for 250 years up until the mid-1800s. They communicate more by feeling and body language than by words. But never make General MacArthur's mistake and say they're like twelve-year olds."

Eilers, who had been waiting for them to get their act together, came over and pulled Joe aside. "My Japanese is a little rusty. Would you mind helping me talk with the hotel manager, confidentially?"

They walked over to the front counter, and in Japanese Joe requested to see the manager.

"A problem, sir?" the clerk asked.

"Yes, Mr. Eilers wishes to talk privately with the manager."

Showing no hurt feelings for being by-passed, the clerk informed them that the manager had left, but his assistant, Nakagawa-san, could see them.

When Nakagawa-san came out, he looked at Joe, who looked back at him. Joe recognized him at once.

"Are you at this hotel now?" he asked. "One of us must be following the other. Since Nikkatsu days, isn't this the third or fourth hotel where we've met? Yurakucho, Osaka, Mitaka, and now here."

"Order in some coffee," he said to the clerk. "I'll talk with them back in the office. Mr. Orimura and I are old friends."

"Please, no drinks," Eilers interrupted. "We had coffee with our supper. This will only take a minute. I know you're busy."

Joe could see Eilers didn't need an interpreter with Nakagawa. Why had he asked Joe to accompany him? Did he need a witness, or was he really unsure of his own Japanese language ability? Eilers looked more comfortable knowing that Nakagawa and he were friends.

"This must be kept confidential," Eilers began in almost a whisper, "so please keep it to yourself. To state it briefly, someone sneaked into my room the last time I visited Tokyo, not at this hotel. This time I did not want anyone getting a hold of the plans I brought with me. I suspected they'd try again; so, I purposely left fake plans in my unlocked briefcase when we came down for supper."

"You certainly fooled me," Joe exclaimed, but Nakagawa showed shock and wanted to know what happened.

"I sprinkled what we in our company call "star dust" around the briefcase on the carpet. It's invisible to the eye and harms nothing. When I returned to the room to get the briefcase which I had pretended to forget, someone already had visited the room and presumably photographed the plans."

Nakagawa stood up and went to the door and ordered the clerk to call the police, *"Keisatsu o yonde kure!"*

But before the clerk could make the call, Eilers stopped him. "Please, no police. We can handle this without them. You have a security man don't you? Have him join us up at my room. I'm sure I can tell you who did it."

Joe looked on in awe, not knowing what to say.

He and Nakagawa hurried after Eilers to the elevator. At the 6th floor the security man was there waiting for them and led them down the hall. Entering the room with him, Eilers slipped on a pair of very dark green glasses.

"Here they are," Eilers said as though he knew all the time.

Eilers went back into the hall and headed toward the elevator as though tracking invisible footprints. A bloodhound could not have done it swifter. Joe and Nakagawa had to run to keep up with Eilers and the guardman.

When they reached the service elevator, Eilers called it up to the 6th floor and they all descended to the basement. Continuing to trace the tracks, Eilers entered a room labeled in Japanese, "Male Employees Only."

Eilers walked straight to locker number 51 and asked Nakagawa, "Do we need special permission to open this?"

He looked perplexed and shrugged his shoulders. "I'm not sure." The guardman assured him in Japanese that every new employee had signed a statement permitting a search of his locker at any time, even without cause. "That's because we've had some drug dealing and thievery in the past. Nowadays we have to hire foreigners. Young Japanese refuse to work as bellboys."

The guardman pulled out a batch of keys and picked the one for Locker No 51. He opened it and felt through the pockets of a windbreaker hanging there. Then he searched a small handbag lying on top of a pair of smelly Mizuno running shoes.

"I think I've found it," he said, as he held up a classy Minolta Capios 115 camera.

"Open it up," Nakagawa ordered

But the security man held up his hand to object. "We'd ruin the film," he warned in Japanese. "Let's check to see if there's film in it. Here on the side, you ought to be able to see if it's loaded."

"Nothing," Joe said. "He's already taken the film out. Boy, he worked fast. Whose locker is this?"

"There's a list on the wall," the guardman said as he read down the names. "Here is 51, name is Lee Feng, a student at Hosei."

Expecting Eilers to want the police called in now, Joe and the other two were surprised when Eilers vetoed the idea. "No need for police. Just warn the young man. Someone probably pressured him or tempted him with quick cash. The PRC students have a rough time making ends meet."

"Couldn't the cadre supervisor have forced him to do it?"

"We shouldn't presume," Eilers explained, "that Feng is politically motivated. He probably just needed money. Mr. Nakagawa, please treat him kindly; he could have been our son, right?"

Joe could see why Eric showed such affection for his stepfather.

Joining the others in the lobby, Eric promptly made out as if he were scolding his father, "Ralph, you said you'd be gone only a few minutes. It took you twenty."

Looking hurt, Eilers pointed at Joe. "It's his fault. He interpreted too slowly."

"Excuses, excuses!" Eric chided.

"Well," Joe asked, "what did you decide about tonight?"

Reardon, spoke as though reciting words memorized long ago: "Tonight we shall let the dead worship the dead, but tomorrow, we must visit the war dead of Yasukuni. Eric claims that will help me understand why the Japanese military in Hong Kong despised the British POWs so much. Let's hope we'll have a clearer vision in the morning. See you here at 8:00."

14

Spirits of the Dead

Upstairs in his room, Joe didn't bother to flick on the television. He'd been holed up at Nojiri away from "civilization" so long he'd broken the TV habit. He took off his shoes and stretched out on the bedspread. Gazing up at the blank ceiling, he reviewed the events of the day, then heaving a sigh, offered up a strange thanksgiving to God, "No fish on Friday like back at Pilgrim Place." He prayed audibly, as though God needed to hear his voice, "Wish I could take those American cooks just once to the Nojiri Asumaro Trout Farm for a real fish dinner."

Unconsciously he reached for the telephone, forgetting that Anita had no phone in the cabin. Instead he decided to send a telegram after he found out which train he'd catch tomorrow. Seeing the mini-refrigerator in the alcove by the door, he walked over and pulled out a can of caffeine-free Pepsi to go with his leftover cheese sandwich. He took two pills to help him sleep, then finished with a handful of Nagano peanuts.

The telephone rang. "Hello, yes, this is Orimura. Who is this?"even though he already knew it was Mei Li Ping.

"Sorry to bother you. You weren't sleeping, were you?" she teased.

"Came in only a few minutes ago."

"Mr. Knight hopes you and Eric will be able to visit us tomorrow morning with Mr. Reardon."

"Yes, we know. We're planning to be there about 11:00 after visiting Yasukuni Shrine. Is that okay? See you tomorrow."

Hanging up, Joe wondered how she had found out he was staying at the Fairmont. With that mystery to mull over, he loosened the sheets that had been tucked too tight. Crawling into bed, he complained aloud, "Why do hotel maids have to tuck in sheets so tight? No one can sleep with them that way."

Finally working it loose enough to stick up his toes, he prayed, "Thanks, Lord for a good day — even though I'm still mystified and unsettled. Amen." He tacked on an afterthought, "I'm not lost, I just don't know where I am."

As he lay there reminiscing about God's unfathomable graciousness, he asked himself what-if questions: What if Dr. Gallagher hadn't discovered his prostate cancer and what if the radiation had proved ineffective, he might never have returned to Japan this summer. He never could have met Reardon, Eric and Eilers, and this Miss Ping.

With such thankful thoughts, he floated off to unconsciousness and slept undisturbed through the night, until shortly before sunrise a soft tapping noise awakened him. It sounded so real he assumed someone was trying to wake him. The rapping continued, yet not in a steady beat, but rather unevenly like a coded message. Sliding out of bed, he padded across the room and pressed his ear flat against the door. He peered out through the security peephole, but didn't see anyone, only a slight movement of what he took to be a shadow cast on the door opposite his.

Leaning flush against the door, he waited and waited, expecting he knew not what. He didn't move until after the first shaft of light drifted through the crack between the drapes and the wall. What further bewildered him was a weird waking dream about Watanabe himself, making him wonder if the pastor's ghost wasn't hovering over him like a guardian angel.

Or was it only auto-suggestion, a mere projection of a desire to capture Watanabe's spirit? Or could it have been a mental trick triggered by what he'd said yesterday about his being enshrined in Yasukuni with the other loyal patriots of the the Great War?

Hoping to sleep at least another hour, Joe scooted back into bed. He turned over on his right side with his back facing the outside and promptly fell asleep, confident his internal alarm would wake him at 6:00.

He didn't rouse till nearly 7:00. When he opened his eyes and saw the clock, he realized he'd been more tired than he thought. Moving over to the window, he flung back the drapes and sat down next to the coffee table. He pulled out his prayerbook from his black handbag and opened to Saturday. The lessons and prayers spoke of the transitoriness of life, and he recalled his early morning jogs every Saturday through theTama Reien Cemetery.

"Lord, you have been biding your time eight long years since I vowed to complete the Watanabe project. You have taught us to believe you hear our prayers, even though sometimes our faith falters. I hope I won't become like one of those farmers who gathered at church to pray for rain, but didn't bring an umbrella."

By the time Joe had showered, shaved and trimmed his shaggy sideburns, the clock read 7:45, time to go down to reserve a quiet corner table in the dining room. When he exited the elevator, he was relieved to see Reardon waiting in the lobby. There was no sign of the plainclothesmen who had been bird-dogging them on Friday.

Everyone was more than ready to eat, especially Eric and his stepfather, who normally would have been eating dinner at this time in the States.

As they entered the dining room, Joe caught sight of the two waiters turning to whisper to each other as Eilers walked by. Word about the theft must have leaked out.

71

Breakfast came and went with little conversation. Each one seemed to be nursing his own agenda, waiting for the right moment to introduce it.

"Did Nakagawa contact you afterward?" Joe decided to ask Eilers. "It would be interesting to know how he dealt with the thief."

"He didn't contact me, but that's all finished. No need to fret over it."

"Last night," Eric said, "the shrine drums were beating till 10 o'clock. Kept me awake. The plaza must be a mess this morning."

"Would you like to join us today, Ralph?" Joe suggested.

"Thanks, but I'm off to more meetings starting at 9:30. Most Japanese don't take Saturday off."

"We're working, too," Reardon declared. "We must put in some solid work today. Can we cut this sightseeing short and get talking before we lose the day? I'll call Knight to tell him we can't see him before 12:30."

"Okay by me," Joe consented. "Why don't you tell them to meet us at International House around 12:30? That's a quiet place to talk and eat."

Reardon excused himself to phone Knight at home. By the time the waiter had poured coffee refills, Reardon was back. "All set," he announced. "The Chinese secretary will join us. You don't think she's got eyes on Eric do you?"

Ralph couldn't contain his laugh. Trying a bit of wit, he said, "Ah, so you're interested in Asian matters?"

Throwing the joke back at his father, Eric said, "Don't worry, I wouldn't marry her without Mom here." Pausing to build up suspense, he added the punch line, "Engagement maybe, but no wedding without mother."

"It looks like we'll have to take Eric to lunch with us after all," Joe laughed. "Not sure when we'll see you, Ralph. Good luck on whatever you're up to."

As they left the hotel, they unconsciously picked up speed. Walking by the Indian Embassy on the left and crossing Yasukuni Boulevard by the South *torii*-gate, they saw tours of elderly pilgrims piling out of buses and queuing up behind their guides' flags.

"If you were to pry open each of those people," Joe said, "you'd uncover a terrible grief over a husband, brother, or father killed in the War. The pain never leaves. Here at Yasukuni the pilgrims go through a catharsis as they enter into a spiritual union with the souls of the dead. It's not inner peace as we know it. Rather, they receive a measure of satisfaction for having done their part by doing the pilgrimmage to Yasukuni. They're proving loyalty to the dead and the Emperor, even though the War ended fifty years ago.

"In D.C. we don't have any memorial to those who died in World War II," Eric said. "I wonder why? Does anyone know?"

"One morning in late August last year," Joe said, "I was climbing up Kudan Hill from the subway station below. The morning sun was casting a glow over Yasukuni's huge cedar trees and the *torii* at the main East entrance. Moved with melancholy, I paused halfway up the hill and tried to capture the moment in a *haiku*, not very good, but I tried.

"Let me see if I have it in my notebook. People who compose *haiku* always carry a notebook. You can never tell when a scene or incident will trigger inspiration. Here it is:

> *"Shusenbi* Armistice Day
> *Kudan no kaidan* On the stairs of Kudan
> *Ashi omoshi* My legs feel heavy"

They had to wait to cross the street which bisects the shrine grounds, so Joe continued to share his thoughts. "I never stroll through here without painful memories of our shared past as Americans and Japanese. How tragic the Japanese were tempted to believe their tribal Shinto religion could be forced onto the rest of Asia. Not all that different from our hubris in believing American-style democracy can cure a country's problems. We all fashion idols in our own image."

"We British never did that," Jack retorted with a face full of sarcasm. "When will we ever learn?"

Walking by memorials to war heroes and under another *torii*, they approached the Divine Gate. Going straight ahead a hundred meters or so, they came to the bottom of the stairs that ascended to the Hall of Worship, the holy of holies. There, a broad 30-40 foot high purple drape imprinted with four huge white chrysanthemums, the imperial seal, concealed the inner sanctum.

"Has anyone pointed out how similar this is to the ancient temple in Jerusalem?" Reardon asked.

"I've never made a study of that, but I know some people have. There are other similarities, too. Whether there actually was Jewish influence in ancient Japan, I don't know. We do know that many Jews settled in China centuries ago, Nestorian Christians also. One Syrian missionary claims the Nestorians reached Himeji, Japan, a millenium ago."

Before entering the path on the right that led to the *Yushukan*-museum which displays memorabilia left by the war dead, they stopped at the kiosk to pick up some picture postcards and an English pamphlet explaining Yasukuni. They also examined the various good-luck charms.

Not bothering to enter the war museum, Joe led Reardon and Eric out a back gate onto the street. Pointing to the dirty beige-colored Belvedere Kudan Building, Joe said, "The Lutheran Hour office is on the second floor of that old building. It's not much on the outside, but the inside is nice."

To enter they had to cut through a ground-level parking garage. The watchman sitting in his cubbyhole next to the elevator was preoccupied with aTV program and didn't take his eyes off the screen. They boarded the decrepit pre-War elevator and waited for the door to clang shut. The floor lurched sideways before the capsule clunked its way up to the second floor. Joe led the way to a covered balcony outside the door to the cramped quarters of the Lutheran media ministry. Switching on the overhead lights and air-conditioner, he invited Jack and Eric to take a seat on the faded-orange couch, while he made a pot of coffee.

"There won't be any interruptions here on Saturday. No one would have thought to bug this room," Joe assured Jack.

Eric pulled out his Walkman, but set it down when Joe began to brief them on how the church used the media. "In the '50s and '60s we used radio drama, but changed to disc-jockey and preaching formats. We had several ventures into television — now a lot with music CDs and the Internet."

Joe went back to the coffee maker, but when he came back and began to pour, the telephone rang. "Probably a wrong number," but he immediately recognized Miss Ping's voice. "How did you know we were here?"

Looking over to Reardon, he whispered, "It's the Chinese woman. What time shall we meet them? Didn't you tell them 12:30?"

"We'll see you at International House lobby about 12:30. We're busy until then."

No sooner had Joe set the phone down when Reardon leaned forward. By his strained look, Joe guessed he had a question he'd been formulating for some time. With measured restraint, he asked, "Why did you try to make a movie in the 1980s about this Pastor Watanabe?"

Taken aback by Reardon's bluntness, Joe fumbled for the right words and retreated to a safe reply. "I've written that up. I must give you a copy. We believed his example during the occupation of Hong Kong could counteract the criticism other nations were making of the Japanese. The vast majority of whom were not monsters or monkeymen as depicted in the wartime propaganda. Our media director in Hong Kong, David Chiang, told us he'd never heard of a Japanese like this Kiyoshi Watanabe. He'd only regarded them as bloodthirsty fanatics.

"Jack, if ever a human being embodied the essence of love and reconciliation, it was Kiyoshi Watanabe. If that's the message you want to give, he's your man."

Reardon responded, "My father had a friend at Shamshuipo. He said the same thing about him."

"That was fifty years ago," questioned Eric. "How can you fit a Japanese into a telecast for Chinese?"

"That's the genius of it. Don't you see," Reardon fired back. "The audience will have to infer the connection. By going back to the War years and telling how a Japanese overcame the dangers under an occupying army, Hong Kong Chinese can find a role model in an Asian like themselves."

"I don't want to pour cold water on that," Joe barged in, "but wait a minute. If Beijing gets upset over this, everyone will conclude it was because they recognized themselves as an occupying force, not a liberating one. It produces a Catch 22 situation for them. Any reaction at all will be wrong, no matter what. They'll have to let the project proceed."

"I follow you," Jack agreed.

"Another end to that scenario might happen, too. Let me play the devil's advocate for a second. Suppose Beijing gets wind of your hidden agenda, won't we be dead in the water? They're clever. They have ways to find out what you're up to. They've got ears everywhere."

"Yeah, Dad found that out."

"Can I assume, Jack, that your backers want Hong Kong to succeed after 1997, or do they have some other motive? You're not funded by the Kuomintang Nationalists inTaiwan are you?"

"Absolutely not! I'll walk out if anyone tries to control me. I've walked before, and I'd do it again. They know that, and I've told them so. 'The ball's yours,' they said."

"But," Joe questioned, "Taiwan money also gets spread around in unexpected places. Are you certain money will be no problem?"

"My sponsors will finance everything within reason."

"Yet," Joe asked, "if you have to build sets and do a lot of filming in Macao or Taiwan, won't you use up the money fast? Will you dramatize part of the story?"

"That depends, but I'm hoping to avoid putting out money for actors. That adds up fast. I want to keep costs to a minimum. Your materials, Joe, are crucial. You musn't let me down."

"I've been thinking, Jack. You'll need someone on the ground in Hong Kong. British TV people won't do. They're too conspicuous. You need a real insider, someone within the TV industry you can trust, a Chinese person who'll be your guide through the mine fields."

"Tall order! How do we find him? Or, her? I'm leary of my old Hong Kong contacts. They'd arouse suspicions. I can't fail, but I'm stymied."

"Coffee. I'll go bring the pot." As he returned, he stopped before pouring refills. "You know what, there's a Chinese TV producer, Andrew Liu. He might be just the man. He's done film work in California, but keeps his Hong Kong base, too."

After a deadening silence, Reardon would only say, "I suppose it wouldn't hurt to contact him. He won't blab about, will he?"

"Absolutely not. He's a pro of the pros. Baptist, I believe. I've known him over ten years, a very open kind of a guy. You'd like him. His wife is experienced in marketing."

"How do we get a hold of him?"

"Let me check my datebook. I've got his phone number in Monterey Park. Let's see."

While Reardon was biting his forefinger, Joe found the number and calculated the difference in time between Pacific Daylight Savings Time and Japan. "It's 6 p.m. on the West coast. Perfect. Okay if I try to catch him?"

Reardon nodded. "Yeah, go on; it can't hurt. Find out if he's available."

Moving back to one of the desks, Joe punched in Liu's number. Maurene, Liu's wife, answered. Joe, not wanting to disrupt the others' conversation, softly explained what he wished to ask Andrew about.

"Andy's out on location near Mt. Baldy," she said. "He's shooting scenery for a new *karaoke*. He'll be home Saturday night."

"Tell him I'll call him about 9:00 your time Saturday night. God bless! *Dzaizyan!*"

Returning to Reardon and Eric, he said, "Andrew Liu won't be home till Saturday night, California time. I promised to call him Sunday 1 p.m., Japan time. Where were we in our talk?"

"If we go the drama route," Reardon said, "it will be hard to hide what we're doing." They continued to muddle along in their talking, then Reardon banged his fist on the table. "We're not getting anywhere."

"I agree," Joe said. "Why don't we go about this differently. It may sound crazy, but I think the most practical first step is to see what of my materials you can use. You have to look over them yourself. I can't decide for you, Jack. Then we can brainstorm more realistically. What do you think?"

"Makes sense, but ..." he hesitated. "What's your proposal?"

Leaning forward, Joe elaborated, "Wild, but I don't think so. Don't laugh! How does this sound? You call Knight and ask if we can take a raincheck on lunch. If he agrees, I propose we cut off discussion right now, run back to the hotels, check out and go for the 1 o'clock train to Nojiri."

"You're crazy!" Reardon looked at Eric for agreement.

"Well, what about you, Eric? Leave your dad a note with my Nojiri neighbor's telephone number on it. You can call him tonight and explain what we're doing. Don't pack much. Leave most of your stuff with Ralph at the hotel. You don't have any must-do dates for Sunday and Monday, right?"

"Nothing that can't wait." But by the strained tilt of his head, Joe knew Eric wasn't sure how his father would take it.

Reardon said, "Let me check with Knight."

"Before you call — I don't know how you can do it — is there any way to ask him how reliable this Miss Ping is? She's been a little too smooth for my comfort — very nosey about what we're doing. Sorry about that, Eric, but we can't be leaking secrets."

"I don't think Knight would hire anybody, especially a Chinese, without a security check, but if it makes you happy, I'll ask him."

While Reardon was telephoning Bill Knight, Joe went back into the corner to check on some reports he'd stored there. Over the sound of the noisy air conditioner, he heard Reardon break out in laughter.

"Get this, Reverend Orimura, your suspicious Dragon Lady turns out to be a Christian. The way Red Knight tells it, Miss Ping's father fought in the Nationalist Army against the Japanese and later against Mao Zedong. The Reds captured him, but he escaped. Some Christian farmers hid him and converted him. He eventually fled and sneaked away toTaiwan. Miss Ping heard about Watanabe from her father, who said he knows you."

"Why didn't she say so?

"At the press club, she was on the verge of telling you, but she was afraid those two *yakuza* types might overhear her."

"Marvel of marvels!" Joe thought for a moment and then asked, "Her Taiwan connections won't compromise her, will they?" Answering his own question, he said, "That's always a possibility, but we could use her Chinese perspective. We can learn how she interprets history. If she's ever lived in Hong Kong, it would be better yet. Maybe she should go along with us to Nojiri." Trying to read Eric's face, he added, "On a three-hour train ride, we can get to know her pretty well."

Reardon called BTV. "Sorry to keep you waiting, Red. We've been talking here. Do you think you could give Miss Ping Sunday and Monday off? We'd like her to go up to Nagano with us. We need a Chinese point of view... 'No problem,' Knight says. She has off until next Wednesday anyway, but he'll ask her."

They waited, surprised at how fast the new plan was gelling.

"Okay," he says. "She needs to run home to pack. Rather than waste time eating somewhere, she suggests we meet in front of the wicket for the 1 o'clock train. Wants us to buy her ticket, non-smoking if possible."

"Will do. Tell her we'll see her about 12:40. Thanks! Red, we can catch up on things when we get back from the lake."

"My watch says, 10:30," Joe said. "If we leave right away, we can make that 1 o'clock train. Let's take a cab to the Fairmont. Jack, you can stay in and go on to the Marunouchi, pack and check out. We'll meet you there outside the front door at 11:45. Since it's Saturday, traffic should be lighter than usual. We'll hang on to the taxi and go together to Ueno. Let's close shop here and be off."

15

Flight to the Mountains

A taxi was parked across the street, with the driver sound asleep.

"I never thought," Reardon said, "a Japanese would get caught asleep on the job."

"You must understand," Joe explained, "Tokyo cabbies often work a 24-hour shift every other day. It's not uncommon to find cabs on side streets with the worn-out drivers stretched out in sleep."

Joe tapped on the door, and they got in. The sleepy driver soon had them passing through the empty crossroad that cuts through Yasukuni and at the second corner turned down a side street leading into the cherry-lined street alongside the Fairmont. Reardon stayed in the car and continued on to his hotel, but Eric and Joe hopped out and hurried up the elevator to their rooms on the 6th floor. Since Joe had already packed, he took a couple minutes to telephone his neighbor at Nojiri to let Anita know three unexpected guests were arriving on the 4:19 train.

Checking one last time around the room, he closed the door and walked down the corridor to Eric and Ralph's suite. The door stood ajar. Eric had not begun packing. He sat slumped over in the big yellow armchair next to the window, his arms reaching out over the coffee table in front of him.

Sensing that something grave had delayed his packing, Joe asked what was wrong. Drawing closer, Joe saw Eric's hands clutching both sides of a large piece of blood-red paper. Peering up at Joe, he asked, "Do you know what this Japanese character means? I think I know, but I'm not sure."

By the squarish calligraphy style, Joe could tell that a Japanese had not written it. There wasn't the customary irregular, flowing grass style which they cherish. It looked like the even, precise work of a Chinese. The simplified stroking suggested a younger person, someone schooled on the mainland since the Cultural Revolution.

"Eric, you have good reason to be frightened by this character. It means, 'Beware,' what a warning sign says if danger lies ahead."

When Joe took the paper from Eric and held it up closer to the window, small Roman letters became visible in the lower right corner. As best as he could make out, they read, "Sub-LRPS."

"Eric, what in the world do these letters stand for? Some kind of secret society?"

Lifting the other armchair opposite from Eric, Joe sat befuddled, not knowing how to re-start the conversation. Following a long silence, he reached across to squeeze Eric's extended arms and stared into his frightened eyes.

"Listen, Eric, this is no prank. Someone is warning Ralph. Do you have any idea what the letters mean?"

Eric looked trapped so that he turned and gazed vacantly out the window over the tops of the cherry trees toward the Martial Arts Building. He didn't seem to be looking at anything in particular. Finally, eeking out grunt-like whispers, as if a demon were strangling his throat, he said he feared what the letters might signify.

Eric began methodically gathering up his toilet articles, clean underwear, shirts and socks. Holding up a pair of brightly patterned swim trunks, he forced a grin. "Shouldn't forget these, should I? To be honest, Orimura-san, I'm worried about Ralph. He's into something dangerous."

Eric resembled a little boy pretending not to be afraid — whistling in the dark. His hesitant, jerky movements showed he wasn't sure he should run off from his stepfather, but he tagged behind Joe anyway, looking like a child who didn't dare be left behind.

From the lobby Joe telephoned Reardon to remind him to meet them outside the Marunouchi entrance. That way they'd save time by holding on to the taxi.

Twenty minutes later as they swung by Tokyo Station, a red light stopped them. Office workers were streaming out of buildings, rushing for seats at noon-time food shops. Those who had Saturday afternoon off were heading across the black-and-white striped safety walk to catch early trains for home.

At the next corner, the driver turned left and pulled up next to the Marunouchi's impressive post-War-vintage marquee, but Reardon was nowhere in sight. After waiting a good two minutes, Joe jumped out to go inside to call his room. As he stepped into the revolving door, Reardon went by him on the way out, so Joe stayed in and followed him back out to the entrance landing. Jack had ripped open a Federal Express packet and was speed-reading the enclosed letter.

"Foul! That's not fair!" he sputtered under his breath and crumpled it up and stuffed the wad into the breastpocket of his safari-shirt. His usual faded-out, tubercular complexion had flushed to a drinker's red, the veins in his neck taut enough to burst.

"You okay?" Joe asked. "Hope it's not bad news."

Joe couldn't keep himself from speculating. If it was such an important message, why hadn't it been faxed? Then he realized it must be something too confidential to fax in care of a hotel, and he suppressed his own curiosity to ask about it.

By the time they had passed Kanda Station, Joe suggested that before they reach Ueno, they ought to map out strategy for the week-end. "We also need" he said, "to talk about how best to fit Miss Ping into the discussions. We don't want to repeat everything to her."

"The only point we need to agree on," Reardon said, "is that Miss Ping must swear to secrecy. We can't have her informing Knight. Bill is an old friend, but he's also a potential competitor, and I'm not 100 percent certain we'll broadcast over British Television. I'll have to satisfy Red somehow with generalities — even though I personally prefer using BTV."

Because it was Saturday, traffic was light. As they walked into Ueno Station, Reardon asked Joe to buy First Class seats, but Joe answered, "Japanese don't speak of class anymore. They use a euphemism, Green Car, because of the green-colored marking on the outside. Joe hadn't ridden in a Green Car since the late '50s. It felt like splurging, but Jack was paying. The upside would be they'd have plenty of leg room and access to Western toilets.

"Four Green Car seats for Nagano on the one o'clock train," he asked at the counter.

"Sorry, all sold out, only Economy left."

"Jack, no Green Car seats. We'll have to go Economy, sorry."

Joe led them over to the wicket. "Wait here. I'll go buy our lunches at the kiosk."

After studying the choices, he picked out an assortment of egg-salad, vegetable, and ham sandwiches, Chinese *shumai* dumplings and two packages of *inarizushi*, a very common sushi made of seasoned rice stuffed inside a soybean wrapping, but with no raw fish. Uncooked fish can cause food poisoning in hot weather. Because of Jack's alchoholism, he avoided beer and bought four cans of hot Chinese *oloong* tea and Diet Cola.

When he returned, Miss Ping, decked out in blue denim hiking shorts and sporting a Chinese-red backpack, came prancing in and shouted above the crowd, "Hope you haven't waited long!"

Gathering up their bags, they squeezed single-file through the narrow wicket and boarded the train. Seeing that Joe's hands were full with lunch goodies, Eric took advantage of Joe's helplessness to lift off Miss Ping's backpack and hoist it onto the baggage rack. With a newly found deference for his seniors, Eric offered Jack and Joe the window seats, which left him face to face with Miss Ping on the aisle.

Instead of concern about the threat to Ralph Eilers, it looked to Joe as though Eric now would have to worry about how to talk with Miss Ping. Nervous twitches suggested Eric's insides were churning over how to sound interesting. He'd have to converse for a long 3-hour ride. That had to be intimidating to a teenager. Besides, he'd have to avoid noticing her long, tanned legs. What happens if Eric's legs rub up against hers?

If they hadn't had food and drinks to handle, Eric never would have been able to surmount his awkwardness. But all four of them soon forgot they'd not known each other from before. The challenge that Reardon had laid out pulled them into a common whirlpool of events, ideas, people and goals. A force stronger than their individual wills had begun to stir them into a single purpose.

Conscious of rumbling wheels beneath them, Joe closed his eyes and repeated God's promise to him. "Let me go forth desiring the coming of thy glory. Let me go forward, for thy glory shall be revealed."

If it was God's Word that created the heavens and the earth, he reasoned, why can't the same Word transform people through this story? If the Ayatollah Khomeni could spark his revolution with mere audio cassettes, why can't we do more — with all the media as our weapons?"

Opening his eyes, Joe looked at each of his cohorts: a stunning Chinese journalist committed to Christ and a proven documentary producer in search of a defining moment of artistic greatness. Joe hoped Watanabe could light the way for millions groping in the twilight of cynicism and despair. Then there was Eric, a 17-year old with eyes open to see how all this might happen.

Suddenly Eric surprised them all. Like a fresh born-again convert, he confronted Miss Ping, "Are you a Christian?"

The spark in her eyes told him, yes, which, of course, he already knew.

"Would you mind if I called you Mei Li?"

Reardon choked on his food and spilled a soy-sauce soaked dumpling over his shirt, but Miss Ping showed no annoyance over Eric's brashness. Instead she looked pleased. "Thank you for asking. Mei Li is fine. As for my faith, do you think I'd want any part of this project if I weren't a believer?"

Reardon rubbed the blotches on his shirt, but avoided any verbal reaction to Eric's questions.

"Growing up in Taiwan," Mei Li continued, "I'd heard how the Japanese oppressed the people during the occupation of Taiwan. That began back in 1895. At graduate school in Hong Kong, I had a chance to see a film that documented Japanese atrocities, like the Rape of Nanking. But my father helped me realize that hate gets us nowhere. Not all Japanese approved of what their soldiers did."

"That may have been the same film I sat through in Hong Kong with David Chiang. Gruesome spectacle!"

"It was only when my father told me about this Pastor Watanabe that I had something of a conversion — or re-conversion."

"Watanabe affected many A-bomb survivors that way, too," Joe said. "Four of the first fifteen post-war converts were *hibakusha*."

"Papa had baptized me as a baby, but I'd fallen away. I thought and acted like everyone else my age. Papa knew I'd been drifting aimlessly, so one night he asked me pointblank, 'Mei Li, if you were arrested for being a Christian, would there be enough evidence to convict you?' Wow! That did it, but I'd better not bore you with details."

Turning their heads, they began to notice the scenery. Speeding by towns and villages, mountains and valleys, forests and streams, the train soon reached Yokokawa. There, a second electric locomotive would be attached in back for the steep, arduous climb up through twenty-eight tunnels leading to the resort town of Karuizawa.

As soon as the train halted, Joe jumped off and raced on the heels of several college-age fellows running toward the queue of travelers lined up at the kiosk. Everyone wanted to buy steaming bowls of Yokokawa hot dish. Joe settled for two bowls, which they could eat along with the other foods. But he'd not anticipated the consequences of dividing two bowls between the four of them.

Carrying a bowl in each hand, he climbed back on the train and returned to the others. While he was shoving the right bowl down into Reardon's lap, Mei Li grabbed the other one. Like an automated Oriental wife, she took over serving chores, but not exactly in the traditional fashion. She dug her own chopsticks into the pungent sauce-smothered rice and slid them into Eric's awe-struck mouth.

Jumping catfish! Joe thought to himself. What's this going to lead to? Before Eric could clear his throat, she stuffed down another mouthful. He gulped the food down noisily and at such a torrid Chinese-coolie pace, he looked helpless.

"Look there!" Joe blurted out to distract her. "It's the new Olympic freeway bridge over the gorge. He was sure if he hadn't distracted her, Eric never could have stopped her, short of brute force. Not hiding her disappointment, she finished off the few remaining mouthfuls herself.

Joe couldn't but wonder how he might contain, or rather harness this bundle of temptation. She could easily divert them from their goal.

At the grandfatherly age of 72, Joe felt responsible. He mustn't shirk from monitoring them. More often than they like to admit, Christians in the name of love and freedom have cut the leashes that hold their libidos in check — with scandalous consequences.

Joe was surprised to see that Reardon handled chopsticks quite well, but didn't imitate Mei Li by feeding him. Instead Jack carefully pushed out some of the hot rice-dish into Joe's *sushi*-box, permitting Joe to use his own chopsticks.

The train speeded up for several miles after reaching the top of the long incline and then slowed down to stop at the resort town of Karuizawa, the highest point on the trip. As the train jerked to a full stop, two *yakuza*-type men wearing dark sunglasses and navy blue suits, which made them very conspicuous among the casually dressed vacationers, boarded. Joe recognized one of them as PeterYu. No mistaking that swagger. Even when carrying two suitcases, Yu kept his arms extended outward several inches on each side. The man with him looked like he might be the same fellow who had tailed them into the tearoom at theTransportation Building.

There was no way Joe & Co. could avoid being recognized by Yu, so Joe decided to take the initiative. Standing up and leaning over Eric, he waved toYu, who was facing their direction.

"Peter, did you stay at Karuizawa last night?"

"No, we came up early this morning. We've been checking on one of the new VIP hotels. Beautiful spot. They've built it along a rushing stream from off the volcano."

Because other passengers couldn't get through the aisle, Yu and his comrade went back to their seats and hoisted their bags up onto the overhead rack. Then a grinning Peter came over to talk.

Smiling so Joe would notice, he said, "Tonight we have to test the Prince Hotel on Lake Nojiri. Is that near your place?

"Not far. It's directly opposite us."

"Say," he began as though he'd just remembered something, "what ever happened to that movie you and David Chiang were working on?"

"It fell through."

Hiding any emotion, Yu nodded and added, "Good thing for you. We Chinese were incensed those days over that Japanese professor who claimed the Rape of Nanking never occured. We'd never accept a Jap as a hero."

That racial slur ticked off Reardon, who jumped up to rebut Peter, but Joe stopped him short by latching onto his sleeve. "Cool it, Jack, a lot of people still call them Japs, but don't realize how offensive it is.

"Peter, I don't believe I introduced my friends to you before? This is Jack Reardon, Mei Li Ping and Eric Gunderson."

"You're quite a mix. Let me guess: an American missionary, a student, a young Chinese lady, and an Englishman. Did I guess right?"

Eyeing Jack like a prosecuting attorney, he began to cross-examine him. "Haven't you been in Hong Kong? You look familiar. Journalist I'd wager."

Yu was getting much too inquisitive, prompting Joe to break off the conversation by suggesting, "Maybe we'll see you at the lake. Drop over. Church meets outside at 8:30 tomorrow on the tennis courts, near the grocery store."

After Peter went back to his seat, Reardon fumed. "Why did you say that? We don't want that fellow sniffing around."

"You're right. I knew I shouldn't have said it the moment I invited him." Thinking about his thoughtless error, he tried to humor Reardon. "You know, Jack, this is the first time I've ever felt guilty for inviting someone to church. Maybe there's a Japanese proverb we could apply here.

"Sugitaru wa nao oyobazaru ga gotoshi.

"Overdoing good is as bad as not doing enough good."

The uncoupling of the train cars shook Joe out of his thoughts. The train started up again and soon was speeding downward at full speed, outdistancing passenger cars on the parallel highway.

Evidences of the new stations for the Olympic Bullet Trains caused Reardon to ask, "How can they avoid gridlock on that road. Olympic traffic will overwhelm a two-lane highway."

"Nagano's economy already is stretched to the breaking point. When the economic bubble burst, it hit this area hard. On top of that the storms of '95 severely damaged the roads. They haven't repaired some of them yet."

"You're too pessimistic," Eric objected. "Japanese honor is at stake. The whole country will rally to Nagano's side."

"You're probably right," Joe admitted. "The *samurai* spirit came to the rescue for the 1964 Tokyo Olympics and probably will bring them through this time, too."

Joe's tone of finality stopped further conversation, and they reverted to private thoughts about the task ahead. But the more Joe thought about it, the more he felt a quiet agitation kicking within him. Small waves of doubt rippled across nerve endings, making his body ill at ease. He asked himself if these waves of doubt signaled a coming storm. *Why such vacillation? Why do we rise to heights of ecstatic faith one minute and fall into unbelief's "slough of despond" the next?*

Joe tried to cover up his anxieties by directing the others' attention out the window like a young tour guide reciting canned descriptions. In a singsong monotone he announced, "This is Nagano City, population 300,000, renowned for the great Zenkoji Temple and headquarters for the 1998 Winter Olympics. On the right they're constructing a magnificent Bullet Train Station. When completed, tourists will reach here from Tokyo in 90 minutes. Many visitors and athletes will commute from Tokyo."

The train slammed its doors shut and haltingly lurched forward straight north for the final ascent through the pass leading to the Japan Sea.

Following close beside historic Route 18, it marks the ancient path over which the silver and gold mined at Sado Island were transported by horse to the capital. Joe bragged overly much about how "civilized" the region had become — with McDonalds, Dennys, Mister Donut and Kentucky Fried Chicken — each offering guaranteed conformity of taste to even this hinterland.

The train crossed a river where a stoplight tried to coax motorists to rest at a mammoth Shell gas station. On both sides of the road, fruit stands stacked high with huge home-grown apples invited tourists to shop. Signs reminded customers to take advantage of the last public toilets this side of Lake Nojiri and Mt. Myoko's hot springs.

From there the train no longer raced along, but lazily wound its way upward parallel with the highway and a mountain stream. Even though a year had gone by since the torrential rains of July '95, work on the road and concrete bedding still lay unfinished.

Joe didn't notice that his spirit was becoming transformed. The winding roadway, rushing rapids, rock cliffs and densely forested slopes kindled memories of exciting family vacations. He realized that more than any other place on earth, Nojiri had become his family's spiritual home.

"I hope my wife found somebody to meet us at the station. Her Japanese driver's license has expired."

Over the intercom, the conductor called out, "Next stop Kurohime, all off for Lake Nojiri. Two minutes to go. Don't forget your baggage."

Reardon kept gazing blankly out the window, gripping the crumpled letter as though he might read it again. His hand pushed against his mouth. His eyes scanned the hillsides like a castle sentry looking for an approaching enemy.

When the doors swung open, a cool afternoon breeze with the fragrance of the ocean rushed in, reviving Joe and his three companions instantly. They paused, then breathed in deeply before stepping out onto the platform.

16

Horatio Chang's Curve

Climbing up the station stairs and down again to No. 1 platform, Joe spied his friend, Matt Collins, stretching his neck over the exit-railing and waving. Matt looked back over his shoulder to report to someone, whom Joe assumed to be Anita. Joe wondered how he was describing what the incoming guests looked like.

On Joe's right came the stocky, fiftyish Jack Reardon followed by Mei Li Ping in her blue shorts and red backpack. She strode with light confident steps unlike that of self-effacing Japanese women, resembling more a Takarazuka chorus girl. Close behind came lean and sinewy Eric Gunderson who could have passed for the actor who played Olympic sprinter Eric Liddell in *Chariots of Fire.*

After introductions, Reardon whispered to Joe, "How'd you ever get married to an Ingrid Bergman look alike?"

"Others have noticed that, too. You should have seen her play Joan of Lorraine in college. Maybe that's why some jokingly say I resemble Yul Brunner," and he patted his balding head.

They boarded Matt's Nissan van. He waited till they were seated, then slammed the broken panel-door shut with a clank like a cell door locking them in.

Instead of driving down Kashiwabara Village's shop-lined street, Matt turned left at the taxi stand, explaining that due to construction on the new Olympic freeway the usual road to the lake was closed.

Eric leaned forward from the rear seat to ask Anita, "Do they still mine gold and silver on Sado Island?"

"I know more about the birds there than about gold and silver. Great flocks of birds fly over Sado on their annual migrations to and from Siberia."

"The mines," Joe said with an authoritative school-teacher demeanor, "were opened up early in the 17th century. They used to produce up to 100 tons of gold a year — about the same time the feudal Tokugawa government tried to stamp out the *Kirishitan* Catholics and forbade contact with Catholic countries. They feared Spain or Portugal would subvert them. The edicts forbidding Christianity remained in force 250 years, right up past the mid-19th century."

Pointing out the Kobayashi Issa Museum on the right Matt suggested, "Joe, you ought to show them some of Issa's *haiku* poetry."

"He's considered Basho's equal," Joe said. "His name literally means a cup of tea. He had a keen sensitivity for small living creatures such as crickets, ants, and frogs."

After cutting across Route 18, they meandered past metal and thatch-roofed farm houses before coming out onto a narrow plain of rice paddies and houses known as Okubo Village. Joe explained that it was a little hamlet like this on Kyushu Island where Watanabe grew up. The place was called "*Nanataki*," after seven waterfalls.

Reardon, at last showing signs of shaking off his smoldering preoccupation with the crumpled letter, spoke up, "No wonder you wanted to get out of that sauna in Tokyo. I feel better already."

"You don't suppose," Eric asked, "any of my old classmates at the American School are here?"

"You can soon find out," Anita answered. "Check the names in the Nojiri Yearbook."

The van wobbled drunk-like over the eroded road by the Summer Store and began grinding its way up the pock-marked gravel hill to the cabin. It lurched across the rock-imbedded ditch and slowed to a stop in the opening separating the entrance's huge pine tree from the uncut bamboo-grass between lot #56 and Matsumoto's below.

"Usually we go through the back doors, but you're company," Anita explained. "Let's go the front way today. We can sit on the porch while we drink some coffee or Cokes. I've made almond bars. You can soak up the late afternoon scenery while I make up your beds."

From the cabin in back, where Japanese renters were living, they could hear children's playful voices and badminton shuttlecocks being whacked about.

"Ani, don't you think Mr. Reardon should have the first-class room with the view? Jack, you're welcome to use my desk. Eric could take the bunk-bed in back and Mei Li the big luxurious guest room out in the rear."

"Luxurious guest room?" Anita mumbled under her breath. "Good thing we cleaned it out last week and fumigated it for grasshoppers. I apologize for the toilets. Sewage system won't be put in for another five years, if ever."

"But," Joe spoke proudly, "we're the only house on the hill with two toilets. This used to be a duplex. In the beginning it was built as a triplex for language students."

"If we had a car here," Anita sighed, "we could go out to the El Capitan for pizza. Wait a minute. Come to think of it, Keiko Matsumoto told me she and her husband are going there tonight. Is it okay with everyone if we have them bring some home for us? Any favorite combinations?"

"Sounds good," Reardon agreed. "We need to stay put where we can have privacy."

Hearing no special requests, Anita offered her choices. "The mixed pizza is good, if they hold the shrimp. Two large should be enough don't you think? I'll get one small vegetarian, too. We can always save what's left over. Jack, why don't you stay here on the porch and get started on your work? It will be at least 7:30 before the pizzas come. Let me spray around your chair, so the ants won't get you. The hornets won't bother you unless you disturb them."

After she served the coffee, Cokes and cookies, Joe decided the mood was right to confront Reardon, but quietly so Mei Li and Eric wouldn't hear.

"Jack, you were not very good at hiding your anger when you read that special delivery letter. It had to do with the TV project didn't it?"

Reardon's dejected face showed up the wrinkles around his eyes and mouth. The morose silence screamed louder than any words he could have uttered. Forgetting his secretive voice, Joe pushed on with, "Maybe it's time to let us in on it. We can't ride a bus with only your one sparkplug connected. We all have to know what's happening. Otherwise, we'll never reach our destination."

Jack peered over at young Eric who had fixed on Reardon's eyes. Looking behind, he saw Miss Ping, too, staring at him questioningly, as though she were about to say, "Go on, out with it. We've got to know what's up — or down."

With deliberately slow pacing, Reardon forced himself to exude pleasantness.

"If this were three years ago," he said, "I would have asked if you have any whiskey stashed away. I'd have drowned my anger in alcohol. Now I'll make do with coffee."

Reaching into his shirt pocket, he yanked out the rumpled letter. Without bothering to open it, he began to relate how the TV mini-series project was conceived. "If I don't tell you that, you won't make any sense out of the letter.

"With Great Britain about to hand over Hong Kong to China a year from now, the world's eyes will focus on it. Hundreds, perhaps thousands, of journalists will descend on the city. Many news organizations already are positioning themselves there. To make a complicated scenario simple, a certain fast-food chain is trying to jump-start a world-wide expansion by riding the coattails of the Hong Kong handover."

The other three looked wide-eyed at each other. "A commercial venture?" exclaimed Mei Li.

"A young Chinese student from Hunan Province by the name of Horatio Chang studied at Oklahoma State University — majoring in business and marketing. Well, this Chang came up with a brilliant idea for a fast-food chain to rival McDonalds and the others. Mao Zedong, you will recall, hailed from Hunan, Horatio's home province. Starting with seed money from a Hong Kong entrepeneur and with provincial backing, he developed what he describes as China's challenge to the Big Mac. He calls it the 'Maoburger.'"

"Holy cow!" Eric blurted out.

"No, not cow," Mei Li corrected him, "holy duck," she laughed. "Yes, duck. I've read somewhere about him. He's built a huge assembly-line factory to process the duck meat. It's located in Hunan within sight of a new rail line connecting Beijing with Hong Kong."

"It seems," Reardon went on to say, "Chang has an unlimited supply of duck meat and Chinese leeks, maybe some of it from forced-labor camps. Horatio is a real operator. He's negotiated with one of the American TV networks to shoot one of his factories when they cover the handover next year."

"You must be kidding?" Joe questioned.

"I swear on the Bible. It's for real. They smother the duck and leeks with a sweet sauce and encase it inside a pancake blanket, replicating Peking duck. That's China's greatest delicacy. It's gone over big in Hunan, then spread to Guangzhou, Nanjing and even Peking, or Beijing, itself."

"Eric, have you ever eaten Peking duck?" Joe asked. "Nothing more delicious! This guy could strike gold."

"There's more. This new food product will kick off its global marketing campaign, June 1, 1997. For their logo they've come up with a Chinese imitation of Donald Duck. Like the Jolibee chain based in the Philippines, the Maoburger will go global, beginning in Hong Kong, June next year. That's when we hope to begin the TV series of 26 programs on the history of Hong Kong."

"So what's the problem?" Eric asked.

"According to this letter, someone in line to be a part of the post-turnover Hong Kong administration told Chang in no uncertain terms that nothing in our programs can even hint at opposition to government authority."

"Where have we heard that before?" Mei Li chimed in. "Maybe they want to be bribed."

"They've even appointed a Chinese loyalist from the mainland to keep an eye on us," Reardon groaned. "What they want is a nice pleasant pro-China series, with plenty of emphasis on Britain's illegal grab of the motherland's territory at the time of the Opium War 155 years ago. Nothing must rock the boat for a smooth handover to Chinese rule."

"Good heavens!" Mei Li shouted.

"They can't do that even before the handover can they?" Eric asked.

"You bet your life they can and will. Oh, why can't problems be simple?" Reardon spouted. "This Horatio Chang is a decent enough fellow. I believe in his heart he wants to do what's right, but Beijing sympathizers are out to stop us."

"Wouldn't you know," Mei Li sneered.

"We think it's to scare Disney off from making Martin Scorsese's movie about the Dalai Lama. On top of that, Horatio tells me a friend in Hong Kong warned him that the CIA and Taiwanese patriots are egging on the pro-democracy movement supporters. They're planning to derail the whole campaign."

"How?" Eric asked.

"I know it sounds farfetched, but they're plotting to start a whisper campaign to get people to call the new burger not 'Maoburger,' after Mao Zedong, but 'Dengburger' after Deng Xiaoping, China's top dog and creator of the 'one-nation-two-systems' policy."

"Unbelievable!" Eric sighed as he shook his head.

"You see how catastrophic that would be?" Reardon said. *"Deng* is pronounced the same as *dung.* Who'd want to eat a Dungburger. The very thought of it would make people puke."

"Yeah, that's right," Eric added excitedly. "I remember when I lived in Japan, some dumb Japanese company named a new sport drink, 'Pocari Sweat.' Who'd want to drink sweat?"

"This letter from Horatio says their management and ad agency are bound up in knots over this. They don't know what to do. Chang wants us to doctor up the World War II episode on Watanabe to make it palatable to the PRC."

Joe could see that this Dengburger news numbed everyone. They collapsed in their chairs dumbfounded. Each of them gazed out at the lake and mountains, searching for wisdom, any wisdom at all.

After several minutes, a quick movement under the veranda roof caught Joe's eye. It was Evangeline, his very wise spider girlfriend. She didn't seem perplexed at all about her responsibilities. She knew that if she wanted supper, she'd better spin out her lair before the bugs started flying toward the house lights.

From inside the cabin Anita called to say the beds were made and the guests could check them out. She'd heated the bath, too, so they could bathe before supper if they wished.

Stepping out onto the porch, she whispered to Mei Li, "Do you know how to take a Japanese bath?" Before she could answer, Anita began with bodily gestures to explain the process. "You wash outside the tub. Afterward you get in and soak, but don't pull the plug when you're finished."

Thoroughly enjoying Anita's demonstration, Mei Li feigned ignorance. Joe wished he'd had a video camera handy. Eric and Joe could hardly keep their calm and almost exploded in laughter, but Anita didn't notice.

She kept on explaining, "We once had a missionary couple from Taiwan visit us. They pulled out the plug in the bath at the inn where they were staying. They didn't know that the other hotel guests had to use that same hot water. Here at our cabin, women and girls go first, not as in most Japanese homes. There the men and boys are at the top of the order."

"See how we men are treated these days," Joe complained to Eric.

"By the way," Anita said to Mei Li, "when we studied Chinese at Yale, one of the teachers gave me the same name as yours. Doesn't the first character mean 'beautiful?' Very suitable for you. I hope there will be a chance for us women to talk sometime. Let me show you the bath and your room."

Joe led Eric to his bunk room, adjoining the study where Reardon would sleep. Next he pulled the boxes of Watanabe materials out from under the desk and told Reardon he hadn't had time to finish sorting. Handing Reardon two English translations of filmscripts, Joe suggested that after reading them he would be able to figure out how to respond to the curve Horatio Chang had thrown at him.

"It's so unlike the Horatio I know," Reardon mused. "So out of character. I can't believe he'd do this to me, unless, of course, they've blackmailed him.

"God help us. I've never had such a tough dilemma. This Watanabe project might be the first test case for 'one country, two systems.' Good God! And we're in the middle of it and don't know what to do.

"This isn't mere self-restraint as the Hong Kong media have been practicing. This is censorship, pure and simple." His eyes strained for some soft, neutral scene to rest on.

They were beginning to grasp the implications of this interference. Inch by inch the authorities would roll back freedom until it eroded to a final collapse. Hong Kong would end up as another Stalinist Socialist region of the Peoples' Republic, outwardly capitalistic and democratic, but completely domesticated to Beijing's agenda.

Reardon and Joe knew they were not up to dealing with censorship, at least for now. They resigned themselves to the quiet glow of sunset at Nojiri, following a dragonfly's final fly-abouts of the day. A long string of crows flew by heading for home. The cooling dampness of the hillside crept in closer, tempting them inside for sweaters, but neither of them broke the soothing spell of the starlit night.

They looked up. A huge moth had flown directly into Evangeline's trap. Without a word, they knew only too well how to sympathize with the innocent moth. He merely had followed the light he saw — and thought he understood.

17

Escaping the Web

The four team members sat in the quiet of their own personal reflections, until Anita called from the doorway. "What do you want to drink with your pizza? Sorry, but all we have is iced tea or Cokes, and milk of course. Oh, and some one-percent Australian beer our son left in the other ice box."

"Can you manage that, Jack?" Joe asked.

"I'm sorry, not even one percent. Any alcohol is poison to me; a disease.You might call it my 'thorn in the flesh.'"

"Okay, then, let's stick to Coke and tea, or milk. Mei Li, can you eat pizza?"

"Of course, don't be silly. My Uncle Stanley inTaipei took me to Shakey's once. After that I was hooked forever. They've even concocted a sweet-and-sour version which is all the rage now."

Fidgety over this wasting of valuable time, Reardon announced that he needed time to think. He wanted to shut himself in the study and start reading the filmscripts and take a quick look through Watanabe's correspondence and memoribilia.

Eric rose and asked apologetically, "Will you excuse me? I should call Ralph. I'm worried about him. I'll be right back. Do you have a flashlight I can borrow?"

"I'd better walk down with you," Joe said. "Those payphones won't take coins; you'll need a plastic card. Besides, I want to speak with Ralph, too. Jack, could use some quiet solitude. Mei Li, why don't you use the bath now?"

Even with a flashlight and the light from the red lantern in back of them, they stumbled a few times before reaching the road. Unfortunately it was only lighted by 20-watt bulbs atop poles interspersed every hundred meters, making walking precarious.

No one was using the phone, so Joe quickly punched in the numbers of the Fairmont and asked for Room 601. "Hello, Mr. Eilers? This is Joe Weaver from Nojiri."

"Oh, Orimura-san, this is Nakagawa. I am so sorry, *sumimasen*. I am very ashamed."

"What do you mean?" But Nakagawa didn't reply. Joe heard the rustling of papers and the sound of footsteps running away.

"*Sumimasen, sumimasen*," he repeated, but couldn't go on. After an anxious pause, he finally managed to speak again. "I have sad news for you." He hesitated as though waiting for Joe to prepare himself for shocking news.

"Some men attacked Mr. Eilers — a few minutes ago when he got out of the taxi."

"Right in front of the hotel?"

"Yes, two men, maybe three, ran out from the alley and shoved him down on the sidewalk. If Okamoto-san, our doorman, hadn't stopped them, Mr. Eilers could have been hurt badly."

"Is he all right?"

"He's in the bathroom washing his face. Here he comes. He wants to talk to you."

"What's wrong?" Eric asked. "Did somebody attack Dad?"

"He's okay. Ralph's on the line. Here's Eric. He's worried about you."

"Eric, listen, I'm okay. No big deal, but I've got to let you in on some things, but not from my phone here. It may not be secure. I'll call you at Weaver's neighbor's cabin after I find a public phone that's safe, in half an hour. Okay? Don't worry, I'll be careful."

Joe put his arm around Eric's waist as they began to stroll alongside the lower tennis court. When they reached the turn, Eric asked, "Would you mind if I sit here on the bench a moment? Should I call you Orimura-san or Weaver?"

"Either is fine."

"After finding that warning in the room today, I didn't know what to think. Dad is into something dangerous, but he hasn't been able to tell me what it is — even though he claims I'll be proud of him."

"I'm sure you can trust him on that."

"Do you think it was right for me to ask God to protect him, or was that selfish?"

"Eric, didn't you say he is doing something you would approve. I don't see why you shouldn't have prayed for him — if God approves what he's doing. From the little Nakagawa-san said on the phone, some people were out to harm Ralph. He might have been killed if the doorman hadn't sent them chasing. Maybe he was your father's guardian angel."

"Dad promised to tell me what's going on. Maybe we'd better go up to the neighbor's cabin and wait for the call."

"I forgot. The Brannigans might be going down to the talent show."

Although their multi-colored lantern cast weird dancing shadows amongst the trees, it gave enough light for them to maneuver the narrow path up to the huge front porch.

"Hello, anyone home?" Both Steve and his wife Ann came out.

"My friend's father is going to call us at your number."

"Come in and wait by the phone," Ann said. "We're on our way to the talent show. Steve is doing one of his silly monologues. Just shut the door when you leave."

As soon as the Brannigans switched on their flashlights and stepped onto the path, the telephone rang. Joe picked up the receiver and handed it to Eric, then he ducked out to the porch to give Eric privacy. But since only a screen window separated them, Joe couldn't help but hear some of Eric's louder responses.

"Where are you? — No one followed you? — What is Sub-LRP? — Who's out to steal it? — The American general from Okinawa, too? — What do you mean they're too late? — We have to keep this TV project a secret, too, at least for now. There was a long pause. "Yes, I'll call Mom in the morning. Take care. See you Monday — probably."

Eric hung up, stood still a minute or two before coming out to sit beside Joe. Their view of Lake Nojiri was spectacular, farming village beyond the lake to the right and Nojiri Village far to the left. Directly across the lake on a hillside stood the Prince Hotel where PeterYu was staying.

"Ralph is safe, only a few bruises. Good thing the doorman was a retired policeman and judo expert. He really sent the two thugs sailing, but Dad thinks they only wanted to frighten him or take their frustration out on him, since he'd tricked them. They'd stolen fake plans. He had delivered the real ones on Friday — signed the contract today."

"Deal?" Joe asked with a tone of surprise.

"Maybe that's the wrong word, but he told me it was so good and significant that he'd stake his life on it. You have to remember that he fought in Vietnam, wounded so badly in a napalm accident that the army flew him back to Japan to recover at Camp Zama. From what I know, he had a profound change of heart in the hospital."

"What was that about?"

"Dad said it had something to do with a visit from the American Ambassador. Meyer was his name, Armin Meyer. He used to visit the wounded on Sundays."

"If Ralph's willing to give his life for this," Joe said, but didn't know what to add. "We'd better get back to the cabin. I think that was Matsumoto's car that went by."

By the time they closed Brannigan's cabin and put on shoes, Dr. Matsumoto had taken the pizza up to the cabin and returned home.

Eric and Joe tiptoed into the house, not wanting to tell the others about the telephone conversation. Anita picked up on their subdued vibes, but chose not to invade their secrecy. Rather, she began to unwrap the hot pizza. The aroma alone was enough to beckon everyone to the table, even Reardon from the next room.

When they all were seated, Joe attempted to ease into an account of what had happened to Eric's stepfather, but finally simply blurted out, "Someone attacked

Ralph outside the hotel, but he's safe. No need to worry," but Joe didn't describe the incident.

"Attack?" Reardon asked. "What kind of attack?"

"I'll tell you later. Pizza is getting cold. Let's pray. Do you mind if we use our old standby prayer? "Come, Lord, Jesus, be our guest, and may these gifts to us be blest." But Joe felt compelled to continue in his own words. "Lord, we've been brought together by unexpected and strange circumstances which we don't fully understand. You have promised wisdom to everyone humble enough to ask. Right now we're asking you. Hear our prayer. Thanks for this food and bless us, and keep Ralph safe, in Jesus' name. Amen."

Reaching back to her Illinois upbringing, Anita invited them to "make out their dinner," which interprets as, "Eat plentifully."

"I've heard that 'Come, Lord Jesus' prayer before," Mei Li commented, but from then on silence descended over the table, not even any sound of silverware because they were tackling the pizza with their hands. No one competed with pizza until well into the second helping.

Reardon looked up, unable to hold back his curiosity. "Eric, are you holding back on us?"

Threatened by Reardon's sudden gruffness, Eric pleaded with his eyes that Joe come to his rescue.

In a matter-of-fact tone, Joe reported. "We were able to contact Mr. Eilers. Truth is that he had been ruffed up by a couple of *yakuza* hoodlums outside the Fairmont Hotel, but he's okay. They won't go after him again, Ralph assured us. They were too late anyway. He had finished his mission. I should add that I'm learning that Ralph Eilers is quite a man, sort of in the Watanabe tradition."

Eric, without looking at the others, and softly, but emphatically, affirmed Joe's assessment. "Rather than torching villages and frying Vietnames peasants with napalm, he's dedicated himself to making such atrocities a thing of the past. He told me he's prepared to die trying."

18

Mei Li Ping's Connection

After a long lull, Anita passed around the fruit bowl and cookies. Eric, seeming to deflect talk from Ralph and himself, said to Mei Li, "On the train today you started to tell us about your family. I take it you were greatly influenced by your father."

Looking pleased to be asked, she replied, "I can't remember where I left off, but since you told us about your stepfather, maybe I should fill you in more about my papa."

"Strange that you don't call him 'Baba,' as in Mandarin," Joe said.

"He may have picked up 'Papa' from the Swedish family he lived with in the States. Only a guess. I really don't know for sure. I've always called him that, but let me go on. During the civil war between Mao Zedong's Communist forces and Chiang Kai-shek's Kuomintang Nationalist army, Papa fought under Chiang and was wounded in the shoulder. The Reds captured him in one of the last battles, but he managed to escape. He's always been a good runner."

"How'd he escape?" Eric asked.

"Luckily, or I should say providentially, he hid in a Christian's barn. He stayed out of sight for three days, but on Sunday morning neighbors began entering the courtyard. When he heard the people singing hymns, ones he'd learned in the Wuhan mission school, he pushed aside his straw covering and crept cautiously into the meeting. He must have created quite a stir."

"I can imagine," Eric said. "They must have been terrified to discover a uniformed Nationalist soldier singing with them."

"You know," she said, "everyone in the congregation agreed he should be cared for. No one wanted to turn him over to the Communists. The Reds would have executed him on the spot. The peasants nursed him for over a month until he was strong enough to flee south. Six months later he got out to Taiwan where Chiang's forces had fled."

Reardon, who had been listening intently, said, "Someday I'd like to meet your father. I want to hear the rest of his story. Sounds like another mini-series in the making — like 'The Fugitive.'"

"Couldn't you call it 'The Chinese Fugitive?'" Eric said.

"Ironically," Mei Li continued, "the Nationalists accused him of being a Red spy and put him in prison. That was in the spring of 1950."

"Whatever for?" Eric asked.

"Someone claimed he was stirring up the Presbyterian Taiwan-born natives. Not many people know it, but the Nationalists massacred 28,000 Taiwanese in 1947."

"I'd heard about that," Reardon said. Looking at Joe, he asked, "I bet your American press never reported that, did they?"

"I can't remember hearing about it "

Mei Li hesitated before continuing. "After the Japanese left in '45, the Kuomintang claimed the native Taiwanese wanted to set up an independent country, separate from Japan and from Chiang's Republic of China. Papa must have said something about self-determination. A lot of former colonies set up independent states after the War."

"You'd make a great history teacher," Eric said.

"*Syesye.* (thanks) He tasted both the Red Terror of the Communists and the White Terror of the Kuomintang. The Nationalist security officer who interrogated him discovered he owned a Bible. Since the Christian General Feng Yu Hsiang had surrendered to the Reds, he accused my father of being a spy and exiled him to Green Island, the prison for political criminals."

"How unfair!" Eric said, looking straight into Mei Li's eyes.

"That's where Papa contracted tuberculosis, and some eye disease ruined his eyes. It was in that period of my father's life that he became disillusioned with both sides. You have an expression in English: 'a plague on both your houses.' I believe that's how my father felt."

"That reminds me," Joe interjected, "of what my friend Taketani-san often says: *Omotemon no tora, uramon no okami* (A tiger at the front gate and a wolf at the back)."

"Papa concluded that Christ was the only way for himself — and for China herself. He received baptism and later felt the call to study for the ministry."

"Haven't I met him somewhere?" Joe asked. "He always held the page up close to his eyes when he read, didn't he?"

"Father mentioned you, I believe. Did you have a friend in Taiwan nicknamed '*Nyou Bobo*'?"

Joe laughed. "That was my nickname. The general secretary at church headquarters in Taipei couldn't stop smiling when he met me for the first time. He began scratching out a cartoon character and asked me, 'Do you know this famous cartoon warrior?'"

"I shook my head when he showed the drawing to me."

"This is *Nyou Bobo,* Uncle Ox."

"I really look that funny? I asked him.

"Your father laughed, too. From then on I'd often refer to myself as *Nyou Bobo* and even sign my letters toTaiwanese that way.

"You won't believe this, but once in a teahouse when I was visiting Taiwan, my Chinese host told the owner, 'That's *Nyou Bobo*,' as he pointed me out. And the owner believed him until I confessed to the false identity. Sorry, go on with your story."

"Once when Papa was on a trip to Hong Kong, he heard about this Japanese pastor, Kiyoshi Watanabe. He told me he hoped more people, not just the British, could learn about what he did for the prisoners-of-war."

"Your father, Mei Li, had a passionate concern for his own people in China, but no narrow nationalism."

"Then it was through your father," Reardon said, "that you became interested in our project?"

"That's right."

Reardon glanced at his watch to hint that it was time to move on to other questions.

"Orimura-san, or should I call you 'Uncle Ox' now, what about you?" and he pointed his finger at Joe's chest. "I've heard only bits and pieces about your Watanabe connection."

Anita's frown fired a warning shot across his bow, so that Joe wouldn't start talking about the Hiroshima days. "No need to tell him about Hiroshima. Start with what you wrote. That will be a great plenty. You always want to tell too much."

"No! I disagree!" Reardon objected as he slapped his hands together. "Hiroshima may be the key to the story. At the press club you assured me that Watanabe was 'the real thing,' but you didn't elaborate."

"Jack, didn't you say that many great people aren't great at all when you come close to them. 'They stink like mackeral,' were your words I think That was not true of Watanabe. He never tooted his own horn about what he'd done in Hong Kong."

Glancing over at Anita for permission, Joe said, "I hardly know where to begin."

"You might as well start from the beginning when he traveled all the way to Tokyo to urge us to move to Hiroshima immediately."

"Jack doesn't need all that story now. We soon learned he was extremely kind. Not until twenty years later when we read Liam Nolan's book, did we fully appreciate how important Watanabe's little favors had been."

Mei Li asked, "How do you mean?"

"Shortly after Watanabe came to the Shamshuipo Prison Camp," said Joe, "the commandant forced him to witness the questioning of a young Brit. Another interpreter, I believe his name was Inoue, punched the prisoner in the face till blood covered his chin. He slapped him with the back of his hand and then used his knuckles."

"Unbelievable," Eric remarked. "Not like any Japanese I know."

"You can check it out in the book, but I think I've remembered it accurately. There was a younger man by the name of Sakaino. He dragged the prisoner into the next room and whipped him across the chest with his belt buckle."

"When we went to Beppu to visit Watanabe in retirement," Anita said, "didn't Watanabe tell us he dashed out of the torture room into the toilet and bolted the door? But he couldn't keep out the sound of screaming."

"That became a turning point for him," Joe explained. "Either he abandoned God or trusted in Him. At that moment, Watanabe told us, God urged him to remember Jesus dying on the cross. In that putrid toilet stall, he fell to his knees. Can you imagine that? He pleaded for God to rescue him.

"As he arose from the filthy floor, he begged God to forgive him for his fearful helplessness. From that day on he prayed for his enemies: Inoue, Sakaino and the other torturers. He prayed the same words Jesus prayed from the cross: 'Father, forgive them for they know not what they do.' I know I am a coward. Help me, God. I don't want to betray Thee."

Looking at Reardon and Eric, Joe sensed that they both were visualizing the scene as through a camera lens. Mei Li, on the other hand, was writing furiously on her note pad.

"Watanabe told us that mental turmoil tormented him for several days," Joe continued, "but on the third day after the beating, he awoke before dawn, and while standing by his window, he peered out across the courtyard to the barely visible prison barracks. 'O God,' he cried in silence, 'give me a clear sign of what I should do.'

"As he waited in the gray morning light, the prophet Isaiah's words came to him as though God himself were speaking:

"'And when you turn to the left, your ears shall hear a word behind you, saying, This is the way, walk in it.' But instead of hearing God's voice from behind, he heard Jesus' voice in front of him. 'Truly ... as you did it to one of the least of these my brethren, you did it to me. Choose to obey me or to obey man.'"

Reardon, Mei Li and Eric could but hold their peace, aware that Joe had hit upon the crux of the story: either obey God or obey men.

"Excruciating as it would be to disobey his military superiors, Watanabe knew in his deepest of hearts that he must obey Christ and follow in his way of agape-love, counting the enemy prisoners as his friends. He resolved that from then on no matter how insignificant a circumstance might seem, he would listen only to God."

99

"There must be lots of examples in that book," Eric said, not realizing the others were watching him as he pretended to line up a scene for filming.

Anita held up her hand to catch Reardon's attention. "I recall," she said, "one scene in the sick ward," Anita said, "after he'd been transferred to the Bowen Street Hospital. One prisoner by name of Rothwell spoke of the many little extra acts of kindness Watanabe had done for the patients. Wasn't he the man who hadn't received any letters from his wife? Watty, that's what he called him, urged him to pray to God about it.

"After supper that night, Watanabe sneaked into the storage room where the undelivered letters were kept. He soon found a big pile of letters addressed to Rothwell. The jealous corporal in charge always excused his cruelty on the grounds that an enemy prisoner shouldn't get more letters than he.

"In the middle of the night while everyone slept Watanabe sneaked into the darkened sick ward with the letters. Rothwell wrote later that he felt movement under his pillow and recognized Watanabe leaving the ward. When he reached under the pillow, he found eighteen letters from his wife. Wouldn't that be an easy scene to do on film? Easier than when the young Canadians finally received their parcels."

"What about after the War in Hiroshima?" Reardon asked. "What can we show from there?"

"Where to begin?" Joe mumbled to himself.

But Anita seemed to know what Reardon was looking for. "I think," she said, "it was more than coincidence that the little house he picked out for us had been built on top of a corner of a former men's dormitory of Hiroshima University. The A-bomb had blown it over. Subtly he wanted us to feel the bomb experience."

Turning toward Joe, she asked, "Remember the twisted girders of the elementary school at the end of the block?"

"He arranged everything for us," Joe said. "Found us tutors. Got a helper for us, even a dog whom we named DiMaggio. Watanabe paved our way for everything. He also was working to open a factory for bomb victims to manufacture imitation pearls."

"His love of children," Anita interrupted, "that's what shined through most. Remember the summer of '52 when we held a Bible camp near the *Sandan Kyo* waterfall. We have a photo of him diving off a rock into the icey mountain stream. He had to do whatever the kids did.

"You also could show him at the apartment of that prisoner's wife, playing with her three girls and asking them to pray for his safety, and the safety of their father."

"I get the picture," Reardon said. "Anita said you'd written about how this wish to do a film came about."

"Let me get the article. It's on top of the filing cabinet. I figured you'd want to see it."

Returning with the magazine in hand, Joe moved his chair directly under the ceiling light and said, "It's too long to read. Let me give the gist of it," but as he began to read he realized there wasn't anything he could skip over.

"In the fall of 1982 many Asian peoples and governments protested plans of the Japanese Education Ministry to revise sections in the textbooks that dealt with Japan's aggressions. When the news leaked out, Koreans exploded in anger, and Chinese in Hong Kong took to the streets in protest. It was clear that even 40 years after the War, the patched wounds had not been healed. They were festering again, poisoning the system we glibly thought was peace in the Far East.

"Without true repentance, we can never have genuine reconciliation between the peoples of Asia. One morning as I was pondering this problem, I remembered Watanabe, the Christ-like suffering servant of God. 'Could he possibly point the way to true peace?' I asked myself.

"When I visited Hong Kong that November I took my copy of his biography, *Small Man of Nanataki*, and lent it to David Chiang, a Christian film and drama producer. That same night, I think as a favor to me, he decided to glance through the book before going to sleep. What a surprise he received! He told me he kept reading until 2 a.m. 'I just couldn't stop,' he told me. 'We must make a movie about what Watanabe did for the people of Hong Kong.'

"I wrote that with some uneasiness because Watanabe had primarily helped save the lives of British Commonwealth military personnel. That included not only English, but also Canadians, Indians, Australians and New Zealanders, some civilians and their families, too, but very few ethnic Chinese."

"We can remedy that," Reardon said.

"Jack, if you do your mini-series right, Watanabe can inspire the people of Hong Kong in 1997 and forever thereafter, even when the honeymoon period ends. His example of courageous love can pre-empt the demoralizing effects of persecution. It can prepare them to meet any worst-case scenario that the police might inflict on the people."

"You do act like *Nyou Bobo*," Mei Li said. "We can learn much from history. There's been a pattern of suppression in China over the last 40 years."

"And from before that, too," Reardon added.

"Two Chinese students arranged for the first date Ani and I had. One of them was Wilson Ai who returned to China, but was purged at the time of the campaign called 'Let a hundred flowers bloom.' Mao never said, 'Let a hundred flowers be planted.' So, when people spoke their minds, the police cut them down and sent them to labor camps."

"I vaguely remember hearing about that," Jack said. "Back in the mid-fifties wasn't it?"

"Don't forget the Democracy Wall campaign in the '70s and then the Tiananmen Square demonstrations of '89," Mei Li inserted.

Joe realized that this review of China's history had cast a dark shadow over the room, inflicting them with a heavy-hearted gloom for they knew it could happen again.

Finally, Anita broke the silence. "If you go out on the porch, you can watch the new moon come up over the pines. I'll clear the table and do up the dishes. Your night off, Joe."

"I can help," Eric offered.

"No, you go outside, I'm okay."

On the veranda they pulled the chairs together into a semi-circle. The faint glimmer of the lake told them the moon was hiding behind the pine trees to the right.

"We know very little," Reardon began philosophizing. "We see but a sliver of the moon, not the whole."

"Seiichi Yashiro, a Catholic playwright," Joe added, "used the moon to symbolize God, but always a full moon."

Mei Li interjected, "The moon is a cold reflection of the sun. If only we could reflect God fully and with warmth."

"We take a story," Reardon said, "or a person's life and present it to an audience by film or drama. I realize how little of the whole truth we are able to get across, but — we keep trying, trying to entice people out of their ruts and pre-conceived ideas."

"Who wants to take a bath next?" Anita called from the kitchen.

"Jack, you ought to go next," Joe suggested. "I'll take a spit bath in the morning after I jog to the lake for the Sunday paper. No delivery on Sundays."

"I'm with you," Eric said. "Do you mind if I run with you? Tonight I'd like to have a look at Nolan's book."

"Sure, but don't stay up half the night like David Chiang. You'd better use the top bunk by the light."

"I want to look through Kagami's filmscript," Reardon said. "That must be Tanaka's professional name, isn't it?" Turning to Mei Li, he suggested that she read through the script the Chinese in Hong Kong put together. "Then we'll be able to compare our reactions and decide what will make the greatest impact."

Mei Li's lips tightened and she sputtered to herself loud enough for the rest of them to hear, "If it only were that simple. Do we have the courage to tell the whole story and show what it means in 1997?" She left the porch, repeating to herself, "I'm afraid... I'm afraid..." But the rest of her sentence was swallowed up by the darkness.

19

All Through the Night

Sensing the poignancy of Mei Li Ping's bedtime fears, Joe couldn't sleep for a long time. He knew Reardon had to be waging a terrible war within his conscience. How many TV or film producers had struggled over his kind of dilemma: either water down the story's implications or risk losing his job and being blackballed forever by the media moguls.

But he knew it was even more than that, for a cowardly decision could betray a whole people, in this case 6-7 million people in Hong Kong and the freedom lovers who had taken refuge there since '89 after the Tienanmen Square Massacre.

Joe couldn't suppress his suspicions that the PRC was buying off the financial leaders of Hong Kong. How many bankers and shipping magnants had sold their souls by kowtowing like swamp reeds before the wind from the North rather than risk being broken off.

Although Joe had shut the sliding wooden doors between the study and living room, it didn't shut out the restless sound of ruffling papers and angry expletives. "The bloody traitors" seemed to be Reardon's phrase of choice, usually followed by the thud of his fist pounding the desk.

Out near the road, Joe heard a badger fussing, and overlooking the hillside, a mother owl, high in the pines signaled that she would watch over them till morning.

Her promise though had no lasting effect on Joe, for what sleep he did get was pre-empted by a terrifying nightmare reminiscent of the dream he had as a child when the doctor cut out his tonsils and adenoids. All he recalled was that after the anesthetist pushed the ether-soaked cloth over his nose, he fell into an elevator shaft and plummeted downward toward the unreachable bottom of a black hole. Down and down, end over end he tumbled in a free fall. But tonight the badger's screech rescued him from the dream.

Close to midnight, Joe made his nightly visit out back to the toilet. As he passed beneath the red lantern, he saw that Eric's reading lamp was lit, shedding just enough light to highlight Watanabe's face framed within a bright-red wartime flag on the jacket of Nolan's book.

Noticing movement outside his window, Eric set the book down beside the wall and strained to see Joe staring at him through the screen.

"Now I can understand," Eric said, "why your Chinese friend in Hong Kong read this story late into the night. And to think that after all Watanabe had gone through, he had to return home to Hiroshima and learn that his wife and daughter had been obliterated by the A-bomb. He couldn't even recognize the street where they had lived. How could God have allowed that to happen?"

A frantic fluttering sound from inside the paper lantern by the kitchen door distracted Joe. A large moth had become trapped. Its wild contortions reflected eerie red psychedelic shadows against the cabin's creosoted siding.

Squirming within himself to avoid a direct answer to Eric's question, Joe hedged his reply: "You're not the first person to ask that question." Feigning humility, he went on to say, "An extra irony was that it was a Lutheran chaplain who prayed for the Enola Gay's crew before they took off to bomb Hiroshima.

"But can we blame God for man's sins? Unless, we're going to blame God for giving us the freedom to disobey him. If we get into that insoluable riddle, we'll never sleep tonight."

At that moment the door to Mei Li Ping's room swung open with its usual scraping sound, and she shuffled barefoot over to see what they were talking about. Although she wore a summer *yukata* bathrobe, her tousled hair suggested she also hadn't been able to sleep.

"Are you worried about Reardon, too?" she asked. "I've seen too many of these British journalists sell their souls away."

"Let's not assume he will," Joe objected. "Give him the benefit of the doubt — at least until tomorrow. He's in a tough spot. Who are we to say what we'd do if we were in his shoes?"

Realizing that his preachy pronouncement had squelched further talk, Joe silently made his way back to bed. He knew that, like him, they'd be fighting back waves of questions and doubts all through the night.

Sunday morning when Joe opened his eyes, he thought he'd just awakened from a quick 5-minute nap, as though he'd idled briefly at a stoplight, but never really fallen into a deep sleep. He felt refreshed and ready to speed off.

As he stepped outside to pull the red lantern's plug out, he lost his balance and banged his right hand against the wood paneling under the kitchen window. The sudden thud plus his pained grunt awakened Eric.

A minute later, Eric wormed his way by the snoring Reardon asleep on the bed in the study, slid open the door and made his way out to the toilet in time to greet Joe coming out.

"How surprising to see a teenager with his eyes open at 5 a.m.!" Joe joked. "Do you want to join me over coffee on the front porch? Tea won't do today; we need strong coffee — and lots of prayer."

"Thanks, but I think I'll walk up to the golf course. I need some time alone. I'm worried about dad. Save me some coffee for later. I couldn't get Watanabe out of my mind. He seemed so real. God, that man was brave, lugging the old threadbare briefcase stuffed with medicines and vitamins across the Shamshuipo Prison courtyard, and in full view of the guards."

"I've been to Shamshuipo with Nolan himself," Joe said. "He described for us Watanabe's defenceless, frightening pilgrimage as he tried to conceal the weight of the suitcase. Did you notice my notation in the margin of the book? I think I wrote Isaiah 53, which tells of God's suffering servant. It's a prophecy about the Messiah who would bear mankind's sins, bringing healing to the wounds of the world."

The squeaking of the bedspring from Anita's room acted like a hushhush signal, so Joe lowered his voice.

"In 1983, Nolan wrote in a letter to me that Uncle John Watanabe, as he knew him, was arguably the gentlest and most saintly person he had ever met, and the bravest. The problem for Reardon will be how to show that on a tiny TV screen when most viewers are looking only for quick escapist entertainment. We must make him try. I don't want to fail Watanabe again."

"You feel strongly about this, don't you?"

"Sorry, but I get worked up. When crunch time comes, we must not let Reardon sell us out like Judas. You go on up the hill. I'll stay on the porch till 7:00. Do you still want to jog with me down to the lake for a newspaper? There's a phone outside the office. It will take an international telelphone card."

"Good, I've got to call Mom, and Dad, too."

When Joe settled down on the veranda, he cradled the warm coffee cup with both hands and breathed in the aroma to draw the chill from his bones.

"O God," he prayed, "today will be a busy one, not a day for Sabbath rest. Do not leave me, do not leave us. Make the impossible possible."

As he opened the prayer book, the British chaplain's prayer Watanabe had recorded in his scrapbook came to mind. He had left it on the sofa, forgetting to hand it to Reardon. Quietly opening the screen door, he went inside to re-read it as his own prayer:

> "Lord of our life, help us in the days when the burdens we carry chafe our shoulders and weigh us down, when the skies are grey and cheerless and our souls have lost their courage. Then tune our hearts to brave music, turn our eyes to where the skies are full of promise and unite us in comradeship with the heroes and saints of every age. For Christ's sake. Amen."

Could a prayer like that, he wondered, quell the fears and despair of the people if and when a crackdown occurs? A flood of scenarios raced through his mind, so many that his mind tired and drifted off into a drowsy reverie recalling what Rothwell had written in the signature book: "I've never been so happy because now I am with a man of God. Thank you very much, Mr. Watanabe."

When Joe came to, he sipped the last drops of cold coffee. Eric rounded the corner of the cabin and came up alongside, saying, "It's almost 6:30."

"Let's go then. Papers will be there. How about a dip in the lake? That'll wake us better than a bath — save time, too, no lingering in the icy water."

"I'm game."

"Do you want to attend the Ecumenical Communion Service? It's held across the road on the tennis court at 8:30."

Eric didn't answer, but his quick move to get his swimming trunks told Joe he would.

Stuffing some coins and a telephone card into his jogging shorts, Joe went out to the back stoop where he and Eric tied up their shoes.

"You boys crazy?" came Mei Li's voice from within her room.

"We're running down for a swim and a call to Eric's folks. Be back in an hour for breakfast and church."

The wet grass brushed their ankles as they made their way out to the rocky, rutted road. Trotting slowly down the hill, Joe wondered if they might not meet the little boy who wasn't lost, but only didn't know where he was.

The downhill road gave Joe the feeling there was an inexplicable force propelling them toward a future they had no way of predicting. They passed the Summer Store and soon sped by Sato Construction's summer office. No one was stirring yet. Except for a barking watchdog by the Chuo University Conference Center on top the next hill, no one met them except a few horseflies.

"They're always lurking near the entrance to Elephant Trail," Joe explained. "Supposedly it's named after the mastodons which once traversed these shores. Nojiri Village has a mastodon's bones on display in a little museum."

Rounding the last curve, the rising sun and towering Mt. Myoko greeted them from out of the mirror-like blue lake. From there it took only a minute to reach the office porch.

Leaving Eric alone to speak with his stepfather and let his worrisome mother know they both were all right, Joe went around front to pick up a newspaper. When he returned, Eric stood facing the phone.

"She's frightened, and my words only made it worse. She's afraid of losing us. Chinese keep calling her about Ralph. The only consolation is that she's glad I'm at Nojiri."

Going a hundred yards farther, the two passed the teenagers' hangout next to the pier. Eric dove into the water straightway, but Joe crept down the metal stairs, wetting his toes one at a time before taking the plunge into the cold water — forgetting all worries about Ralph, Reardon and Mei Li's premonition, even about Peter Yu.

Eric sufaced from his dive, and Joe shouted at him, "Isn't it great how cold water throws cold water on our worries?"

107

20

Foretaste of Glory

Joe struggled up the ladder halfway across the swimming area and walked back to where he had left his shoes and T-shirt. Eric swam to the opposite pier and pushed off to return to where they'd started. Only then did Joe realize they had forgotten to bring towels. Worse than shivering from the cold was his fear they'd have no weapons with which to fight off the hornets on the path up the hill. By the time they'd reached where the hornets usually orbited, their bodies began to perspire, just what the hornets like, but it seemed the hornets had called a truce for the Sabbath.

When Joe and Eric reached the top of their climb, they stepped up into the front lawn, drops of sweat glistening on their bodies from the hot sun. Heading straight across the yard up onto the porch, they entered the living room quietly, careful not to let the screen door slam shut. Anita already had set the table and laid out boxes of Grape Nuts and Kellog's Corn Flakes for breakfast.

They could hear Reardon stirring behind the sliding doors where he'd slept, and Anita reported that Miss Ping was dressed and waiting to be called for breakfast.

"I'm playing at the Communion Service," Anita explained, while pouring some sugarless granola for herself out of a plastic container. "Excuse me for eating first, but I need to be at the tennis court by 8:15. No one has told me yet what hymns I have to play."

Joe called through the *fusuma* wooden doors to Reardon, "Eric and I are going to the 8:30 service. Do you want to go with us?"

Mei Li had circled the cabin from the back and come in the front door. She answered Joe's question, "Maybe I'll come later, but first I need to compare notes with Mr. Reardon. I think we need to clear up some matters. No use to sit in church and fret over loose ends."

The doors scraped open and a haggard, unshaven Reardon, tripping on the door runner, stumbled in, grasping a chair to keep from falling.

"Pardon me, but I didn't sleep very well. That Watanabe was close to being shot — for treason," but he seemed to know that label missed the mark. Joe guessed that Reardon might be reading his own dilemma into what happened to Watanabe.

Both Mei Li and Eric looked at Joe, but neither was up to rebutting Reardon before breakfast. Mei Li's abrupt stiffening around the shoulders and the way she jabbed at her cereal bowl convinced Joe that she was fuming about something. Eric, too, caught the signals, but Jack, pretending not to notice, hurried past her and on out the back door.

"What was that all about?" Eric asked with a puzzled expression, not addressing anyone in particular.

Working hard to be charitable, Joe defended Reardon. "Don't forget that Jack is an artist. Creative work is like birthing a baby. He not only has to make something out of all his fermenting ideas, but also must make some hard choices soon — like today. I think you're right, Mei Li, to stay with him, difficult as that may be. He must have someone to bounce ideas off."

"I think I can understand that," Eric put in. "When you're groping for the way, you can become all out of joint. My mom always says that about me."

"Mei Li," Joe said, "I guess we've appointed you to bear the brunt this morning. Do you mind?" as though they could influence what she'd decided to do already. She nodded resignedly.

Eric and Joe ate only cereal quickly, since swimming and the hot climb had dampened their appetites.

Reardon didn't return until just before Eric and Joe headed through the backyard out to the road. Several families were walking ahead of them, and others were coming from behind, followed by a PriviaVan bumping along carrying what looked like somebody's parents visiting for the summer.

"See that little boy down on the road?" Joe asked. "Remind me to tell you about him. Usually he carries a tennis racket, but not to church."

From the hill, Joe and Eric could see Anita playing on an old pump-style reed organ. Folding chairs and long backless benches were lined up eight or nine deep in a semi-circle facing a portable altar in front of the net. Steeple-like pines shaded the whole area and separated it from the two tennis courts below.

"When I visited here before," Eric said, "the service was held in the auditorium by the beach."

"They still have them there, one at 8:30 and another at 11:00. We prefer the outdoor service, where Communion is offered. It's more intimate and combines elements from various liturgies, even from the Orthodox, but it's also informal enough so that free prayers aren't out of place. Several Catholic couples attend, too."

As Eric and Joe drew closer, they avoided the stone stairs. Instead they hopped onto the small play area between the road and the tennis court. From there it was but a few steps to an opening in the wire backstop. They stooped through the breach, then rather than sit in back where they'd be bothered by latecomers, Joe led Eric down front where they'd be least distracted. Joe wanted to concentrate on the words spoken. After the opening hymn he closed his eyes to pray. He had so much on his mind he couldn't remember much about the first part of the service, except the woman lector trumpeting a scripture lesson from

Paul's Letter to the Romans: "You know what time it is. Now it is time to wake from sleep... Put on the Lord, Jesus, and make no provision for the flesh..."

Try as he may, Joe found himself drifting away from Joshua McDuffy's sermon back fifty-five years to a dimly lit room at Shamshuipo Prison. Stench from the latrine at the end of the barrack permeated everything. From across the field came the groans of dying prisoners and through the open window, he saw the drooping outlines of what were once robust young men like Eric Gunderson by his side. He watched the walking skeletons, bodies ravaged by dysentery and diptheria, as they hobbled slowly to view the scene outside.

From the far end of the field the mournful notes of last taps drifted in softly. Even the sick tried to stand at attention as a gun cart piled high with corpses passed, escorted by a scraggly honour guard of prisoners leading the way to the burial site.

Then Joe saw Uncle John Watanabe slouched over on his cot, his head in his hands, heaving with grief. As though he sensed Joe's presence behind him, he turned his head and looked right at him. With the careful diction of a man who had recited English phrases until he sounded like a Gettysburg Yankee, Watanabe questioned Joe: "What else can I do for you? What do you want of me?"

"Only your forgiveness," Joe sobbed. "When we worked together in Hiroshima, I never knew what you had suffered in Hong Kong. It wasn't until the BBC brought you to London for the "This Is Your Life" show, that we learned of what you'd done. If only you had told me, I would have been more patient and understanding. Why didn't you tell me your malaria aftereffects got you down? How could I have been so arrogant as to argue with you over Japanese grammar. I wanted to say that creation is possible for God, but instead my hertical grammar made it to mean that we create God.

"If I had truly caught your message of love, I would have realized why you kept repeating *subeshi* (must do) with the word for *love*. You told us your favorite book was *Agape and Eros*. You knew the cost of God's love. You enfleshed its meaning for us.

"Now, God is giving me another chance to tell your story to the world. Will you pray for our success?"

Then, Joe thought he heard Uncle John say to him, "You have already won the struggle."

McDuffy suddenly toned down to a whisper. He spoke directly to Joe: "Don't leave this place before you've cast your lot to become a soldier of the cross — living and dying for others. Don't be afraid. Jesus has won your battle. He will help you take your stand and strengthen you to do his work, always. Amen."

Joe again went back in his mind to Shamshuipo, until Eric tugged his sleeve. It was time to stand up and move forward for Communion. As they filed up front, a large circle of men and women, boys and girls, from many countries, formed. Joe knew and Eric knew, too, that they were about to experience Christ's presence and his promise never to forsake them.

"Take, eat, this is my body broken for you.

"Take, drink, this is my blood shed for you for the remission of sin."

While Joe made his way back to the bench, who should be standing in line but Peter Yu, waiting to go forward to the altar.

Lord, help me be open to him and not let the past control the present. But how, Lord, can I handle him? I can't just invite him to the cabin, he'll sabotage everything.

At the close of the service when visitors were introduced, Joe had Eric stand up and told how his young friend hoped to meet former classmates from the American School.

"Also," Joe continued, "there's one more guest I must introduce. We met by chance on the train yesterday. Mr. Peter Yu is a journalist from Hong Kong checking out Olympic facilities for the New China News Agency, *Xinhua*."

Without soliciting remarks from him, Peter strode up to the front of the congregation and launched into some flattering praises of Joe. Then without warning, he changed demeanor to what sounded like a memorized propaganda piece praising "our Peoples' Republic of China." He spoke glowingly about how overjoyed the Chinese in Hong Kong will be when China liberates them from the yoke of British colonialism and welcomes them back to the motherland.

"Deng Xiaoping has pledged that Hong Kong can continue its capitalistic system unchanged for fifty years, one China, but two systems. This successful reunion will also pave the way for Taiwan's return to China."

From two rows in back, Joe heard a man's voice mutter, "Won't that make the Taiwanese happy!"

As Peter returned to his seat, Joe thought he saw Yu's traveling comrade standing beyond the backstop netting. The congregation broke up into small informal groups, renewing acquaintances and greeting newcomers, but several conversations must have been about Peter Yu because they kept looking in his direction as they talked.

Joe didn't dare take Peter home. Even if his doubts about Peter's reliability were mistaken, he couldn't risk it. He feared his perplexity was showing because Eric edged closer and whispered, "We're not going to invite him to the cabin, are we?"

"Joe," Anita called from the organ, "Matsumotos have invited us over for coffee. They said to bring our guests, too."

111

"Whew!" Joe breathed out. "Peter, can you join us at the neighbors for coffee? Dr. Matsumoto is a science professor. You'll find him very interesting."

Peter looked at his watch and shook his head, but accepted the invitation. "Our driver is going down to the lake and will be back at 10:00.," he said. He's to meet my companion and me by the parking lot beyond the store. Before we go for coffee, Joe, could I speak with you privately."

"Ani, would you take Eric with you? I've told him about Dr. Matsumoto, and I think he wants to ask him some questions. Peter and I will join you shortly."

A long bench under the trees and away from the road near the practice court was open, so they walked back there to talk.

"Ten years ago," Yu began, "didn't we bump into each other at the Church Centre on Waterloo Road? You were trying to launch a movie about a Japanese pastor who had been posted to Hong Kong during World War II. Do you remember what I told you?"

"Refresh my memory," *but how can I ever forget?*

"The idea was absurd." Yu emphasized. "The Japanese still denied the Rape of Nanking. How could you hope to sell a Japanese hero to Chinese?"

Lifting his eyebrows and tilting his head as if to get a better look at Joe's face, Yu began to grill him. "I trust you gave up that foolish idea? It would never work. I bet no Chinese encouraged you."

Not sure of Yu's intent, Joe resorted to his Japanese poker face and countered with, "Didn't you know? I would have thought you would have heard from the Hong Kong staff."

"You'd never get away with that film once the Chinese take over. What are you working on now?"

"We're simply playing around with some ideas. Nothing concrete yet."

"Just wondered, since that British TV fellow is with you and the Chinese woman from Taiwan. I wouldn't trust her. What do you know about her?"

"Oh! That does look strange, doesn't it? Only a coincidence; we met in Tokyo, and I invited them up here to get away from the heat."

Yu appeared to believe him, but Joe couldn't be sure. "We'd better get you a cup of coffee before your driver comes back."

I wish I knew someone from Hong Kong who has kept track of Yu. Maybe Andy Liu knows about him.

Peter scowled at his watch, "It's after 10:00. I've got to go. We're due at Myoko to see a hot spring resort in thirty minutes. I'm sorry to run. As he headed down the road, he slowed his pace and put his right hand up on his head. He stopped and looked back at Joe. "Be careful!" Making sure Joe had heard him correctly, he shouted again even louder, "Be careful! Next time my boss may be with me."

Joe knew he meant it as no mere formality. The two had always gotten along well — perhaps because Joe wasn't British, or was it because he never had authority overYu?

After indulging a while at Matsumotos, Joe excused himself. "Ani, you stay. I want to walk down and buy some Obuse cinnamon rolls to take back to Mei Li and Jack."

What Joe really wanted was to have some time alone. Eric stood up, too, and said, "I'll go along." The two of them backtracked to the Summer Store. On the way home, however, Joe regretted the detour to the store, for by now the mid-morning sun had burned off the coolness. Even the cicada were crying for the sun to show mercy. Butterflies and dragonflies had taken refuge in the leafy trees and were nowhere in sight. By the time they turned in toward the cabin, beads of sweat were rolling down Joe's forehead. Instead of yearning for coffee he now wanted something cold.

Drawing near the back door, angry shouts from the front of the house stopped them dead in their tracks. Eric and Joe looked at each other. Incriminating bursts of temper cut the thick morning air like lightning bolts. Any dream of consensus was exploding in their faces. On and on Mei Li and Reardon thundered. Eric looked at Joe and held both palms skyward, hoping Joe could explain this.

"What do you think we should do, Eric?" They stood motionless in the shade of the pine tree, feeling like helpless fools.

"We've got to go calm that storm," Joe said. At that very moment, Mei Li's high-pitched scream split the air. It pierced so loud swimmers across the lake must have heard it.

21

The Blowup

Embarrassed for having heard Mei Li and Reardon's argument, Joe purposely let the back screen door slam shut. Thus, he could warn them to cool it before he and Eric joined them.

"Anyone ready for cinnamon buns and coffee?" Joe shouted to them on the porch.

"Eric, why don't you go out and tell them I'm coming with coffee and rolls. That might calm them down," and he thought it had, but the moment of quiet proved to be no more than a break between rounds of a prize fight. Offering of refreshments rang the bell for the two to go after each other again.

"Opium War?" Reardon bellowed. "What does that have to do with us now? That was 155 years ago. The Commies are just throwing that up again to justify their power grab."

"Oh, you English, you don't understand anything. If you fail to mention how your British merchants — Jardine and the others — corrupted South China by selling opium to pay for imports, no one will listen to you. Chinese television is playing that War up big these days. They're even going to telecast a serial drama about it."

"Don't try to mess up the Watanabe story. You can't say everything in a one-hour program. TV's not a newspaper."

"But if you don't," she rebutted, "no Chinese in Hong Kong or anywhere else will take you seriously. Theyre not dumb. To make Watanabe credible, you mustn't whitewash the British. They're not victims, the Chinese of Hong Kong are. Can't you get that through your head? You've been the imperialistic oppressors for 200 years. I'd be willing to bet you've never even heard of your British Mt. Davis Concentration Camp in Hong Kong."

"You're distorting history," Reardon retorted. "The British government didn't sell opium to the Chinese."

"You're copping out, and you know it," she hissed back. "Your government backed up its traders all along and finally sent troops to protect the greedy merchants."

Joe turned to Eric and suggested they sit on the living room couch till the storm blew over. "They're letting out some pretty strong feelings, but it's good that Mei Li confronts him."

"I don't know anything about the Opium War," Eric admitted. "It never came up in any of my history classes. In fact, we don't learn anything about

Asian history. Crazy, isn't it? Our country's future lies in Asia, and we aren't teaching anything about it. Did you know that Los Angeles is a busier port now than New York? Much of that trade is with China, and more than half of it passes through Hong Kong, Dad told me."

Circling in on Reardon for the final knockout blow, Mei Li raised her voice, accentuating her every word. "The British built Hong Kong on top of the opium addicts' graves. They fathered the addicts, fed them and ended up murdering them."

"You're hysterical now. Settle down," Reardon cautioned. "I get your point. No need to get so excited."

"Who's excited? I'm merely reciting history that your schools censored. Exactly as the Japanese did after the War."

"We're back to Japan, are we?" Reardon acknowledged with disgust. Then remembering that he'd heard Joe ask about coffee and rolls, he called in, "Hold the coffee and rolls until Ms. Ping and I straighten out some things."

"That's where this whole business started," she went on. "Don't you remember the '80s? The Japanese Ministry of Education decided to sanitize the historical accounts of Japan's invasions of Asian countries. They wanted to re-name them 'incursions' or something benign like that."

Mei Li paused, then with a strained voice she said, "It amounted to a whitewash. They didn't want the children to learn what the fathers had done. One so-called scholar even made an attempt to deny the Rape of Nanking — although we Chinese had films of it. That infuriated us."

"Wasn't that when Weaver lent Nolan's book on Watanabe to their media director in Hong Kong?"

"That's right."

"The book," Reardon continued, "moved him so much he insisted on trying to make a movie of it. You read their screenplay last night, didn't you?"

"It was a first draft, but even so, very powerful," she replied. "I was in Hong Kong then working part time. I was a student intern in the office of a Chinese film company specializing in documentaries. The company had a sharp young film maker, by the name of Ann Wei from the mainland."

"Your point?"

"Well, she came into the office one morning, fuming about something. The night before Wei had met with Mr. Weaver and David Chiang. They had proposed that she do the film about Watanabe. She felt uneasy about it. The very thought of glorifying a Japanese bothered her, so she politely told them she already was committed for the next two years. Anyway, she couldn't consider directing a film until she'd seen the script.

"You could verify that with Mr. Weaver. At the time, Wei felt no Chinese would do a film praising a Japanese. You have to remember that was about the time the theaters were featuring horrific documentaries on Japanese atrocities in China."

Inside the cabin, Joe nodded with understanding, remembering how upset Chinese congregations would get when he said anything good about the Japanese.

"What I think I hear you saying," Reardon said in a tone of resignation, "is that we should drop this TV project. It's too hot to handle."

"That's exactly what I don't mean," Mei Li shot back. "I'm saying the opposite. Oh, you English are so dense. You don't grasp anything. You're worse than Americans. You look at truth always from your own warped self-righteous interpretation of history."

"That's not fair, and you know it."

Reardon's plea for fairness had thrown Mei Li off balance. Joe could see her through the window. She stood up and gazed off toward Mt. Madarao and the lake, as though she was drawing wisdom from their likeness to Victoria Peak and Victoria Harbour. He suspected she was marshaling more arguments for one final counterattack, but before she could turn around and cut loose again, Reardon pre-empted her.

"I've decided to trash the TV project."

When he announced that, Mei Li's face flushed red with rage. Her fierce dragon-lady frown out-scowled any face Joe'd ever seen, even in Japanese horror films. Her livid countenance could have been mistaken for a volcano spilling out fiery-red lava.

"You chicken!" she screamed. "You're a coward! Talk about a paper tiger! You're all big and tough on the outside, but inside you're a wet noodle." She turned from him and walked away. Spitting out at him one last time, her every syllable cutting into him like a two-edged sword, twisting on every word as she thrust deeper into his heart. "No wonder your wife wants to leave you."

Reardon's face writhed with pain. Joe could see she had cut all the way to the core of his being. Eric shut his eyes and squirmed empathetically. Joe dropped his head and groaned.

Realizing she'd crossed the bounds of civil speech, Mei Li's voice cracked and went hoarse again as she apologized and shifted to a reconciliatory approach: "But you have to live, I suppose, if this Maoburger man threatens to cut off his sponsorship."

Trying to humor her, Reardon forced a smile and said, "We've lived without Dengburgers up to now, and we can jolly well keep on living, in spite of being dung-deprived."

That gross joke offended her. Joe could see Mei Li's face flush red and the tense shoulders signaled an iminent attack on Reardon again.

"Write that Horatio Judas off! You can do the TV program about Watanabe, but can't do it by selling your soul to the devil. Better to do what's right and fail than succeed with a lie. Your only hope is to stick to the truth. My father pounded that into me. When the KMT imprisoned him, he could have made up something and gone free. Instead he stuck it out until truth won out — though he almost lost his sight doing it."

Reardon clapped his hands to applaud her speech, then looked at Joe and Eric through the window and raised his voice. "Sounds very noble, but — I don't know. You talk about obeying God rather than men, but when it hurts your pocketbook, I wonder..."

Staring Joe down, Reardon stood there watching for his reaction. Joe recognized in Reardon's eyes a weary sadness when he struck at Joe with, "Aren't you having a world assembly of Lutherans in Hong Kong the week after the takeover? Just wait till the Communists get wind of your stand on human rights. When Beijing threatens to cancel the assembly, what will you do? You won't be any braver than the World Bank. They're forming contingency plans to move their meeting out of Hong Kong."

"Oh, you're impossible," Mei Li scoffed and jumped up again. Forgetting where she was, she leaned against one of the poles holding up the veranda roof. It lurched out, releasing a three-meter section of roofing, which crunched out a warning that it was collapsing. Reardon saw it falling. He jumped up, grabbing Mei Li with his left arm as he pushed his right hand up under the roof to stop the fall. He held it up long enough for Eric to rush out to rescue them and force the roof and pole back up into place. Then he grabbed Mei Li's shoulders with both hands. Looking her in the eyes, he asked, "Are you all right? Sit down over here."

"Whew, now's the time for coffee and rolls," Joe sighed.

"What on earth could you two have been talking about so long?" Joe queried with enough smile to dull the impact, but it let them know Eric and he had overheard the argument. That would make it easier to start up discussion for the next round, for which the bell was about to ring.

22

An Invincible Enemy?

When Joe began to pour coffee into the cups, a familiar voice called from the opening in the bushes, "Isn't it *Ruteru Awa* time? It was Dr. Matsumoto. He always jokes about liking *Ruteru Awa,* which he makes a pun out of since *Ruteru* means Lutheran and *awa* means both hour and foam, as in *Lutheran Hour.*

"Oh, only coffee, no beer?" he complained. "There was a telephone call to Brannigans from a Ralph Eilers. He wanted to tell his son that everything is okay. He's decided to take the 11 o'clock train that arrives here at 2:15. He has some important news which he wants to tell him in person.

"He says not to worry about meeting him. He'll take a taxi."

"That's wonderful," Joe said, before remembering about a bed for him to sleep on.

Noticing Joe's worried look, Eric rescued him by reminding him that the bunk bed under him was open. Then he added, "It sounds as though Dad finally is ready to explain what he's been up to."

Matsumoto sheepishly excused himself, "Only coffee? I have to go home. Our kids are coming from Tokyo."

"Oh, Paul, could I beg a favor of you?" Joe asked. "I've promised to call someone in the States at 1:00 our time. Would you mind if I used your phone? I'll put it on my card."

"No problem. Any time."

"Thanks. I'd hate to go down the hill again to the public phone."

Fearing further distractions, Reardon resumed the role of director and called the meeting to order, reminding the team members that they must try to wrap things up that afternoon.

Looking accusingly at Mei Li, he began what was to become a rambling review of what he thought were the salient points to keep in mind. His haggard, unshaven face made Joe suspect he was about to take them on a long, circuitous, defensive wild-goose chase that could only wind down to a jerking halt when he'd admit he couldn't go on.

Joe turned off his ears rather than suffer Reardon's fumbling excuses. He feared the explanation would reek of resignation and outright defeatism. Like an alcoholic beaten down by one too many lapses, Reardon's bleary eyes looked tragic. He stared blankly at the mountains becoming hidden by dark threatening clouds.

Joe wished he could whisk Eric away from Reardon's pessimism, but there was no escaping. On and on he listed insurmountable obstacles in the way. "We can't succeed," Reardon complained, "because the government has forced Horatio Chang to agree to putting a PRC Chinese in as executive producer over me. He'll make us dilute the message.

"The Commies will restrict location sites for shooting background footage.

"They'll never let us show Watanabe defying authority, even if its Japanese imperial tyranny.

"China's new propaganda chief, Ding Guangen, will kill us, if not literally, then by subtle sophisticated tricks."

Hoping to shut Reardon up, Joe lifted his left hand to look at his watch, then said, "Excuse me, I'll run in and get some coffee." That broke Reardon's stream of thought, giving Mei Li her patiently awaited chance to drag Reardon away from the pit he'd dug for himself.

Mei Li looked and sounded like a different woman. The stormy typhoon of the morning had swept through, leaving her calm as a waveless lake. Gone was her shrill, accusing soprano voice. Now she spoke with a pianissimo tone. Her eyes emitted a kindness that matched her new melodious contralto voice.

Reminding Joe of an experienced psychiatrist, minus a white coat and the smell of leathery couches, Mei Li reflected back to Reardon the images he had been projecting onto the cloudy screen engulfing him. One by one she handed back to him proofs of the photos she'd taken of him in her mind. Ever so gently she needled him by reminding him that the photos she'd taken didn't lie.

"So," she began, "let me see if I heard you correctly. Horatio Chang has created a new position of executive producer and appointed a pro-communist Chinese to that position. You think he'll dampen your style, right?"

Reardon sat motionless, intent on this new, kinder Mei Li Ping he was hearing. "You fear he'll cut your production budget. You won't be free to shoot on locations too sensitive to the PRC? That's what you implied, wasn't it? You're not clever enough to shoot shots without official approval?"

More silence.

"Watanabe," she continued, "has to be shown as a loyal Japanese and in no way defying his superiors, even ruthless ones? Is that what you meant? You're not able to make it possible for a Chinese, or foreign viewer to uncover the implications of the story? You don't trust the audience to figure it out?"

"Well," he stammered, "I didn't quite mean it like that."

"You believe this new propaganda genius in the PRC is invincible? There's no way for a veteran documentary producer and journalist like you to outwit the Chinese bureaucracy? If you are saying that, my boss Bill Knight's opinion of you is way off the mark. He told me if anyone is up to this job, you are the man." Catching herself, she rephrased the sentence in the politically correct way: "I mean you are that person. According to him you're the best in the business."

"Red said that about me?"

"For God's sake, and I do mean for God's sake, Mr. Reardon," she scolded. "Pull yourself together. I'm not against you. I really believe in you — down deep I believe in you. Forget my bad mouth earlier. We're all behind you."

Looking first to Joe, then to Eric, "We are, aren't we?"

Scanning each of them with a hurting sadness in his eyes, Reardon asked them, "Did I sound that bad? You actually believe we can pull this off?"

More silence.

Then, Joe asked him, "When the road is blocked, what do you do?" As he said that, Joe happened to look through the study window. Hanging on the wall next to his desk was the cartoon-like drawing his son had given him for his birthday many years before.

"Eric, do me a favor. Go into the study and bring me that golf picture next to the desk."

Reardon, irritated by the very word *golf*, glared at Joe. "Is this the time to talk about golf?"

"But, Jack, you think visually don't you? Even if you hate golf, you can identify with that picture."

"Yeah, I saw it last night. It thoroughly depressed me."

Eric handed it to Joe, who placed it upright on the window sill, so all could see a hopeless golfer peering down over the lip of a 15-foot-deep sand trap. Next to his ball buried in the sand lay the bleached bones of animals who had fallen in and were unable to escape.

"Hopeless isn't it? But do you know the name *Phil Mikelson*, the left-handed pro golfer? He's famous for inventing fantastic recovery shots. I saw him once on television illustrate how you can hit out of an impossible sand trap, like the one in the picture."

"That's impossible!" Reardon laughed. "No one can hit out of that."

"The ball is embedded in that sand slope which is about 45-degrees steep. Phil took his 64-degree sand wedge and aiming straight into the embankment below the lip struck the ball along the line of the bank in the direction of the green, but instead of going forward the ball shot high up in the air and landed 10 feet behind him, safely beyond the backside of the sand trap. Then he was able to hit his next shot safely onto the green."

"I'm not a golfer," Reardon grumbled, "so what's the point?"

"Very simple, the moral of the story is to bang straight ahead and land the ball behind on the grass. There you'll be able to see what you should do next.

"In non-golf language, this means you need to step back from the pit. Then you'll be able to see the way ahead — clearer than you could see in the bunker."

"That's a long way to make my point, I admit, but let's blast straight ahead with our most lofted club. Ironically that throws us back ten or twenty yards farther from where we want to go. But it positions us to see how we can cross over the trap and hill in our way.

"My son gave me that picture when we were failing to get enough money for the film project in the '80s, but I kept believing that some day we'd succeed. God in his own good time would provide us with a 64-degree lofted wedge."

Joe couldn't decide whether Reardon was bored or taking the lesson to heart.

"An old Chinese friend said something similar to Anita and me on our wedding day: 'With God all things are possible.' It was a wall hanging. You can see it on the wall in the back bedroom. I pinned under it a poem titled, 'Never Quit.' Go back and see it yourself."

"I just can't believe," Reardon confessed, "but isn't there a place in the Bible that says, 'I believe, help thou my unbelief?'"

"That's okay with us," Mei Li assured him with remarkable feminine intuition, "but that doesn't keep us from believing in you. You blast the ball. We'll stand behind you, won't we?" she commanded Eric and Joe.

For a minute, no one spoke. Eric seemed to be daydreaming. Joe worried about how this arguing and vacillating were affecting him. Was he making any sense of the struggle? If Joe had failed ten years ago, how could he be sure they'd succeed this time?

Questions about what was God's will poured through his mind. What are his intentions? How and why had that will been thwarted before? Are these circumstances in life merely detours which faith can overcome and turn into a better good? How can we attain certainty that what we're about to attempt is part of God's ultimate will for Hong Kong — and the Chinese people?

"How do we know? Is there some sign God can use to show us the way? I wonder if Andrew Liu's connections in Hong Kong might not prove to be our trump card."

Joe looked over at Mei Li, who astonished him with a most un-Chinese gesture. She had raised her fist as though she wanted to shout to Heaven, "Let's go for it."

Yet, in spite of her demonstrative affirmation, Reardon stayed seated in what could only be interpreted as a gloomy skepticism. He was either unwilling or unable to respond.

Eric had been facing out toward the lake and had taken no notice of Mei Li's militant gesture to go forward.

"Excuse me a minute," and he ducked around to the back of the cabin. The door banged shut and later the hand-washer clicked a few times, but Eric didn't come back.

George L. Olson

The other three remained in frozen inaction. Joe got up and went to fetch more coffee and a fresh bag of Nagano peanuts. He knew crunching peanuts could arouse flagging spirits.

While returning through the living room, he caught sight of Eric beyond the bushes, standing by the road, deep in thought. Eric punched his right fist into his left hand, turned around and ran back toward the cabin. He pushed his way through an opening in the bushes and hopped up onto the veranda. His worried look had vanished, replaced with a cheerful, but determined appearance.

He burst out, "Mr. Reardon, may I say something?"

Jack gaped out of his tired reddish eyes. The contrast between the pale worn-out TV journalist and the ruddy bright-eyed 17-year old struck Joe. Mei Li looked astonished, too.

Joe's eyes met with hers for an instant of mutual understanding that felt like a plus-minus shock. They both realized that this young man just might rescue Reardon and the whole project.

"Maybe it's time for you to help us out, Eric," Joe said. "What's on your mind?"

"Well," he said cautiously, "I thought of something. I don't think Mr. Weaver even knows this, but a high school buddy and I back in D.C. won an amateur film award. That we won wasn't important, but how we won."

"Your mother," Joe said, "never mentioned that to us. Most mothers would have told everybody."

"My Mom never bragged about me, or Dad, for that matter."

"Go on, we're all ears," Joe said, "but no bragging."

"While I was outside thinking, I remembered how discouraged my pal and I felt when our media teacher vetoed our plans. He put us down by saying our proposed project was not only impossible, but dangerous. He couldn't take responsibility for us, and besides that, he was frightened by what the school's financial supporters would think."

This point caught Reardon's attention. "What were you cooking up?" he asked.

Swallowing his nervousness, Eric haltingly began to outline what they'd done. "You know where the White House sits — right smack in the middle of an area bordered by almost slumish housing. There sits this beautiful white mansion, the epitome of luxury, standing in a sea of poverty. Drug dealers and muggers roam at will, and the homeless lie strewn about, huddling to keep from freezing to death. It's better now, but used to be pretty awful."

"What did you do?" Mei Li asked. Reardon moved forward in his chair, his mouth open in disbelief as Eric's enthusiasm built up momentum.

Eric talked faster. "We'd heard that we could get free footage of past inaugural celebrations. So, all we did was edit some of those films in with some

122

of our own shots of the neighborhood, plus some good stuff the church-run shelters had been using for promotion."

"Good grief, Eric, how did you get the courage to do that?" Joe asked.

Ignoring the question, he continued faster. "Then at the end we showed the estimated $48,000,000 inauguration budget next to the annual budgets for these Washington shelters. That shook people up. The father of one of our classmates worked at the *Washington Post* and happened to be in the audience when we showed the video. He wrote it up for the paper, and then, of all things, President Clinton called to congratulate us. He even joked with us. He said he didn't care how small the inauguration party budget was as long as he could play his saxophone."

"He said that?" Mei Li said. "You should have sold the story to the Republicans."

"Our teacher," Eric continued, "whom we had run an end-run on, suddenly took credit as our producer. The school board organized a petition to the President and Congress. They asked that future inauguration budgets be cut in half, with the other half going to the social agencies within three miles of the White House." Eric was out of breath when he finished.

After the four had settled down and each grabbed a last handful of peanuts, Reardon looked around at each of them one by one, saying with his eyes, now coming alive with expectancy, what each of them thought. There was no way any of them could say, "No," to the project and expect to live without guilt — no way at all. Thus, that Sunday morning they vowed to blast ahead, come what may.

Reardon smiled broadly and glancing toward Joe, asked, "Do you own a 64-degree sand wedge? I think we need one now. We'll back up a bit for now. When we come together this afternoon — shall we say at coffee time — we can rationally decide how we shall move ahead.

He stopped, looking as if he was about to say something extremely important. Like a Marine sergeant he barked to Joe: "Orimura-san, don't forget your sand wedge."

23

Edge of the Pit

As they separated, each to his or her own corner, the faint sound of "Praise to the Almighty" drifted up through the trees from the lakeside. The 11 o'clock service had begun. The four retreated to their invisible cubicles to think about future scenarios, but a sudden fatherly inspiration overcame Joe. He pulled Eric aside to tell him he had something to show him.

Leading him to the backyard, they headed out under the clotheslines to a thicket of scrubby bushes, grass and small trees. "Watch out for the red-stemmed plants. They're poison lacquer." The growth was almost impenetrable, though Joe said he'd whacked a path through it two weeks before. Holding their arms up to avoid thorns and cobwebs, they pushed back through the brush much like drawing apart clothes hanging in a huge wardrobe closet.

"Remind you of C.S. Lewis' Narnia? Remember the boy Edmond who discovered the secret door to the enchanted land?"

Eric caught on at once. "Is this your secret Narnia?" he joked.

"I dunno," Joe answered, "this is not exactly the door to a pleasant kingdom."

Pointing to two half-rotten doors leaning against the hillside, Joe said, "This is our old snowpit. As late as the early '50s, the caretakers would fill this deep pit with snow, so we could keep food from spoiling in the summer. I've filled it up now with tree branches and trash. We keep it covered so that no one can fall in."

"That would be scary," Eric said.

"There's a classic story among the Nojiri legends about a pompous fellow, whom for the sake of the story, I'll call 'Schulz.' He preached a super Barthian Calvinism while his neighbor loved to spout out the latest modernistic fads.

"One day Schulz fell into his snowpit. As the story is told, the two had had an acrimonious argument about the neighbor's unruly son. During a tennis tournament, the neighbor's son accidentally stepped on Schulz' brand-new white shoes. That made Schulz furious. He accused the boy of dirtying his new shoes on purpose. He demanded that the boy come over to his house and not only apologize, but also clean and polish the shoes.

"That same afternoon Schulz went out to his snowpit to get a bottle of cold beer, but the door swung shut and bumped him down into the pit. There was no way he could climb out. Schulz yelled and yelled, but no one heard him until his liberal neighbor did and came running to rescue him. Just as he was stretching down to grab Schulz' hand, a gust of wind blew the door shut again and knocked the neighbor down on top of Schulz — hilarious reconciliation under duress."

"What a story!"

"They kept screaming for help, the neighbor in English and Schulz in German. The irony of the story is that it was the neighbor's son and two of his rowdy friends who finally heard the cries and came to save them."

"Beautiful! That's a great story," Eric howled.

"But did you recognize yourself in the story?"

"Me?"

"This morning weren't we all stranded in a pit? We were tied up in knots about what to do. Did you realize Reardon was on the verge of giving up? When you came running back, you boosted us up out of the mire. I don't think it's a mere accident that you've come to Japan this summer."

"I didn't know if I should speak up or not, but when you looked so helplessly bogged down, I don't know why, but I felt I had to speak up."

Pausing for a brief interlude, Joe then dared ask Eric, "You don't suppose that someone who pushed you today was God, do you?"

The question didn't surprise Eric. He nodded as he though he already had concluded that.

"This Pastor Watanabe, you knew him didn't you? If you don't mind my saying, it would be very dishonest and hypocritical to his legacy if you guys didn't at least try to act like him."

Eric had said "you," but Joe knew he really meant the four of them.

Not wishing to leave this sharp challenge suspended in mid-air, Eric added, "Money and politics shouldn't be everything. There comes a time when each of us must stand up and be counted. Dad would want me to anyway, because he is... He choked a moment as he groped for the right words. "When I explain this to him, he'll understand — I'm sure, even if Mom can't — for now."

"Whew! It's hot back here. Let's get out of the sun. Eric, why don't you try jotting some of your ideas on paper."

As the two emerged out of the brush, Mei Li was watching them from her back window. She drew the curtain closed and came outside next to the bath heater.

"What have you fellows been up to, hiding out there in the bushes?"

Joe and Eric blushed. "Did you think we were peeping Toms?" Joe asked. "I swear I'm innocent."

"Well?" and she decided to hold her tongue.

"Orimura-san was showing me the snowpit they used to use for an icebox. He told me a cool story of how some teenagers saved two grumpy old men who'd fallen into one and couldn't get out. I think he was trying to teach me something."

"God knows we need it!" she exclaimed, "but maybe Reardon is beginning to come around, don't you think?"

"He's leaning toward trying, but he knows how risky it will be," Joe said. "It's never easy to swim against the stream of those who gave him the chance in the first place.

"Your views, Mei Li, might prove decisive. What part of the story will mean the most to Hong Kongers? That Chinese script could give us help on that. Kagami's screenplay can show which facets Japanese and non-Chinese Asians would be most moved by. Eric, you can speak for youth." He waited and then said, "But where does that leave me?"

"Your generation, of course," Eric said. "It was you guys who survived the Depression and the War. You must have a special perspective which shouldn't be overlooked."

"And we mustn't forget children," Joe added from his grandfatherly point of view. "What about Reardon? What's his role?"

That question stumped them for a moment, but Eric had an idea. "How about wily quarterback? He'll call the plays."

"We shouldn't sack him." Joe said. "We've got to back him all the way, especially if they go after him."

"Sounds like a football game, doesn't it?" Eric laughed. "And all along I thought we were playing golf."

24

Forward, No Matter What?

Over lunch, they ate like Trappist monks under a rigorous discipline of silence. Halfway through the meal, Reardon abruptly reached across the table and stabbed his fork into a piece of blood-red salami.

After several minutes, Anita broke the silence. "This brown bread is baked in Obuse. If I'd thought of it earlier, I could have ordered one of their blueberry pies. These rolls are from there, too." But no matter how hard she tried, she couldn't jump-start a meaningful conversation and soon dropped her head in quiet resignation.

Joe tried to comfort her by saying, "Eric's father doesn't need to be met. He's taking a taxi from the station."

Not being sure he could guarantee a cool breeze on the porch by 2:00, Joe suggested they meet in the larger living room in back, which is shaded by the pines to the west. "We can move out to the porch later if the breeze comes in. By then shadows will cover the plastic roof. I'll straighten things up here and stack the dishes. Why don't the rest of you stretch out for a while?"

Anita looked on in surprise as Joe picked up in the living room. He arranged the chairs to form a semi-circle facing away from the inner plywood wall and toward the soft wicker chair in front of the outside door leading to the porch. He could rest his materials on the window seat. Everyone would have a clear full-face view of him, but more importantly he'd be facing the opening to the back bedroom where hung the framed Bible verse a Chinese friend had presented to the Weavers on their wedding day. It read, "With God all things are possible."

A half hour later, Joe sensed that Mei Li was still awake. He went over to the couch where she was stretched out and whispered in her ear, "Would you mind going next door with me to phone Andrew Liu. He hasn't heard from us directly about what we hope he can do for us."

They slipped out quietly and walked down to Matsumoto's cabin. Mrs. Matsumoto let them in and led them to the phone resting on an end table separating the dining and living room.

Punching in the international operator's number, it took less that 10 seconds for Liu's telephone to start ringing. Andrew himself answered. Joe asked if he had understood his wife's explanation correctly. Andrew proceeded to repeat what she had told him, which sounded right. *No garbling here, thank goodness.*

"Andy," Joe said, "we've got a woman here from British TV in Tokyo. Her name is Ping, Mei Li Ping. I'm going to let her talk with you in Chinese."

Handing the phone to Mei Li, she and Andrew jabbered on and on in Mandarin, each sentence more animated than the last. Although Joe couldn't understand the conversation, he intuited that she knew Andrew, or at least knew of him. Finally she wound down and excitedly repeated, *"Dzaizyan"* twice, which meant, "See you again."

Handing the phone back to Joe, she exclaimed, "I know him. His Chinese name is Liu Shih-Feng. I took his television course at Hong Kong Baptist College. He's tops and will help us all he can. I asked him about Peter Yu. He knows about him, but went dumb when I suggested asking for his help."

"Hello, Andrew. Mei Li says she knows you. You realize what we're asking could be dangerous?"

"Anything really worth doing in Hong Kong is dangerous," he replied, but added, "There's a brief honeymoon period for at least a year. After that, we don't know what'll happen. We should do the project as soon as possible, before the honeymoon sours and people want to file for a divorce."

"What about your wife Maurene? Is she willing to go along with you on this?"

Andrew didn't answer quickly, but seemed to be struggling to word his reply in the most accurate way. "Joe, or should I remind you that you're *Nyou Bobo* to us? Don't we live by faith? Maurene agrees that I should help. How can we say 'No' when believers inside China told us to broadcast the gospel, no matter who opposes. 'Even if we're arrested for listening, that's okay,' they say. 'The gospel spreads anyway. The more they oppress, the more our numbers grow.'" This led to a long description of what the future in China might hold.

Joe couldn't add anything to Andrew's evaluation, but thanked him and said, "With you on board, I believe we'll be able to move ahead. I'll be in touch. *Dzaizyan, dzaizyan.*"

It was a few minutes before 2:00 when Mei Li, Eric and Joe gathered quietly in the back living room and took their seats. Jack Reardon came in and as planned took the open seat in front of the outside screen door. Joe plugged in the coffee pot and placed it on the table at the end of the room near the entrance to the study. Everyone was too tense to think about eating and drinking. Like dogs pulling at their leashes, they were set to jump in and start talking.

"The good news," Joe announced cheerfully, "is that Andrew Liu is coming aboard. Maurene, his wife, backs him wholeheartedly in the decision even though he admits the project will be fraught with dangers. 'Working in a den of lions,' he says.

"Liu predicts Hong Kong's honeymoon may last only a short time. "A Hong Kong cartoonist," he says "has drawn China as the Sugar Daddy from the North, suggesting that he'll take over the household throne in Hong Kong. Like a feudal Mandarin he'll demand servitude. At the least sign of an independent spirit, he'll denounce her infidelity and abuse her. He'll beat her down and rape her. He'll do it so often that the Hong Kong we now know will die. She'll become a sex slave, her master's concubine."

"I've seen a cartoon of that," Mei Li said. "Overdrawn, but that's what cartoonists do."

"Andrew thinks we must act before it's too late," Joe explained. "Everyone who can must live their faith. 'Even if Hong Kong is raped,' he insists, 'Chinese believers must stand firm. God won't forsake them.'"

Deferring to Reardon, the strained faces of the three couldn't conceal their anxiety. Squatty Reardon, his forehead wrinkles pinched together, sunk deep into the padded chair, filling it tight to the sides. He frowned at each of them. As though he hadn't heard a word Joe said, he began his bad-news speech. He held a cheap black-and-white ballpoint pen which he kept tapping on his writing pad. He gripped it so tightly that his reddish hand accentuated whitish knuckles, and Joe wondered if he might not suffer from high blood pressure.

Although usually a fast talker, more like a used-car salesman than a TV producer, — but then again, Joe had known church artists who could explode, too. When Reardon eventually spoke, he wouldn't look at them, but kept staring downward, "I think you all know," pacing his words slowly, "that I received an express letter from Horatio Chang. He's the Chinese fellow who proposed the TV series in the first place. Well, some appointee by Beijing in the new Hong Kong Assembly has pulled the rug out from under Chang. They've forced a quality-control supervisor on him. That's a euphemism for a security police watchdog who has power to censor whatever we do.

"Friends, Hong Kong's political and economic life is supposed to remain unchanged for fifty years, but few believe it. The rumor is that Beijing's appointees will revise the 1984 turnover agreements. Frankly, I don't know what to do. I'm sorry for dragging you into this and wasting your time." He scanned their faces to see reactions.

"Bullshit!" Dragon Lady Ping spouted out. "You've chickened out," and Joe promptly dropped his papers all over the floor.

Ashamed of his groveling around on the floor, Joe began sorting his papers. He knew he must say something, anything at all. Waiting for his inner batteries to become charged, he finally confronted Reardon and spoke up from the floor. "We may be knocked down, but we've not lost the fight. Before you even begin to think of throwing in the towel, why don't we go back to Plan A and see what program ideas or angles each of us has? Let's not call it quits until we've had our say. That's only fair, don't you think? Let's not go down without a fight."

"There's the money problem, too," Reardon grumbled.

"Hear us out," Joe pleaded. Before Reardon could reply, Joe struck first. "Mei Li, what struck you in that script the Hong Kong staff prepared?"

"The very name they titled it: 'Christmas at *Shamshuipo*.'"

"I've been there," Joe said, "grim place, even without sword-wielding Japanese soldiers all over the place, and prisoners dropping like flies in the barracks.

"You know," Mei Li reminded them, "Hong Kong fell on Christmas Day, 1941, so Christmas in Hong Kong during the Occupation had a double-barreled impact on people. The Christmas angle is worth exploring. Audiences can relate to Christmas any time."

"For my part," Joe put in, "I've always empathized with the anguish Watanabe felt when he learned the Americans were bombing the Japanese homeland. His family in Hiroshima was trying to survive without him. The A-bomb news about Hiroshima must have crushed him. How could he face up to going home? By the end of the War even his own people in Hong Kong had disowned him. They threw him out as a traitor. He had to survive on the streets, surrounded by bitter, hungry Chinese and enemy aliens."

"Sorry, but I disagree." Eric piped in. "I don't think that's the core of the story. When I was reading last night in bed, I tried to see the story through a camera lens. That always helps. The most unforgettable picture, the one I can't erase from my mind, is that first time he lugged medicines and vitamins into camp. The suitcase was stuffed solid, and little Watanabe, no more than 120 pounds sopping wet, struggled across the open clearing. Repeating Bible verses under his breath — I bet from the 23rd Psalm. I looked it up. 'Yea, though I walk through the valley of the shadow of death, I will fear no evil, for thou art with me, thy rod and thy staff they comfort me.'

"Frightened to death that one of those guards would cut him down, his hand raw and shoulder socket and elbow aching, he staggered past the sentries, afraid even to switch hands, crossing a 100 yards of open no-man's land of courtyard. That's a scene no one will forget." Eric choked as he tried to complete the sentence.

No one could say a word.

Breaking the silence, Joe finally said, "Earlier I had started to interrupt Eric's appeal, but stopped short. I didn't want to dampen his enthusiasm. But I need to make one small, but important correction."

"What's that?" Reardon, Eric and Mei Li 'trioed' in unison.

"Eric, your instincts were right," Joe said. "I think we too would have guessed Watanabe recited those famous words from Psalm 23, but we were mistaken. Later he revealed that what he actually kept repeating was a verse from Isaiah.

"Jack, would you hand me that Bible under the window? The verse he always recited under his breath was Isaiah 41:11. Let's see, Isaiah comes right before Jeremiah. Here it is. 'Fear not, for I am with you.'

"He cultivated the habit that whenever he approached the gate at Shamshuipo, he'd repeat that verse to remind himself that he wasn't alone. The Lord was walking with him."

It took several minutes for them to let that sink in.

"How lonely the walk would have been without God by his side!" Mei Li said as though she had known some lonely walks herself.

"But," Joe added, "we mustn't overlook that Watanabe had the integrity to admit that when he carried the briefcase full of supplies, he never had a moment without dreadful fear, not so much fear of death, but of torture. He'd seen how the *Kempeitai*, Japan's Gestapo, inflicted excruciating torture on victims. This fear terrified him. Yet, he willingly chose to face it day after day and week after week, deliberately meeting it head on."

Reardon then spoke up. "The title Kagami gave to his version of the story was 'A Brave Man of Love.'"

"That title almost says it right," Eric questioned. "It's more than that though, but what?"

"I sensed that, too," Mei Li said as she groped in her mind for what would fit. "How about this: 'Terrifying Bravery with Compassion?'"

"That's close to it," Eric responded, "but too long."

"Details like that will come later, but you've hit an important fact," Reardon said to move the discussion along.

"As a pastor," Joe said, "Watanabe certainly knew the context in which Isaiah had uttered those words. So, when Watanabe spoke them, it was as if he were Isaiah, in the same situation in which Isaiah had been. The Lord said to them, 'be not dismayed, for I am your God; I will strengthen you, I will help you, I will uphold you with my victorious right hand.'"

"Go on," Reardon said. "Go on, keep reading. What comes next?"

"Behold, all who are incensed against you shall be put to shame and confounded; those who strive against you shall be as nothing and shall perish. You shall seek those who contend with you, but you shall not find them, those who war against you shall be as nothing at all. For I, the Lord your God, hold your right hand; it is I who say to you, 'Fear not, I will help you.'"

"No wonder he chose those words," exclaimed Mei Li.

"Although Nolan would object to being compared with Watanbe," Joe continued, "those of us who visited Shamshuipo with him in '87 can never forget how he portrayed his mysterious affinity with Uncle John Watanabe. Nolan, you see, had discovered in 1969 that back in 1956 as a young British Army officer, he had bunked in the very same room Watanabe had used in 1942.

"When Nolan stood in the open field halfway between that room and the barracks to which Watanabe had to haul the supplies, he could barely speak; he was so shaken up.

"Another important point Nolan made to us was that he believed Watanabe was as relevant for our time as Joan of Arc, Martin Luther King, or Mother Teresa had been in their times."

"They are all non-Asians," Mei Li pointed out. "Even Mother Teresa was Albanian. Watanabe was an Asian saint we could celebrate. He was one of us."

"That's a valuable insight," Eric said.

"Over and over again," Joe continued, "Watanabe trudged that lonely stretch, believing in his heart that Christ was with him, helping him carry those love gifts to prisoners who lay dying."

To hide his tears, Eric had listened to these last words with his head down in his hands. Slowly he lifted tearful eyes and looked straight at Jack Reardon. Like a resurrected Old Testament prophet or a protaganist from a Morality Play, Eric lashed out, "Mr. Reardon, I'm only 17-years old, and I don't pretend to know everything about right and wrong, but I can't help it but say, 'Isn't it time we act like Watanabe? Good God, they can't do more than jail or execute us." The words seemed to have shocked Eric himself.

"I remember that scene, too," Mei Li chimed in. "The Chinese script told it graphically."

"Did you notice 'Isaiah 53' written in the script's margin?" Joe asked. "It's a picture of God's suffering servant bearing the weight of all mankind's sins."

They knew God's Spirit had blown in upon them, transforming the cabin into a tabernacle of light. As though on cue, a shaft of sunlight broke through the curtain of trees, flooding the center of the room.

Each of them knew that God had wiped away their despair. It had taken the youngest of the team to rouse them to the truth. Without a word of careful reasoning, Eric had acted with faith. They knew now the only direction they could go was forward.

25

The Pre-emptive Strike

Like a concert audience waiting for the conductor to appear, they sat quietly ready to applaud. Suddenly Eric stood up. "What's that?" he exclaimed and hurried out on the veranda. Far off in the distance the wailing of police sirens floated in from beyond the golf course.

Sirens on a sabbath afternoon at Nojiri were close to blasphemy. The eerie wailing was coming closer and closer, until Joe guessed someone really important must be getting V.I.P. treatment. No mistake, it was police sirens. Neighbors down below were running out to the road to see who was coming. The Governor of Nagano Prefecture visited once a year, but never on Sunday.

Joe jumped into his outdoor slippers and ran toward the road as two escort motorcyles approached from along the tennis courts, followed by an oversized black limosine flying flags on its two front fenders. One was the Japanese flag with its reddish orange sun and the other the Chinese flag with its large yellow star and four smaller ones surrounded by a sea of bright red. Behind came a second car displaying the 1998 Olympic flag and what they recognized as the new flag Hong Kong was going to use after turnover.

The motorcycles slowed and turned right at the #56 sign, bouncing across the shallow drainage ditch and into Joe and Anita's yard. They swerved to the side, making room for the two luxury cars to park under the pine tree, one on each side.

"Good grief!" Joe shouted to Eric who had joined him. "Peter Yu wasn't kidding about bringing his boss to Nojiri."

Taking responsibility for this intrusion, Joe mustered up some instant protocol humility. He recognized Peter Yu in the backseat of the second car. With him sat none other than the two Japanese men who had sat near them at the press club.

"This can only mean trouble," Joe whispered to Eric. But after Peter and his *yakuza*-types removed their extra large black sunglasses, they didn't look nearly so menacing.

Peter ran over to the first limo and opened the backdoor on the right, and who should step out but Mr. Hong Kong himself, Anthony Loh. The chauffeur opened the left backdoor, and Joe recognized the former governor of Nagano, who, he concluded, must be doing public-relations duties for the present governor.

George L. Olson

Peter introduced them, and Joe quickly pulled two "emergency" business cards out of his wallet, but Loh made no move to reciprocate.

Drawing up all the sugary phrases he could recall, Joe put on as unflustered performance as he had ever done. Bowing and scraping in deepest humility, he apologized for not taking Peter Yu's words seriously.

"I had no idea whom Mr. Yu might be escorting here. If I had only known, we could have been better prepared." Attempting a joke, Joe added, "I could at least have cut the grass before you arrived."

"Please don't apologize," Loh replied respectfully. "The governor assured me that you Nojiri people are very informal and gracious toward visitors, so I have presumed on your reputation."

"Your speech at the press club on Friday impressed many in the audience," Joe complimented with authority, covering up his honest opinion.

Loh glanced up at Anita, Mei Li and Reardon who were looking down on the scene from the veranda. "May we serve you some coffee or tea? We're out of Tsingtao beer," Joe offered with proper deference to the guests.

"Please, we had refreshments at the hotel only half an hour ago. We need to hurry on."

"Well then," Joe replied, "permit me at least to treat you to our private view of Hong Kong Harbour and Mt. Victoria."

Thinking he must have misheard, Loh looked befuddled.

"Please come over here by the slope. A few days ago I was struck by the similarity between this view and what you see from the Kowloon side of Hong Kong Harbour."

"You've quite an imagination."

Since the ex-governor had distanced himself from them, Anita came down to strike up a conversation with him in Japanese. But Loh abruptly grasped Joe's arm and forcefully pulled him farther away. As self-conscious short men often do, Loh pushed himself up as tall as he could get. His eyes turned irate as he raised his eyebrows and began to speak with a gruff voice, like what traffic cops use on teenage speeders to intimidate them.

Right at that moment, the children from #58 pushed through the bushes separating the cottages and ran up to Loh with paper and pens for him to sign his autograph. He smiled as genuinely as a politician could and wrote his name in Chinese characters first, then English. The kids were thrilled and ran back to show their mother who was watching from the yard next door.

Loh's demeanor quickly changed. The eyebrows stood up again, and his eyes glistened with freezing tears. "To be very frank, Reverend Weaver," which he pronounced to emphasize Joe's Anglo name, "we want to clarify some matters. We know a great deal more about you and your plans than you realize. Shoving his right hand down toward the ground as if he were pushing an unruly

134

dog's head down, he barked out, "This John Reardon could get you and your people into real trouble. We Chinese will not tolerate any outside interference in Britain's turnover plans for Hong Kong. The Colonial Era is finished. Don't second-guess us. Our people are very sensitive."

He repeated himself, only this time with special emphasis on *very.* "I mean they are very sensitive, touchy and excitable. We don't want to squash any legitimate functions, but our people will not permit cultural pollution from the outside."

Loh paused to catch his breath and looked right through Joe. "Are you listening? You get only one warning. Don't forget we have long memories. You step out of line with this Dengburger plot, and you people will pay for it."

"I don't quite understand," Joe whispered with a confused look.

"As a starter, we'll cancel your Lutheran World Federation Assembly in July. We might revoke recognition of your schools and torch your new seminary complex at Tao Fong Shan. Shall I go on?

"You wouldn't? Who gives you that right?" Joe pleaded. "That all cleared Beijing."

"Right? There are no inalienable rights for Hong Kong people. Rights are allowed only so long as people follow the government's policies. No Martin Lee or other lawyers, or Emily Lau can prevent that. It's not the Chinese way."

Heaven forbid. Here's a Hong Kong leader delivered straight out of Mao's Cultural Revolution. Like a new convert, he's swallowed Mao's little red book hook, line and sinker.

"Better distance yourself from Reardon before it's too late," he said with deliberate firmness. "He'll only be trouble for you. The Taiwan journalist is no better."

"Yes, yes," Joe replied like any astute Japanese politician who means, "Yes, yes, I hear you talking," but he didn't agree. He merely used one of the recognized 16 ways Japanese have for saying, No, without saying No.

"Thank you for your kind advice, Mr. Loh. You have gone to much trouble today, and I respect you for your forthrightness. It is reassuring to know that the ethnic Chinese of Hong Kong are unabashedly Chinese. I pray that your future will be as prosperous and happy as you deserve."

Beyond Loh he could see three anxious faces staring down at Loh and him.

"O Lord," Joe prayed in his heart, "is this my time to follow Watanabe? Jesus' promise came to his silent lips: "for I will give you words and a wisdom that none of your opponents will be able to withstand or contradict." (Luke 21:15) "O Christ, bestowe on me, on us, the wisdom to reply wisely and in faith."

With the pounding of Joe's heart came a sudden surge of courage filling him as he opened his mouth to speak. "Mr. Loh, I think I can remember what you have told me today. I shall strive with all my heart for what I believe best for

Hong Kong and for China, for I can see you at heart are a true Chinese patriot. May I have your business card so that I may write you my reply carefully. I would not want you to misunderstand me."

Loh reached into his inside breastpocket and pulled out a long leather wallet, the kind that sell in Tokyo for US$500, and handed Joe his card.

"If I fax you, is that all right?"

"No problem," Loh answered and turned to walk away toward his limousine, but he swerved too close to the slope on the left and headed toward some poisonous red-stemmed lacquer saplings.

"Be careful," Joe shouted after him. "Those plants with the bright red stems are poison lacquer." Unable to resist a pun, Joe repeated his warning, "It's the red ones you need to fear," but whether or not Loh caught the double meaning, no one will ever know. The "Gang of Three" on the porch got the point. Jack nodded while pointing his thumbs skyward as if to say, "You did it. Good for you."

What happened the next few minutes, Joe couldn't recall, except that it reminded him of a grave-site burial service. The bereaved boarded the undertaker's hearse to procede home in funereal reverence. Not until far down and onto Friendship Road did the police turn their sirens back on.

Joe let out a loud sigh and called out to the others on the porch, "We've won the battle, but can we win the war?"

26

Time for Decision

Reardon snapped his fingers, then rushed inside to Joe's desk and grabbed a large Manila envelope full of loose letter-size papers. He leafed through them swiftly and lifted out one of the pages.

He held up the paper with a reverence similar to the way the prison chaplain held up the communion chalice to the Shamshuipo prisoners.

"In these pages, I believe," he announced, "I've discovered the sign we've been looking for. At least it's the sign I need. Now this pompous prig, Anthony Loh, has re-confirmed for me how important our task is. It's not merely an interesting job. It's our mission."

"Was I hearing right?" Joe asked Mei Li.

Reardon continued. "I think I may have mentioned to you earlier that I had a personal connection with Watanabe, not that I ever met him in person. Am I repeating myself?"

"No, go on," Joe said.

"As a boy back in England, I recall going with my father to visit one of his cousins, a Jim Anderson, who'd been a P.O.W. at Shamshuipo. I sat in the corner as Anderson told about those cheerless years in Hong Kong and about a brave and gentle Japanese saint whom they called Uncle John Watanabe. I remember because Anderson, a Baptist, used the word *saint* about him... The way he spoke of him excited my curiosity. Ever since then I've felt an inner compulsion to someday tell Watanabe's story."

To Joe and the others this was all news to them.

Reardon went on explaining. "As you know, by lunch time today, I'd pretty well given up, but it was only fair to hear out what the rest of you thought. I know I'm impulsive and tend to make foolish mistakes. I needed your imput. I had to be sure. I couldn't trust my feelings. Then that ridiculous ass, Anthony Loh, appeared. That made me mad. We couldn't give in to him."

"So what happened?" Mei Li asked.

"While you people rested this afternoon, I didn't sleep. Instead I pursued my search for a sign. I thumbed through Watanabe's Autograph Scrapbook. I tried to hear those prisoners speaking to us now through what they'd written 50 years ago. Their words made me realize that we could not let them down. Their suffering must not have been in vain."

Joe heard Eric breathing into his hand, "Yes, yes."

"Best of all," Reardon continued, "I discovered what James Anderson had written for Uncle John. It was then that I knew for certain we can't quit. Listen to what he wrote:

> 'But bear today whate'er today may bring,
>   'Tis the one way to make tomorrow sing.'

"We must make tomorrow sing. And there was that chaplain's prayer Roger Rothwell recorded in the book. We ought to memorize it and repeat it like a mantra every day.

> "'Lord of our life, help us in the days when the burdens we carry chafe our shoulders and weigh us down, when the skies are grey and cheerless and our souls have lost their courage. Then tune our hearts to brave music; turn our eyes to where the skies are full of promise and unite us in comradeship with the heroes and Saints of every age. For Christ's sake. Amen.'"

Reardon stood by the table, resembling a mannequin miraculously impregnated with life, and began to soliloquize, speaking his innermost thoughts aloud, more to himself than to the others, who sat speechless because of his sudden change of heart.

"Just suppose," he said, "we make Watanabe so real, so genuine that everyone who hears his story will catch a vision for a new Asia — a vast stretch of territory with more than half the world's population, finding in one of her own a symbol of reconciliation. As Gettysburg, Watanabe's school, became the place where the two Americas, North and South, became reconciled, now, we must summon the peoples of Asia together in forgiveness for a new beginning — that those who died may not have died in vain."

Because of everyone's absorption in the story, no one had heard a car drive into the yard. When the door slammed, Eric jumped up, exclaiming, "That must be Dad!" He scurried out back to check, with Joe close on his heels.

"Hello! I'm here!" Mr. Eilers shouted. Eric and Joe slipped clogs on and scampered out to welcome him. Eric ran toward Ralph, so fast one clog fell off so he stumbled headlong into his stepfather's outstretched arms.

Wrapping his arms around Ralph, Eric blubbered out, "O Dad, it's wonderful here, and you're safe."

Father and son embraced a long while, before Eilers was calm enough to speak, "I'm sorry, son, but I didn't dare tell you on the phone. I knew you'd understand. I think I can say this in front of Pastor Orimura, too. But it must be kept secret."

Joe drew closer, surprised to be included in such a tender and confidential moment.

"Those letters I found on that red paper in the hotel room — they did mean something, didn't they? Sub-LRPS, wasn't it? I guessed 'Sub-Liminal Reversible Propulsion Screen.' Was that pretty close?"

Realizing that Eric had deciphered the acronym, Ralph began to explain. "Those letters are an in-joke the lab scientists used — no significance, but they helped keep us focused. I don't want you to tell anyone, not even your Mother, even though the formulas have passed into safe hands."

"I don't quite get it," Eric said.

"Separate from our research, the Pentagon and the hawkish armament lobby in the Congress constantly call for the creation of a Theater Missile Defense. Terribly expensive and provocative. The truth is no one knows if it will work. Their arithmetic is way off, but the munitions industry doesn't care as long as they profit."

Eric and Joe listened, waiting for Eiler's explanation of his Sub-LRPS.

"Our research took a unique approach. Costs only one-twentieth of a TMD system. Of course, all the media focus on the expensive system the industry wants to profit off of. Good side of that is that it's diverted attention away from us."

"I'm confused," Eric confessed. "What is it you've got?"

"There's a story behind it. Several years back, a Chinese defector was inspired to turn Japanese *judo* principles into a scientifically feasible defense weapon. This weapon not only can repel an enemy's missile attack, but can return the missiles to their launching sites. Fantastic idea, but so simple no one thought of it before.

"Do you realize what this means, especially for Hong Kong and Taiwan, Tibet and the Koreas. It gives everyone in Asia breathing room until the tensions subside. We have gained time to make peace."

"Good God!" Eric shouted. "No wonder they were after you."

"I don't think they know what we have, but they do know they want to know what it is. That's why Congress is so upset over the leaking of scientific secrets to China, but they don't know about our secret."

Not knowing how to react to this news, they entered the cabin and fell into bland chitchat over coffee until Reardon set his cup down, signaling serious talk was about to commence. He stood up, clearing his throat to let the others know he was going to pronounce his offical verdict on the deliberations.

Looking at Ralph Eilers, who had joined the confab in the living room, Reardon spoke with excessive dignity, almost Winston Churchillian, as though there were an audience of several hundred dignitaries present: "You should be proud of this young man of yours. He's saved us — or, excuse me, I guess it's about time I credit God. He's saved us.

"It seems clear, as Eric challenged us, we must go on in spite of all obstacles and dangers, in the spirit of Kiyoshi Watanabe. I've decided to push Horatio Chang and his Communist watchdog all the way to the limit. If they insist on opposing us, I say we do the project anyway — money or no money. We'll find a way."

Mei Li looked over at Joe, then butted in and stopped Reardon in the middle of his sentence. "We mustn't forget we have Liu Shih-Feng. He goes by Andrew most of the time. He's ready to help. Andrew Liu's the greatest."

"Will he help us?" Reardon asked, "and is he someone who can get along with me?"

"Don't worry about that," she snapped back; he's not just an artist, he's also a people person, but he did question me about you."

"About me? What did he ask?"

"He said you may have heard about the TV series he produced about British colonial rule. Andrew came down hard on English foibles, but as we talked I realized his anti-British reputation would be a big plus for us. The Chinese Communists would find it hard to label him anti-China, and he is a past master at working Hong Kong's media systems."

"You forgot to say," Joe interrupted, "that I clearly warned him of the danger in doing the Watanabe project. He discussed it with Maurene, his wife, and they both committed themselves to help us."

Reardon broke in and asked, "You told him television isn't the only medium, didn't you? We still have radio, video, fax and Internet possibilities, you name it."

Ralph Eilers had been taking in the conversation with a seriousness that showed all over his face and in his body language. Then he commented, "I'm not exactly sure I know everything you're attempting, but I know enough to say 'I'm with you.' My own secular mission is finished."

"Don't say secular," Joe objected. "You've been carrying on what we call the work of God's left hand while we do his righthanded work of forgiving love through the church.

"Watanabe was God's right hand in Hong Kong, but the War Crimes Court at Hong Kong in '46, did God's lefthanded work. It sentenced the commandant and chief medical officer of Shamshuipo to be hanged. Later they lessened the sentences to twenty and fifteen years. They even convicted one interpreter on eight counts of extreme brutality and another by the name of Inoue with twenty-seven acts of cruelty and high treason, so they hanged him. I think Inoue must have been a Canadian citizen because of the treason verdict."

Looking befuddled, Eric asked, "You mean the Court distinguished between crimes done by Japanese citizens and Japanese who were Commonwealth citizens?"

"That's right," Joe said. "Although they all were judged guilty and sentenced, I believe Watanabe would have wanted to confront them personally and offer them his own forgiveness, and Christ's. We must realize that a pastor's role is to be forever hopeful about people. He looks beyond guilt, shame and punishment. These war criminals didn't realize how severely humanity would judge them. Watanabe said it best: 'War made them crazy.' I'm sure he would have forgiven them. Forgiven, but not excused them. He wouldn't have given up on them."

Nodding approval, Eilers continued, "What I'm trying to say is that I'm free to help you on this. I'll get you the money. I've got friends. Many former Vietnam GIs feel as I do, and some of them have money to spare."

No one had mentioned money before that, but by their relieved looks, everyone must have been thinking that sooner or later financing could make or break the project.

"Mr. Eilers, you're very gracious," Reardon responded. Pausing as he groped for the right words, he asked, "May I ask another special favor from you? Could you lend us your son over the Christmas holidays? I need his talent and insight. He's invaluable to me.

"What about you, Mei Li? I think I can twist Knight's arm enough so that he'd release you for a few weeks if we promise him a big scoop."

Feigning hurt pride, Joe whined like a neglected child, "And what about me?"

"What about you?" Reardon retorted, with emphasis on the *about.* Then turning toward Anita, he pleaded much too seriously, "Would you be willing to let your dear husband go to Hong Kong, too?"

"Absolutely not!" she scorned back. "Without me, not on your life."

"Of course, what good is Joe without you? You'll keep his feet on the ground."

Reardon's sudden jocularity caught everyone by surprise. With an exaggerated flare he raised his right fist and roared, "We'll do it; we'll do it. All in favor say 'Aye!'"

"Aye! Aye! Aye! Aye!" everyone hollered in laughter.

"Tonight, I propose," Joe declared solemnly, "we celebrate two victories: Ralph's and ours. I'll call the fish farm. Tonight like true disciples, we must eat fish — and for Jack's sake, chips."

Still pontificating, Joe offered one final proposal a la Reardon's final speech. "On this gorgeous, clear-blue day, when we can see far beyond the usual horizon, I want to escort you down to a special spot on the western slope. From there we can gaze at the sun setting in the crimson sky over Korea and China. Resembling the closing scene of Japanese epic movie, we can walk arm in arm into the golden sunset

"Yuk!" Anita scorned.

"I'll order two cabs to meet us at the waterfront by Hiratsuka's store and take us to the trout farm to celebrate what we're going to do."

They looked at each other, amazed at what Joe had said. Anita stood in the doorway and announced her own conclusive verdict on the day: "You sound too happy. What's gotten into you?"

But Reardon, needing to say one more final word and speak it with traditional English dignity, took the floor. Waiting to be sure each of them was listening, he pronounced his conclusions. "Next December our paths will cross again in Hong Kong, crossroads of the 21st century"

To make certain he had heard himself correctly, he repeated himself. Next Christmas we shall meet our cross in Hong Kong, crossroads of the world...

The others had closed their eyes. The ensuing silence was deafening. They had heard the final verdict on the day, but what did it mean for them? Each of them in his or her own way was counting up the cost this decision inevitably would make on them.

Joe couldn't remember when he had experienced God's presence as powerfully as at this moment. Opening his eyes, for a moment he thought he saw another figure standing in their midst, and he didn't need to question who it was.

27

On to Hong Kong

At Christmas time, six months before the turnover, Joe, Anita, Eric, Mei Li, Andrew and Maurene Liu rendezvoused with Jack Reardon at the Waterloo Road YMCA in Hong Kong. The Y was conveniently located across the street from Truth Church and a mere 10-minute walk to Shanghai Street, where the Lutheran Media Centre was located. The latter had kept its original name in spite of the China Christian Council's abolishment of pre-war denominational names.

When the team members gathered in the lounge to meet Reardon, he began the conversation in a very serious tone. "For security reasons I don't want any of us walking the streets alone. Make sure you know where you are and keep on the watch for persons who might be tailing you. When we have to ride in cabs, we'll never take the first one that stops, lest we be carjacked. Any questions?"

Andrew spoke first. "I've mapped out a work schedule on the basis of Mr. Reardon's instructions and cleared it with Hong Kong Television. I had to modify his ideas to fit the new political situation. You may think nothing has changed in Hong Kong, but you'd be terribly mistaken. Outwardly everything seems the same, but internally things have been re-shaped by invisible strings. These usually are disguised under what is called the "trend to Chineseness," sometimes exhibited negatively by tirades against the old British colonialists."

"For location shooting," Reardon then continued, "rather than film only scenes in Hong Kong, we'll go to Macao. That's because certain Chinese neighborhoods there haven't changed in fifty years and show little Portuguese influence."

"Smart idea," said Mei Li.

"We'll divide into three groups. I'll go with Eric as if he's my son."

"If people doubt that, we'll say he takes after his mother," Joe said.

"Very funny," Reardon responded. "Maurene and Andrew will pretend to be a Westernized couple on their second honeymoon. Mei Li, you can pretend to serve as the Weavers' interpreter.

"Anita and Joe, try to look like pious pilgrims visiting the grave of pioneer missionary, Robert Morrison, and the ruins of the 16th century Catholic church built by Japanese artisans. The Lius will head for the back streets. Eric and I will manuever around the temptations of the casino areas. I suggest we all meet back at the pier to catch the 5 o'clock ferryboat and cross the bay where I've booked our hotel rooms.

Day 2, they went sightseeing nearby and met at a waterfront cafe at noon to compare notes. Between Andrew and Jack's video cameras and Joe's still shots, Jack concluded they had gotten what they needed for background, so they took the 3 o'clock hydrofoil back to Hong Kong.

For the next morning Maurene had arranged through Caritas, the Catholic charity organization, for them to tour Mother Teresa's Sisters of Charity work among the elderly destitute who lived inside the former Shamshuipo Prison Camp.

When Joe had been there before, Nolan had pointed out the barracks where Watanabe slept. Today as they walked toward the middle of the parade grounds, Joe tried to re-live in his mind and body what Watanabe must have experienced back in 1942. From that spot they could survey the whole camp. They stood between the old Japanese military barracks and the ramshackle ones for the prisoners-of-war.

As Joe put himself into Watanabe's shoes, he tried to speak. "It was over these 100 yards that Watanabe had walked, lugging the medicines and vitamins." Strangely Joe felt a sudden tingling in his arms which moved downward through his chest and abdomen — even into his feet. In his innermost soul Joe thought he could hear taps being played by a distant bugler. Eric must have heard it, too, for after a few seconds he slowly dropped down onto his knees.

The Hong Kong policeman who had been keeping an eye on them started their way, but thought better of it and went back to his post.

"Eric, what are you doing?" Joe asked.

Not responding, Eric began scooping dirt into an old plastic bag. Turning toward Joe with a puzzled look, he asked, "Didn't you feel it?"

Rubbing earth between his fingers, he mumbled, "This is holy ground. I've got to take some home. I'll never forget this day, the day when we walked on the same dusty plaza where Watanabe had walked. It was here where he kept reciting those words from Isaiah: 'Do not fear, for I am with you.'"

All this happened while Andrew and Reardon were filming the area, making it overly obvious they were producing a special program about the sisters and their charitable service. By getting this genuine footage of the camp, Reardon believed he wouldn't need to build sets. By mixing film shots with what was available through the BBC library and Japanese military archives, viewers would see Shamshuipo and Hong Kong about as it existed during the war.

The next morning they visited the old Bowen Road Hospital, which Youth with a Mission now occupies. They also went out to Repulse Bay to see St. Stephen's Church and the hills where the Battle of Hong Kong ended on Christmas Day, 1941.

That was the evening they discovered they hadn't gone unnoticed, for inside the front door of the YMCA sat none other than Peter Yu. Seeing them turn away from the front desk and head toward the elevator, Yu confronted Joe with a look of surprise, reminding Joe of the overplayed shock a Chinese opera singer might show.

"Weaver, Pastor Weaver, not again," and P.Yu's eyebrows stretched low, pushing his eyes out wide, signaling that he'd soon throw invectives Joe's way. Singling him out with a stare, he angrily spouted, "You'll never get away with this. Go home. Reardon can only mean trouble for you. Don't think Andrew Liu offers you any safety. We know him," and as though wishing to add an extra dimension to his threat, he tacked on, "and his lovely wife, Maurene," overemphasizing *lovely*.

From out of Joe's distant past the famous Japanese pop singer Misora Hibari's face came up on his mind's screen. *Yakuza* gangsters had thrown acid in her face, almost ending her career as Japan's most famous post-war pop vocalist.

We men are cowards enough, but when someone threatens to mutilate our wives or children, who of us won't tap into a hidden reservoir of bravery?

Afterward that evening the five plus the Lius gathered in Reardon's room before supper to compare notes. They needed to make sure each one of them was still committed. What was most surprising was that P.Yu's threat hadn't surprised any of them. Or, Joe wondered, hadn't they overheard him in the lobby?

Andrew spoke up first: "Yu's all blustering hot air."

"But it's not only you, Andy," Joe retorted. "Yu distinctly threatened Maurene and by implication your two sons."

Anita, sensing it was time for a woman's perspective, said, "Maurene, you have a valid passport and U.S. visa, don't you? I think you should get out of Hong Kong right away."

"We carry multiple-entry visas, but I can't leave my husband here alone. We're in this together."

"But, Maurene," Mei Li offered, "it's not just you and Andrew. You're responsible for your boys, too."

Except for the humming of the heater and an occasional honk of a passing car, the room had fallen deadly silent. No one knew what to say about this dilemma.

Eric diverted their attention to other issues. "Mr. Reardon, won't you have to interview former prisoners in England or down under in Australia and New Zealand — also Japanese. I've heard that some veterans of the Rape of Nanking are coming forward to confess. They want to make peace before they die. We ought to be able to find some old soldiers who remember Watanabe from Shamshuipo.

"Mr. Director, am I right in thinking we could leave Hong Kong now and not damage the results of the final production?"

"You're right on," Reardon agreed. "We could do more here, but it's not absolutely necessary."

Then Andrew spoke up, "Let's cut this off and get some supper. We can decide our next step in the morning. We shouldn't make hasty decisions about leaving."

As he stood up from his chair by the window, he reached his hands into the bouquet of artificial flowers on the coffee table, pulling the stems apart. He held up both hands to stop their departure. He pressed his forefinger to his lips. From out of the bouquet of artificial flowers he plucked a minuscule green-colored microphone. Wrapping it in his handkerchief, he set it down under a pillow and motioned for the others to huddle in the corner.

"They've heard everything we said. Let's not eat here, but go out somewhere where we can talk freely."

"I'm hungry," Eric said loudly. "Can't we go eat?"

Without hesitating Mei Li whispered, "I know just the place, a little hole in the wall around the corner. It's called 'The Henan Castle.' Refugees from Henan Province run it. They make the best *jaudze* (potstickers), and their other dishes are as spicey hot as *Sichuan* food. My father always took me there, cheap and good, nothing fancy. Best of all, it's very noisy."

"Yeah, I know the place," Joe said. "No one stands on ceremony, but food is great. No one could overhear us there. We may not be able to hear each other, either."

Without returning to their rooms, they walked down all five flights of stairs rather than attract attention in the elevator and lobby. They exited through the employee's back door, which led out onto a narrow curved lane, the kind of dimly lit alley a tourist never would dare walk alone at night. It proved to be a shortcut to the Henan Castle, which they reached within five minutes.

Hurrying by the rotting garbage stacked along the road, they turned right at Nathan Road. From there the pungent fragrance of genuine northern Chinese foods filtered through the plethora of smells from the sidewalk stalls, indicating they had arrived at the Henan Castle.

Winding past noisy tables, they ended in back where nostalgic music from a television set blared loudly, drowning out even the customers' boisterous frivolity. They seated themselves at the empty round table beneath the TV. Dirty dishes and chopsticks lay strewn over a soy-sauce stained oil cloth.

Recognizing Mei Li, a short robust peasant-type of man wearing a dirty yellowish apron came over to welcome them.

"This is the owner, Mr. Oh," she announced.

"Oh?" Joe asked. "The *Oh* for *Europe*, or the *Oh* for *king*?

Mei Li translated the question. Grabbing a leftover napkin, he wrote the character for *king* on it.

Trying to Impress Mr. Oh, Joe said, "The Chinese in Taiwan call me *'Nyou Bobo'* (Uncle Ox)," and Oh guffawed heartedly. Pointing at Joe's balding head, he laughed and shook his hand like a pump handle.

"You call this 'Henan Castle?'" Joe asked. "That makes it King Oh's castle. *Hen hau* — very good. How about beginning with a big platter of *jaudze?*" Joe gestered by illustrating a pile a foot high. "What do you think, Mei Li?"

"Some peanuts to munch on." At least that's what he thought she'd told him in Mandarin. No sooner had she spoken when one of Oh's waiters came running in with tea and peanuts.

"Why don't you order for us," Anita suggested to Mei Li. "Andrew and Helen are too pre-occupied to think about food."

"Not that pre-occupied!" Andrew countered with, "But go ahead. Best to have one person do it; otherwise we'll be here all night trying to decide."

King Oh had cheered their spirits, turning gloom into a fleeting respite of merriment.

After Oh had left with the order and disappeared beyond the metal swinging door to the kitchen, Mei Li leaned in close. Covering her mouth on the kitchen side, she lowered her voice to tell them about Oh.

"He's a member at Truth Church," she said. "He fled here with his family in '57, the year of Mao Zedong's crackdown known as 'the blossoming of a hundred flowers.'"

"Yeah," Joe said, "that's when our good friend, Wilson Ai — remember, Ani? He was one of our matchmakers. The police shipped him off to labor camp for it."

While they waited for the food, Andrew poured *oolong* tea for everyone, and they began testing chopstick-skills on the peanuts. Reardon struggled to hold his right, trying to imitate Andrew, but he almost poked his own eye out.

Watching young Eric succeed in downing peanut after peanut, Jack's cheeks were flushing red. In disgust he snorted, "I used to be good at this."

His fingers tangled with the chopsticks, causing him to drop one on the floor. He reached down with his left arm, but couldn't retrieve it. Groaning in defeat, he came back up and threw the other chopstick on the table, then darted his right hand out to grab a handful of peanuts, refusing to look at how the others were giggling over his ineptness. He jammed all the peanuts into his mouth. While still chewing, he tried to mouth some words that sounded like, "Let's carry on where we left off."

After his jaws stopped grinding the nuts, he gulped them down, helped by a swig of tea. He now was ready, or so it seemed to the others. He spoke, "We have lucked out with the weather. I believe Eric is right. We have enough film footage. How do you feel about it, Andy?

"You can never shoot too much, but if you're asking if we have enough, the answer is 'Yes.' I can get more later if you find out we need it, but we shouldn't let PeterYu's warning influence our decision."

"But," Mei Li interrupted, "let's not let bravery becloud our minds. I think Mrs. Liu and the children should get out of here fast, don't you? Go back home to California. You can research from there using the Internet, if we need it. You've got your house there in Monterey Park, and the children have friends in school. Why risk both you and the boys, Maurene? Don't you agree, Andrew?"

"Yet," — she tried to object, but no words came out. Her lips contracted, eyes batting rapidly with tiny tremors racing across her cheeks, but she held back the tears.

"Where do you stay in Hong Kong?" Mei Li asked.

"We use a friend's little apartment off Nathan Road, a block or so from the Waterloo intersection. The church's middle school is directly above us."

"Let me get you plane tickets," Mei Li insisted. "I've got a friend at Northwest. She can book tickets for me anytime if it's urgent," and she felt around in her purse for a note pad.

"I think she's right," Andrew nodded. "I'd constantly be worried about you here."

"Couldn't the rest of us," Joe proposed, "go about like any other church tourists — no need to fret about formal appointments. Maybe tomorrow we should drop in at the new seminary out in Shatin and shoot some tourist footage. A shot of the Buddhist-style altar at the Christian Mission to Buddhists church would be worth getting. Great background — the big Chinese characters over the altar are from John's Gospel, chapter 1. The Chinese literally says, "In the beginning was the way," not *word* as in English and Japanese. That adds a real contrast to the usual understanding, but …"

Oh himself came running from the kitchen carrying a huge platter, big enough for a 20-pound turkey, heaped high with *jaudze*.

In their absorption with food and conversation, no one had noticed that Mei Li had slipped out toward the restrooms by the kitchen. When she returned to the table, she pretended to be angry.

"Is that all the *jaudze* you saved for me?" Snatching up her chopsticks, she stabbed the mass of dumplings, coming up with two. At first tempted to stuff both into her mouth at once, she thought better of it and laid them both down before taking up only one.

"Andrew," she said, "I've got the reservations for all three of them on the morning flight to L.A. — one stop in Tokyo."

Turning to look straight at Maurene, she warned, "You'd better figure out a way to elude Yu's men. They could be staking out your place."

"Is it really happening?" Joe asked. "I've read that Hong Kongers are worried that the PRC occupation forces will get bribed. Their pay is far less than the Hong Kong average — a sure recipe for corruption. Even before turnover, one rumor goes, the Peoples' Liberation Army has lined itself up with Hong Kong secret societies and their allies among Japanese *yakuza*. Is it true that the locals call the alliance 'The Troikaites?"

Mei Li's voice cracked as she tried to speak up, "Don't leave anything to chance. Take only what you'd carry to the grocery store. Stuff the boys' clothes in their school bags."

Anita grabbed the side of the table and mumbled to herself, "Is this then our Passover meal? May God protect us all, each and everyone."

"If you want," Joe offered, "I can monitor your escape. I go jogging in the morning, so no one should suspect anything. If there's a path up to the school from behind your flat, I can go up the hill from the side of the church and watch for you on top at King's Park. You could fit right in with the early birds there for *tai-chi* and aerobics."

"I like this," Reardon whooped. "You trying to be a James Bond, Orimura? Or are you really CIA?"

"Never!" Joe retorted. "Never CIA. KCIA maybe, but never CIA."

Eric's eyebrows jumped up half and inch, his mouth hung open.

"Wear slacks, Maurene," advised Mei Li. "Pretend it's just another day beginning with calisthenics with the neighbors. You can pick up the air tickets at the airport. Be sure you have your travel documents. Do you have enough U.S. dollars for the limousine home?"

"What about the phone?" Reardon interjected. "Don't phone anybody. They've no doubt tapped it. Don't even discuss this in your apartment. That may be bugged, too. God, are we going to have to hire an electronic expert? If I stay off the bottle, it'll be a miracle. How'd I ever get into this mess? Damn it!"

With nerves stretched taut, they ravaged their last supper together, but at least, Joe believed, no Judas was sharing the meal with them. His pastoral inclination was to close the meal with prayer, but that would have been superfluous. Each in his or her own way had fallen deep into reflection and prayers without words.

As they shouted *dzaizyan-dzaizyan* farewells to King Oh, they split up to walk separately to the Y. No one chose the shortcut via the alley.

The Lius walked alone ahead up Nathan Road, with the rest of them straggling thirty steps behind like an entourage of mourners.

Anita nudged Joe's side and pointed with her chin toward Maurene and Andrew as they crossed Waterloo Road. Andrew had gripped his wife's hand in lover's style and didn't let go when they reached the other side. Even so, Maurene stumbled on the curb and lunged toward Andrew who kept her from falling. She didn't pull away when he wrapped his left arm around her waist. The two walked close together, leaning in toward each other more like newlyweds than a fortyish couple with boys in middle school.

Or, would it be more true to the mood to say they walked deliberately, like young parents facing the last evening with their children?

The rest had agreed that the next morning they'd make a protocol visit to the Media Centre — assuming Maurene and the boys escaped safely. Reardon wanted to meet Josephine Sum, the woman who'd written the first screenplay for the film about Watanabe.

"No breakfast together," Joe said. "Let's rendevous at 10:00 on the 8th floor of the Shanghai Building — God willing."

28

The Escape

Weighted down with care, Anita and Joe returned to the Y with only one stop. That was to buy some Taiwan bananas and Mandarin oranges to eat later with their nightly chocolate.

No sinister-looking characters lurked in the lobby. No one stared at them as they hurried to the elevator and waited to be jerked and rattled up to the 5th floor. The lift's operator was the same crippled man who had been on the job from the '60s when Joe first stayed at the Y.

The elevator job must have been a great find for him. Boring as it must be sometimes, he always seemed alert and cheerful, usually humming a Chinese pop song. If Joe had been he, could he have stuck it out this long, day in and day out? Or were there fringe benefits? Constantly meeting new people, eavesdropping on unusual conversations? Maybe it's more interesting than people realize.

Anita looked morose, Joe presumed, because their room might be bugged. Prying mikes squelch thoughts of romance. Gazing at the ceiling, trying to figure out what was safe to talk about, they turned to family matters such as how the kids' families would spend Christmas, but shared nothing of what they really were thinking.

About 9 p.m. they ate the snacks, brushed and flossed, and set the alarm for 6:00. Joe extended his hand over to Miriam's bed and held her, praying in a low voice, "Lord and Savior, keep us in your tender care. Protect us, especially — but he caught himself before mentioning Andrew and Maurene and their two sons. Instead, he inserted the words *friends, and any enemies if there are any.* May your will be done. Amen."

Joe was maddened about how he would feel if he had to flee with his children, or grandchildren. The side next to his heart abruptly tightened, and a twinge of pain shot up his left arm. He started to reach for aspirin to unclog his arteries, but decided it was a false alarm, likely indigestion from all the *jaudze* and spicy dishes.

Rather than rely on a sleeping pill, he decided that commiting everything to Christ would be a more appropriate relaxant. Only noisy guests laughing in the hall and a rumbling water pipe disturbed his sleep. Otherwise they both slept soundly until an hour or so before the alarm went off, when rain pelted the window for several minutes.

Knowing that Maurene and her sons would be heading for King's Park around 6:30, Joe put on his running shorts and shoes, then read the lessons and prayers for the day.

Since Joe had no reason to be sneaky, he exited as usual from the main entrance and crossed Waterloo at the crosswalk in front of Truth Church. After running uphill past church headquarters, he fell in behind several old grandfather types carrying bird cages up to the park, much as old people in Europe and America lead their pet dogs for a morning walk. He followed up the hill steadily for a good 10 or 15 minutes. When he heard the lively beat of pop aerobic music blaring over a loud speaker, he speeded up, curious to know if *tai-chi* or the Falun Gong had gone modern.

Off in the back right corner of the park, he saw men, women and children dancing solo to the music's rhythm as if at a disco hall. The morning sun shone through the waving tree tops, simulating psychedelic flashing lights to transport the dancers out of themselves. He thought what a strange cross section of Hong Kongers were assembled here: portly women in house dresses or work slacks, skinny model-types in jeans or shorts, old men with Mao caps, and children in drab blue school uniforms. There was even a little sheltie sheepdog pretending to keep the dancers in bounds.

To Joe's left in the middle of the plaza a similar hodgepodge of humanity, dressed more conservatively, were slow-motioning their way through stylized isometric *tai-chi* movements. Joe had been told that as long as people can remember, these traditionalists have held center stage here. That's why the aerobic enthusiasts have had to resign themselves to the margin of the park.

Winded by the climb, he moved over behind the aerobic class to rest and stay out of sight on a bench from where he had a full view of the park. Hardly had he sat down when Maurene and her two sons appeared from the west entrance and made their way toward his end of the grounds. They played their parts well. No one would have guessed that they were about to break for it down the opposite slope to catch a taxi for the airport.

They didn't wave or stare at each other, avoiding any eye contact at all. Without removing their knapsacks, the three squeezed in between the back and the second to the last row of dancers. For about five minutes they kept pace as though they did this everyday.

Suddenly Maurene yelled to them loud enough for bystanders to hear, "Time for school. Better go to the toilet first." The boys followed close behind her while Joe made a sweep of the park with his eyes to check for any stalkers.

Maurene and the boys entered the unisex W.C. entrance, and half a minute later went out through the back and started trotting down the hill as though not wanting to be late for school. Joe leaned into a tree for several leg-stretches and then began a slow jog about 100 yards behind them. As far as he could see, no one left the plaza to pursue them. Nevertheless, he continued all the way down until he could confirm that they'd boarded a taxi on Gascoigne Road and were safely on the way to the airport.

Needing exercise and also relief from emotional stress, Joe decided to run a wide circuit that took him below theYWCA on Pui Ching Road and out onto Waterloo for a tailback-style zigzagging run over the congested sidewalk safely back to theYM.

Nothing untoward happened to Reardon and his five remaining cohorts until the day before Christmas Eve. They'd had three days of innocent-looking protocol visits. Andrew and Eric shot up about 10 video cassettes of film, including interviews with the presidents of the seminary in Shatin and Concordia Seminary and the general secretary of the Hong Kong Christian Council, as well as some spontaneous ones with ordinary people they met on the street.

Hong Kong's world-wide reputation for outward calm six months before the turnover outwardly appeared well founded. The pundits may be right after all, and Hong Kong will keep its semblance of democracy, but Joe couldn't help wonder if the fad to make everything Chinese trendy might undermine personal liberties.

His old friends involved in Media Awareness Training and Bible distribution confided to them that they sensed that residents of Hong Kong had an underlying anxiety. "Because no one," they agreed, "even before reversion feels free to publish anything critical of China or question the newly appointed Hong Kong officials who were rolling back democratic policies." Church leaders were ambivalent and looked concerned about what the future holds.

Although Joe knew they were busy with Christmas rallies and preparations for the LWF Assembly in July, he did manage to get one very important appointment for a brief interview. But only when Joe was able to draw aside one of the women leaders for a private conversation, did he get a true sense of how much some of them were apprehensive about the future.

"Several delegates from the former East Germany," Joe told her, "were gathering support to push through a resolution on human rights — even condemning the PRC by name."

"That worries us," she admitted. "We're building up a rebuttal so that our churches won't be jeopardized. We must convince the Assembly to delete China's name from the resolution, but we may fail. The Germans carry a lot of weight. Other Europeans and the Americans don't understand how serious our predicament could become."

After the interview, as Joe and the others rode back to the Y, Anita and Joe were sullen with feelings of ambiguity. They didn't share their misgivings with Mei Li and Josephine Sum, who rode with them. The people's trepidation over the future had undermined every optimistic prediction Joe and Anita had read about.

29

Dzaizyan Dzaizyan

When they got out of the taxis, Andrew took out his wallet first, but Reardon insisted on paying for both fares.

As Joe turned toward the YMCA entrance, he saw someone peering at them from behind the drapes left of the door.

Joe had everyone imitate early American pioneers by circling the wagons against attack. They huddled near one another next to the curb. No one headed toward the entrance — each one sensed an awkward dilemma. The public sidewalk was no proper venue for deciding how to bid farewell to Andrew. They couldn't just say "Goodbye" here and be done with it. He deserved more than that.

Covering up his own indecision, Reardon played around with the papers in his briefcase. He looked up at Mei Li and tried to defer the next move to her Chinese judgement. But she missed the signal. Ignoring him, she leaned over and whispered in Eric's ear. Whereupon he shrugged his shoulders and threw up his hands, palms upward as if to say, "Why ask me?"

Andrew sided up to Reardon and breaching oriental etiquette reached out and grasped his arm — preventing Reardon from heading toward the entrance. Andrew's strained face looked as though he was holding back a leashed pitbull.

The day before in the taxi Andrew had confided about a nightmare he'd had the night before. Maurene and the boys had been abducted, and the prison guards were torturing them.

When Joe told Anita about it, she pondered the meaning for a moment and proffered one interpretation. "The three," she explained, "likely represent Andrew himself — a sort of unconscious projection of his own fears onto family members."

Joe wanted to kick himself for being so insensitive. Why hadn't any of the others picked up on Andrew's nervous signs earlier?

Andrew panned the scene with his eyes. Then he dubbed in his own voice. "The decisive turning point for us," he began, "was the night at the Henan Castle. Don't you agree? So, tonight you must be my guests there." Hesitatingly and with funereal heaviness he added, "It may be our last time together."

They looked at each other, speaking with their eyes, "He really is worried, isn't he?"

Taking silence as assent, he asked, "Is 6:30 agreeable to everyone?"

Josephine Sum shook her head and made a counterproposal, "Could we make it 6:00 instead? The Centre closes at 5:30. I wouldn't want to show up at the restaurant alone. You understand, nice Chinese girls like me don't do that — especially if we're married."

Looking at wide-eyed Eric, she added for emphasis, "You knew I was married, didn't you?"

"You're not as Anglicized as I thought," Mei Li chided. "In Taiwan, and the mainland I'm told, women in Hong Kong have a loose, aggressive reputation. We're still very traditional."

"Traditional?" Reardon chuckled, "not what I hear," implying that her boss in Tokyo had been snitching on her.

Quick to seize the opening, Eric jumped in. "You don't look too corrupt — to me, anyway." Mei Li answered him with a jerk of the neck and a coquettish flip of her hair.

"Chalk one up for Eric!" Reardon laughed. "Six is fine with me, but if I eat as much as last time, I'd better bring some Alka Seltzer."

"You're not used to the spices?" Anita asked. "It could be the grease, you know, or MSG seasoning. Some people are allergic to it. They break out in a rash and get dizzy."

"Beer would help cut the grease, but ..." Joe'd forgotten Reardon's drink problem, so stopped in the middle of his sentence.

"Are we all agreed, 6 o'clock?" Andrew asked. "I'll meet you in the lobby about 5:50. That way no one will mistake Josephine for a pick-up. Oops, that didn't sound quite right. No offense." But Josephine blushed, though flattered.

Motioning to her, Mei Li drew her out of earshot and jabbered something in Mandarin. Joe assumed it was about foreigners' misconceptions of Chinese women.

Andrew drew back and headed toward the crosswalk. Reaching the other side of Waterloo Road he turned right by Truth Church. The Church bulletin board caught his attention. He slowed down to think about what the big 10-inch tall Chinese characters said. He lifted his sagging shoulders and walked on very erectly.

"Did you see that?" Eric pointed out. "What do those characters mean?"

"I think I recognize what is *osore* in Japanese, the word for fear," Anita said. "Can you make it out, Mei Li?"

She stared hard at the sign, writing imaginary characters on her left palm and mumbling to herself. "Some Bible verse, I'm quite sure it's from Luke, I think, but I can't read the numbers."

"Well," Reardon pressed her, "what do the characters say?"

"Isn't there a saying of Jesus that goes, 'Fear not, little flock?" she asked.

"For it is your Father's good pleasure to give you the kingdom," Joe added.

Andrew had gone halfway down the block, shoulders still upright and his step steady. For a moment a similar scene flashed back to Joe. It was when Pastor Watanabe had led him and Anita through throngs of shoppers on the main business street of Hiroshima. He was taking them to visit the Kikkawas, who operated the A-bomb souvenir stand next to the skeletal remains of the once magnificent Industrial Promotion Hall.

Fixed on Andrew's departing figure, Reardon motioned to Eric, "That's an angle we must not forget. There's reality, the pathos of living people in Hong Kong. Families divided. Children uprooted. Fathers alone. Masses of people, people happy on the outside, but crying on the inside."

"How can you portray that?" Joe asked, not expecting Reardon to respond.

"In their eyes — where else?" he snapped back, as though even a numbskull should know that.

In spite of being in full public view, Joe locked his right arm with Anita's left. Over-dramatically he confessed something he'd never admitted before.

"Many a morning I wake up frightened. Suppose I'd reach over and discover your arm stiff and cold — like a mannequin's."

"Don't talk like that," she scratched at him.

"Sorry, but that's how I feel."

Frozen in silence, they followed Andrew's figure as he shrunk from sight, lost amidst the rush-hour crowd.

A bicycle sped by, a gust of wind accelerating it dangerously fast. Loose candy wrappers and scraps of paper flapped about in the street. The fresh scent of salt water filled the air. At the next blast of wind, Joe grabbed his hair, pretending the wind would blow his wig away.

The two women snickered, but Anita tired of seeing that joke shoved him through the doorway and toward the reception desk.

From the far corner at the left a derisive voice accosted them, "Welcome back. How's your visit going? New seminary at Shatin looks glorious, doesn't it? Like an ancient Roman fortress, don't you think?"

"*Shimouta!*" Joe muttered in the Hiroshima dialect, his way of saying "Shit!" with no one knowing it. "He's kept tabs on us all along."

Joe's hand trembled as the desk clerk handed him the room key.

"Peter Yu, again. You weren't waiting for us, were you?" Deciding to strike first, Joe asked, "What's the latest?" But he couldn't quiet his facial twitches.

"Latest news? I thought you'd have news for me," he smirked. "I see you've met Josephine Sum. Good girl! Too good. Could go far if she'd quit wasting her talents. Don't you think so, Director Reardon?"

"I wouldn't know," he replied. "We've just met."

"No money in mission work," Joe said. He speculated about how much the police were paying Yu.

"Good to see you again," Joe lied, as he remembered Jesus' serving the bread and wine to the traitor, Judas Iscariot. *God, it's so hard to be nice.*

"We leave for home tomorrow. If you ever come to Los Angeles, look us up. We're only 50 miles from the airport." *O God, he made me lie again. I don't want to lie, but he gets to me, Lord. He's treacherous. I can feel it.*

Peter Yu's eyebrows pinched together closer. Joe felt defenceless against the sarcasm he knew was coming.

"Who'd ever choose to live in Southern California — earthquakes, windstorms, drought, brush fires, landslides, flooding. Why'd you ever pick California? Why not back in Indiana?"

Pitiful ignoramus!

"It's the weather," Joe fired back at him, tempted to tack on *Stupid.*

That would have been only too true. Instead he bit his lip and held his tongue.

"See you when we see you," refusing to shake hands, but merely tipping his head. He'd put Yu in his place — as a Japanese boss would have dismissed a tea-serving flunky.

As the elevator door rattled open, Joe breathed loudly enough for Anita to hear him say, "God, I hate to act like that. Why can't I put a charitable construction on Yu's words? I had to go stick him with ridicule."

Wanting to absolve Joe's guilt, Anita assured him, "God's probably up there laughing at all this."

But Joe felt like spitting at Yu, not laughing. "Shit, Iago pales in comparison." Angry with himself and circumstances, he walked ahead of Anita to catch the elevator.

That evening the little flock of five fearful sheep gathered in the lounge at 5:45, anxious to confirm their commitment to Reardon — to Andrew and to each other. The price on their loyalty had risen far higher than any of them could have anticipated the summer before.

Everytime the door swung open, they'd expected Andrew — only to be disappointed and increasingly alarmed. Time passed slowly, 5:55, 6:00, 6:05 and still no Andrew.

The telephone at the front desk rang.

"Yes, I think they're here. Reardon? I'll call him."

Reardon burst out, "Something's gone wrong! I knew it! Damn!" banging his hand against the side of his chair.

He rushed over and grabbed the phone. "That you, Andy? Speak up, I can't hear you. What do you mean you can't tell me? Got you. We'll meet you there — in 10 minutes. Be careful." Slowly he put the telephone back on its cradle.

"Are you all right? I hope it's nothing serious," the clerk said.

Reardon didn't respond, but hurried back to their corner. He hesitated as he suppressed his angst by scratching his cheek, then he ordered the others, "Hurry! We meet Andy at the restaurant in 10 minutes."

Never had Joe seen Jack Reardon so worked up. He rushed through the door, setting his face toward Nathan Road, the wind howling at his back and pushing him faster and faster. Like a line of frightened ducks the others chased after him, Eric at his heels with Mei Li and Josephine running to keep up. Far behind, Anita and Joe puffed just to keep the others in view.

By the time Reardon turned the corner at the light, they lost sight of him and his scurrying entourage. Realizing they would end up at the Henan Castle, they slowed to catch their breath and walk at a normal pace.

By the time they arrived, Reardon and Eric already had commandered the same big table as four nights before.

King Oh had been expecting them. He was sporting a clean white apron, not the yellowish, soiled one. Tea and peanuts graced the sparklingly clean table, damp from a good scrubbing.

Joe was concerned about why Andrew couldn't explain to Reardon over the phone.

"Could something have happened to Maurene and the boys?" Mei Li questioned aloud.

"Some kind of threat? That's what they always do," Josephine suspected, but Anita tried to calm them.

"Likely nothing at all!"

However, Reardon remained upset. He'd heard the panic in Andrew's voice. It couldn't have been a mere trifle. Jack's stolid face had unglued.

On the street a sign blew over. The wind had turned into a winter gale.

"Andrew better get here before the rain," Mei Li said. "Hope a typhoon isn't coming."

"The radio reported only a quick squall," Josephine said as she flopped her long black hair away from her cheeks. "It shouldn't last long."

The two young women calmed nerves by pouring tea and passing the peanut dish around. Crunching peanuts helped relieve their tension, or at least channeled it into manageable eddies. Yet no one was up to chitchat. To the other customers their soberness must have looked out of place amidst the rowdy partying and blaring of music from the TV overhead.

Pointing to the door, Eric said, "He's here!"

A wind-blown, disheveled Andrew Liu shuffled through the door, neglecting to shut it tightly. It immediately blew open and let more cool air in. His shoulders again sagged. His face was drawn and had on a wet ruddiness from the wind and rain.

Lowering himself into the one remaining chair, Andrew reached over to get the teapot, pouring out some hot tea for himself as he began his report.

"Sorry, if I upset you. I was very troubled on the phone, Mr. Reardon. When I arrived at the apartment, at first I hadn't noticed anything peculiar because I'd gone straight into the bathroom to clean up. But when I went into the living room everything was strewn about. Somebody had ransacked the place."

"Go on," Reardon urged. "We're all ears. What did they take?"

"That's it! I don't think they found anything. I had my camcorder and camera with me, and last night I'd locked up our film and notes at the station, but still it's scary."

"Can we help you straighten up the apartment?" Mei Li offered, with strong affirming nods from Eric.

"Thanks anyway, but I can manage. In our house I'm the tidy one."

Anita frowned at Joe, making no effort to hide her envy which in silence shouted at Joe, "You could be like that if you'd only try!"

"Here's something that may cheer you up," Josephine announced, "a fax came in from the States before I left. It was from Paulene. Who's she?"

Andrew grinned as he opened the envelope. "Paulene is Maurene's code name." He scanned the page and breathed out in relief, "Good news. She and the boys are safe. She closes with, 'Greet Mr. Reardon, Eric, Mei Li and Orimuras with Phil. 4:13, 19-23.' Just like her to add a Bible passage. Anyone carrying a New Testament?"

"There's one in my bag, Gideon one a friend gave me for travel — King James Version, but very small print. I don't have my glasses. Maybe you can read it, Ani. Loudly, so we all can hear."

"Philippians 4? Verse 13?" she asked.

"Then skip to 19-23," Andrew said.

"I can do all things through Christ who strengthens me.' Then verse 19. 'And my God shall supply all your needs according to His riches in glory by Christ Jesus. Now to our God and Father be glory forever and ever. Amen. Greet every saint in Christ Jesus. The brethren who are with me greet you. All the saints greet you, but especially those who are of Caesar's household. The grace of our Lord Jesus Christ be with you all. Amen.'"

"*Caesar* refers to the Roman emperor, right?" Mei Li asked. "Does that have some special meaning for us?"

"I doubt it. We're usually a little touchy about emperors," Andrew answered.

With his exact meaning left unexplained, they settled into their final meal together, wondering whether or not they'd all ever eat together again. Without anyone saying a word, the Henan Castle had become like the Upper Room before Passover. The solemnity had muffled the merriment surrounding them. The fortune cookies and orange slices became the substitutes for bread and wine.

Reardon pried open his fortune cookie first and read it to himself. A smile spread across his face. "Listen to this. You blokes didn't plant this one for me did you?"

"Should we have?" Eric joked back.

"'A smile is your passport into the hearts of others.' Not bad, eh; I could use a good smile about now."

"We all could," Andrew answered, with the rest of them agreeing. "We'll welcome good cheer even from a fortune cookie."

Before everyone had cracked open their fortunes, Reardon interrupted the fortune-telling ceremony.

"Josephine, I'm curious about why you focused your filmscript on 'Christmas at Shamshuipo.' Have we missed something? I don't see how Christmas connects to a prisoner-of-war story."

"Yeah, that confused me, too," Eric chimed in, anxious for the chance to agree with Reardon.

"You Hong Kong people," Reardon pressed on, "you must know of a special reason that the rest of us don't get. What is it?"

Josephine shook back her hair, but seemed unable to reply.

Sensing Reardon had put her on the spot, Andrew tried out an answer. "I haven't read your script, but were you trying to link Hong Kong's surrender to the story? If I remember right, didn't the British surrender to the Japanese on Christmas Day, 1941?"

"That's right," and Josephine took over from there. "Whenever we'd talk with oldtimers who'd been here in '41, that date stuck in their minds. Many believed the Japanese held off their final assault until Christmas Day. The commanders wanted to rub British noses into the dirt — on their great Christian festival day."

"Hmm, I see," Reardon nodded, "so by linking the story to Christmas, you'd increase the impact on people in Hong Kong and the British?"

Nodding affirmatively, Josephine replied, "That's how we saw it. I think it was Rev. Chiang's idea. He had a great sense for the dramatic. We used to kid him about wanting to play the villainous Japanese commander at the prison camp. You'll have to meet him sometime. He and his wife Annie emigrated to New Zealand."

While she was talking, Oh himself came in with more tea and fortune cookies for those who hadn't received propitious ones. He looked uneasy and kept glancing around. When he set the fresh pot of tea down, he slipped a note under Andrew's sleeve.

Shielding his face, Andrew read it, then slid it over to Mei Li. As soon as Josephine had read it, she leaned over to Anita and me and whispered, "We're being watched. Hold your tongues."

161

Reardon pushed his chair back from the table and stood up. "The storm's going to get worse. We'd better break up before we get stranded. Tomorrow's busy for us all. You must have packing to do, so let's go back for a good night's sleep. We have early morning flights. Two taxis should do it. No need for Andrew and Josephine to see us off."

"Not on your life," Andrew protested. "We'll see you off. After all, we're Chinese."

"If you insist," Reardon agreed. "How does 7 o'clock sound?"

"Wouldn't 6:45 be safer?" Joe countered with. "Could have a flat tie or an accident on the way."

Anita shook her head, but kept quiet, except to say to herself, "We're always too early."

"Planes serve breakfast, but you may want something at the airport," Andrew advised.

Thus, with uneasy relief at the Henan Castle, their last evening came to a close. They scurried back to the YMCA in the rain and made preparations for departure.

The next morning, they left the Y at 7 o'clock. By 8:00 they'd checked in and gathered outside the Security Checkpoint at 8:30.

"Andy," Reardon said, "I'll contact you as soon as I can about returning to Hong Kong."

"Don't wait too long."

"Let's go in," Reardon ordered, not wishing for them to draw attention to themselves.

"Wait a minute!" Andrew said. "Have you forgotten? We're sending you off. We do things right in China, and we don't care what others think. We always sing a hymn at times like this..."

"You do that, too?" Joe asked. "Japanese Christians see people off by singing "God be with you till we meet again."

"We don't always use that one," Mei Li said. "We know it, don't we?" She beat the time for them, "One, two, three," then Andrew and Josephine joined her in singing, with the rest of them falling in behind and trying to recall the words.

Singing with choked up throats, Reardon, Eric, Mei Li, Anita and Joe headed toward the baggage check. Before passing through the metal detector, Andrew called after them.

"*Dzaizyan, dzaizyan.*"

They stopped and turned around to wave. "*Dzaizyan, dzaizyan.*" So long till we meet again.

30

The Betrayal

Back home in California, Joe, feeling like a patient waiting for the oncologist to announce the result of a biopsy, constantly scanned the newspapers and even the internet for any news about Hong Kong. The rumors of media self-censorship worried him. No veteran journalists in Hong Kong dared speculate negatively about the impending turnover. Only the latecomers, who had no personal stakes in the future of Hong Kong, reported about the people's misgivings. The Chinese-language media suddenly had discovered their Chineseness and loyalty to the homeland.

God, I wish I knew what was really happening.

Joe wanted more than anything to return to Hong Kong when the mini-series would be broadcast, but he knew he might cause more trouble than good. Although he'd always believed he was more patient than most people, he hated the waiting.

Finally the dam broke and news from Hong Kong flooded in. On Wednesday, June 4th, newscasts reported that a commemorative candlelight vigil had been held to mark the eighth anniversary of the Tiananmen Square Massacre. That very afternoon UPS delivered to Joe a parcel from the Media Centre in Hong Kong containing a tape of Reardon's telecast of June 1st. The attached note read: "High viewer ratings and great impact." There was no signature. By the writing Joe guessed it was from Josephine.

She wrote, "The live radio and TV talk shows are being overwhelmed. Some callers are furious about featuring a Japanese. Just as many rave about how inspired they were. Your friend Taketani's *Dai Hodo* staff really had a stroke of genius in orchestrating that Letters-to-the-Editor campaign. Ratings can only skyrocket higher."

Two days later on June 6th about 5:30 in the evening, a hysterical Josephine telephoned. As soon as Joe lifted up the phone, he knew something was wrong.

"Andrew's dead!"she shrieked. "We found him this morning at the bottom of the office stairs."

Joe backed away from the kitchen counter gripping the phone tightly. Collapsing into a chair, he yelled, "What? Dead did you say?".

"Andy had been editing the video version with Helene Lim. The police think he tripped and fell down the stairs, but I can't believe that."

No words formed in Joe's mouth. He was so dry, he couldn't speak.

Anita heard Joe's shout and came running to see what had happened.

"Helene's delirious," Josephine continued. "She'd been with him working the console. She's in bad shock, can't talk. The doctor sedated her and put her in the hospital."

"What happened?" Anita asked.

"Andy's dead. Fell down the stairs at the Centre."

"That can't be!"

"Sorry," Josephine said. "All we've been able to get out of Helene is that she'd been recording with Andrew on camera. She stepped into the next room. After that everything went blank. When we learn more, I'll call you."

"I don't know what to say," Joe stammered out. "Please convey our sympathies to Reardon and the others. Do you want us to contact Maurene and the boys? Maybe her pastor, Reverend Wei, could go with us. I don't think I can handle this alone. Let us think about this and call you back. *Dzaizyan.*"

Shaking her head and biting her nails, Anita spoke up, "Sounds fishy. Think for a moment. Reardon and Andrew's TV program attracts a big audience, right? Have the Hong Kong papers and wire services run stories on the program? BTV probably carried it."

"There's a controversial debate over it on the talk shows," Joe replied…

"It's greatly encouraged the viewers," Anita conjectured. Two days later, the Chinese director of the program dies, falling down a flight of stairs he'd used many, many times before. That's no accident."

"You've watched too many murder mysteries," Joe said, but quickly squelched his sarcasm by adding, "but you could be right. The timing is too much of a coincidence, but what can we do? Let's call Hong Kong tomorrow. They may know more by then."

"What about his wife and kids?" Anita sobbed. "How can we tell her?"

"I'm going to contact Pastor Wei. It's best that he be with us. He can talk to Maurene in Chinese."

The next evening Joe phoned the Media Centre. It was 10 a.m. there. An out-of-breath Josephine answered. "Good you called. I just climbed those stairs. There's no way Andy could have tripped. He must have been shoved."

"Can't anything be done?"

"Here's Mr. Reardon. I'll let him talk. He saw Helene this morning."

"Hello, Joe, we've got a touchy mess here. Things don't add up."

"How's Helene? Could she talk with you?"

"She's still too shaken up, but she did remember something. She says when she stepped out of the control room to get some papers, someone stuck her in the arm. Knocked her out till morning. That's when the staff found her — completely out of it. No one knew she'd been there all night."

"Does she have any scar on her arm?"

"Clear as day, so we're sure she didn't dream it, but dumb me, I never thought to check if anyone had tampered with the film. When I phoned Eric in the States, he took the news terribly hard, but, bless him, once he recovered from the shock, he asked about the tape. Good thing I caught him. He was about to leave for home in Washington. Sharp boy to remember it. A lot smarter than I was."

"You mean you might have the actual murder on tape?"

"I'm going to check on it now."

"If you've got something, send me a copy right away. We need to keep it safe. Can't let the evidence be lost. Okay? Do it before the police think of it. They may be in cahoots with whoever murdered him."

"Will do. I'm mad as a hornet. Damn fools will pay!" He banged the receiver down as though he were blaming Joe.

For two days no new word came from Hong Kong, leaving the Weavers to stew over their worries. Then on June 9th, Joe spied the big, brown UPS van entering their cul-de-sac.The suspense had been unbearable. Nothing had come on the second day after Joe'd spoken with Reardon, so, he was certain UPS was coming to their house.

The friendly delivery man, dressed in his khaki uniform with shorts, jumped out of the driver's seat and ran up the walk. Joe met him at the curb.

Sporting his customary smile, he held out a small video-sized package and handed it over. to Joe, who already had concluded it wasn't merely another mail-order parcel from Lands' End or Miles Kimball.

"Ani, it came. Come here," he yelled toward the house. "It's the tape. I'll get it ready to see."

"Be there in a second."

Grabbing a letter opener, Joe ripped open the box. A note was stuck on the video container.

"Here's the key section of the video. We caught them in the act. Murder *verite*! Scary viewing!" Josephine's signature was scrawled at the bottom...

Joe pushed the start button. Andrew appeared on screen, promoting the Watanabe Story. "You will find this program useful for large public audiences, small house meetings and for personal viewing. When used with the study guide, you will discover that the video throws inspirational light on many crucial problems of our time. For instance, should we obey God or man?"

As he finished uttering those words, a masked thug with mere slits open for his eyes sneaked up behind the unsuspecting Andrew — his steps muffled by background music. He struck him on the back of the head with a blackjack. Andrew crumpled to the floor, motionless.

A voice Joe had heard before shouted in Cantonese, and the attacker and another accomplice dragged the body out of the studio. Again that voice in

Cantonese ordered something, followed by the thumping sound of the body bouncing down the stairs.

"That's enough!" Anita ordered. "Turn it off. I can't stand it." She ran out of the room, crying.

Joe sat frozen. As the video kept running, he slumped lower and lower, finally burying tear-drenched eyes into his hands. The video continued to run, its dull humming sound was Joe's only comfort, so he let it drone on and on. The screen showed only the back wall of the studio with several Chinese posters and one in English. Ironically they read: "Life in the New Millenium. Joe let the video run itself out, knowing it would re-wind automatically.

Anita called from the kitchen doorway, "Hasn't it finished yet?" Pointing at the screen, she shouted, "What's that? Someone's entering the studio?"

"*Yappari!*" Joe yelled in Japanese. "I thought so! It's our old friend, Peter Yu. We've caught him dead to right."

"Traitor!" Anita spouted. "I always felt he'd betray us."

"We've got him now," Joe said as he thrust out his fist and swung it downward. "But will the judicial system be free to work? Will a judge have enough courage?"

"Can a judge convict him?" Anita quipped back. "Beijing won't allow a conviction. They'll figure out some loophole. 'No tapes allowed,' they'll say, or 'The pictures don't show P. Yu actually killing Andrew, that voice can't be proved to be his, etc. etc. It'll never go to trial.'"

"You're too negative," Joe complained. "We shouldn't give up on this."

"We'd better call Eric," she proposed. "Let him know about the tape — Maurene, too. They need to know."

Unfortunately Eric had left Pepperdine and was enroute home to the East coast, but they reached Maurene and arranged to meet her the next morning in Alhambra. Pastor Wei gladly agreed to come, too.

At the Kairos office, housed in True Light Presbyterian Church, they sat around the long table in the conference room. A large 4-5 feet-wide viewing screen rested on a shelf at the end of the room, making it possible to sit around the table and view the screen.

Broad-shouldered Pastor Wei, whose English name was Lincoln, wasn't wearing his usual Sunday smile. His roughly chiseled face suggested a life that had known suffering. His silvering gray hair gave him a sharp, but wise appearance. By contrast Hong Kong-born and bred Maurene's face looked as pale as Wei's was ruddy. She sat opposite him.

"Sorry we're late," Joe apologized as he and Anita entered the room. "Road repairs on the I-10 by Rosemead."

"Is Eric coming?" Maurene inquired.

"We missed him. He's already left for home in Maryland." Acknowledging Pastor Wei, Joe bowed halfway Japanese style. "Glad you could be here, Wei *Mushr*, emphasizing the word for *pastor.*

Stalling for time to drum up courage, Joe veered left over to the serving table.

"What would you like?" he asked, but Maurene, true to her upbringing, pushed her chair back and came over to do the honors.

Silently, except for the slurping, they sipped the tea. Johanna and Esther from the Kairos staff appeared at the door to inquire if they could be of any help.

"Thanks, we can manage," Joe said, and Pastor Wei said something in Chinese that probably meant that they needed to be left alone.

Joe called the women back and asked, "Do you know how to work this VCR? It's different from ours at home."

"It's easy," Esther replied. "Just push the Play button when you're ready. I'll stick the tape in." Then she tested the picture and sound level, rewound it back to the beginning and set it on Pause.

As soon as Esther shut the door, Lincoln Wei bowed his head and said, "Why don't we pray." Apologizing to Anita and Joe, he said, "Forgive me, but God needs to hear this in Chinese," and began to boom out in his deep preacher's voice. He prayed for Maurene, but not quite with the accent the Weavers had tried to learn at Yale 48 years before. It must have been his Henan dialect, Joe concluded.

All four of them had bowed their heads against the table, as though they needed its support. On and on Pastor Wei prayed. Among the melodic intonations, only a few words stood out in the fervent crecendo of petitions.

"Liu Syensyeng" (Teacher Liu).

"Reardon Syensyeng" (Teacher Reardon).

"Watanabe Mushr" (Pastor Watanabe).

"Liu Taitai" (Mrs. Liu).

"Wode pengyou" (our friends).

O God, Joe prayed in his heart, *let my fervent prayer be answered. Pastor Wei is claiming your promises. He sounds as if he's grabbed you around the feet and won't let go till you bless us. O God, let it be so.*

Wei stopped, unable to go on. He was sobbing deeply, his shoulders heaving with each breath. Yet, his tears were not only of sorrow. They also glowed with a joyous confidence. The Lord had spoken to him. Joe looked toward Maurene. She no longer looked pale and weak. She emitted an almost golden luster of strength.

Anita glimpsed at Joe. Their eyes met. She confirmed what Joe had felt. Jesus had come into their circle and answered the prayers of their hearts.

167

Again, Pastor Wei began, but this time in a quiet melodious tone as though he was placing his hands on each of their heads and blessing them in English with, "May the peace of God, which passes all understanding, guard your hearts and minds in Christ Jesus."

"Amen," he trumpeted, and they all repeated after him, "Amen, let it be so."

"Shall we view the tape?" Joe asked.

"Yes, please," Maurene nodded consent.

Joe set the tape in motion, and there as large as life stood Andrew looking straight at his wife and us.

"O God," she moaned in English. "I can't stand this."

Joe pressed the mute button.

"No, that's all right. We need to see it," she said.

As in a horrible nightmare, they witnessed the silent assasination. With the remote control set on mute, they watched the lengthy no-action section. Before, Joe hadn't realized how long that had been. It reminded him of when a pastor calls on the congregation to pray silently for three minutes. It always feels like like thirty. Joe glanced over at Maurene, but to his surprise no morbid or distraught signs showed. They continued to stare at the blank wall of the studio and the three posters hanging there.

"I'll fast forward," Joe said, and they kept watching. Gloom blanketed their room, made even darker by ominous clouds advancing from the San Gabriel mountains. It seemed to Joe like a re-play of how darkness had once descended over Jerusalem on Passion Friday.

And over Hiroshima, too, when black clouds of radioactive dust settled over the city, creating complete darkness. Then nine days later at noon on August 15, the Japanese people huddled around their radios and loud speakers to hear the Emperor say, "We must endure the unendurable and bear the unbearable...my own vital organs are torn asunder."

Maurene wiped her eyes with the back of her hand and looked over at Pastor Wei. Then turning to Joe and Anita, she spoke slowly in a deliberate cadence.

"You want to ask me what I'm going to do, don't you?"

They couldn't hide their questioning looks. "What are you going to do?" Anita asked.

She gazed away from them, gathering up her memories. "That night before the boys and I escaped from Hong Kong, Andy and I faced up to the possibility that the police or their hirelings would kill him for doing the program on Watanabe. We accepted that possibility."

"You accepted that?" Anita reflected back. "You knew the potential cost and chose to go ahead anyway? You two decided that together?"

Maurene's nodded, then looked at Pastor Wei.

"May I ask a favor of you? Could you write to Peter Yu?"

"PeterYu? Whatever for?" a confused Wei responded.

"Tell him I'm sorry about what he has done, but I'm not going to prosecute him, that I know he didn't know what he was doing. But one day he will know."

"God!" Joe groaned.

She continued. "Tell Peter that I shall pray that, like his namesake, he'll experience Christ's forgiveness. Would you do that, pastor," and she emphasized *pastor*. "It may be Peter's only hope."

31

Everything Changed

The days of grieving passed quickly, until the last week of July. Joe and Anita suddenly realized that their departure date for Japan was upon them. Since they stored summer clothes at the Nojiri cabin, they needed only one day to get ready to leave on the 24th. As usual procrastinating, Joe didn't start packing until the evening of the 23rd.

Anita and he were eating a late supper and planning to watch PBS' Thursday-night mystery at 9:00. Settling down in the sofa with a homemade salsa-lined burrito and a beef chichimanga, Joe flicked on the TV just as the telephone rang.

"Wouldn't you know it! Why do people call us when we're eating? I'll get it." Struggling to stand up without spilling the tray of burritos, he hurried into the study and picked up the phone.

"Weavers' residence. Ani, turn the TV down. It's Andrew's wife. Maurene, we should have called you. Ani and I are leaving for Japan in the morning. What? Say that again. You're going to Hong Kong next week? I don't understand. Reardon sent you tickets? What's he up to? Hold on a second. Ani, get on the other phone. Reardon's asked her back to Hong Kong. He says she has to go."

"I'm on now. What's this about Reardon? Why does he insist?"

"He says it's a surprise. Let me read you his E-mail."

'Forgive my silence. Everyone here in Hong Kong still grieves over Andrew's death, but we have good news for you. Trust me! Just get on the plane and come next Thursday. Tickets are on the way to you c/o the Kairos office. Can't say anything more. Just come. Very sincerely, Jack Reardon.'

"What shall I do?"

"That's easy. Reardon wouldn't do this if he didn't have a good reason."

"You must be needed over there," Anita said. "I'd say you've got to go."

"It's that clear, is it?" Maurene asked rhetorically...

"Yes, and be sure to let us know what happens. We'll be at our cabin in Japan. Our son's set up his computer with a telephone line, so you can E-mail us there. Let us know what happens."

After Anita gave her their son's E-mail address, they chatted a while, but Joe couldn't follow the conversation. All he could think about was this bizarre order for Maurene to fly back to Hong Kong, now under China's wing. *I hope Reardon knows what he's doing.*

Anita and Joe returned to the sofa, but muted the TV so they could absorb this news and speculate over its meaning. Up to now they'd had only one letter from Hong Kong since the murder. Josephine Sum had written that the police were dragging their feet, but life at the Media Centre was back to normal. As for Hong Kong itself, she philosophied that "Nothing had changed; yet, everything had changed," — whatever that meant.

They reviewed what news they'd heard or seen on television and tried to analyze it. The first Watanabe telecast reportedly had gone smoothly on June 1. To Reardon and Andrew's astonishment, the new Chinese executive producer had been so elated over the turnover, he didn't object to anything in the broadcast. With overconfident generosity, he stamped his seal of approval on the entire script without altering a thing, like when Chinese customs officers look straight at a suitcase full of contraband Bibles and never see them.

"God does answer prayers," Joe nodded. "Press reports say that the Hong Kong administration has been abiding by the letter of the turnover agreement, which, of course has become the official interpretation."

"Yes, but hadn't some foreign correspondents released stories about Pro-democracy critics claiming the plain words of the Basic Law had come to have strange Chinese nuances."

"You're right," Joe responded. "Come to think of it, wasn't there a story saying that 'our old friend' Anthony Loh often acted as the official spokesman. Some have claimed Loh might be the real brains of the Hong Kong government."

"Joe, just think if the video camera and recording equipment in the studio had not been left on that night, no one might have suspected foul play. No one would have doubted the police report that Andrew stumbled down the stairs and hit his head on the doorknob."

"The police didn't listen to Josephine," Joe added, "when she pointed out that Andrew's fatal bruise had been on the back of his head, not the forehead. Thank God the video confirmed her testimony."

Again the phone rang.

"Now who's calling?" Joe wondered. Since the cellular phone was on the coffee table, he answered quickly.

"Weavers' residence. Jack!" Joe turned to Anita, "It's Reardon. Are you okay, Jack? Maurene just called to say you wanted her back in Hong Kong. What gives? We're all confused."

Reardon chuckled. "Sorry, I can't tell you, but please make sure she comes. Don't let her refuse. How are you doing?"

"Better than I could have hoped for. PSA is so low I kidded the nurses that I'm going through a sex change."

"Wonderful! When you're up to it, be sure to come to Hong Kong again. Say, you couldn't change your tickets and come now, could you?"

"O, Jack, that sounds tempting, but we're locked in for a few weeks at Nojiri. I've got to preach next Sunday."

"I'm hanging around here till September. Maybe you can come while I'm still here. I hope so. You're sure Maurene is coming?"

"Positive."

"Don't let her back out."

"Ani and I leave for Japan tomorrow. Maurene has our son's E-mail address, so let us know when your secrets become disposable."

"Disposable — sounds like diaper talk," he chortled.

"I'm sorry, I meant exposable."

"I'll stay in touch this time, friend. Oh, I forgot to tell you the video version of the telecast is selling like wildfire. The foreign media picked up on the story, so it's become something of a tour de force."

"It was worth it then, except for Andrew, but...

"Another interesting development. Do you know the name *Ann Hui*?

"Sure, the famous Hong Kong film director. I met her once."

"Listen to this," Reardon continued. "Her new film premiered at the Berlin International Film Festival. Now get this. It played up an ordinary worker and a young boy lighting candles in the midst of a rally commemorating the pro-democracy heroes of Tiananmen Square. The authorities haven't shut her down yet, so maybe there's still hope for long-term freedom in Hong Kong."

"Let's hope so," Joe agreed, "but we're still in the honeymoon stage. Don't get careless. We don't want to lose you, too. You really ought to have Eilers and Eric with you."

"Why didn't I think of that?" Reardon said to himself. "I'd better call them. They should be here. Mei Li is coming — on assignment, so it should be easy to talk Eric into it."

Reardon stopped the conversation, as though speculating about the great camaraderie between Mei Li and Eric. "Greet Anita. Hope to see you, if not here, then on my way back to England. I'll need some R&R about then. You'll be home in September, won't you?"

"We'll look forward to having you. Let's really celebrate, but be careful there. *Dzaizyan, dzaizyan.*"

Exhilarated by the two calls, Joe and Anita fell into a quiet, pensive mood as they chewed their cold burritos. Drifting into a self-flagellating soliloquy, Joe thought aloud, "Why didn't we make Andrew return to America with his family? His sense of commitment blinded us. Why had we forgotten that night when Andy treated Eric and us to pizza by the Star Ferry pier?"

Turning to Anita, Joe asked, "Remember Reardon's blunt question to Andrew? 'Shouldn't you drop out? If Peter Yu and his gang go after anyone, won't it be you?'"

"Pious me! I had felt compelled to sermonize with "There's nothing that infuriates a Judas as much as seeing a genuine disciple willing to give his life for Christ. If I'd only known — would I have said that? My big mouth again!""

The next day on the plane flying west across the Pacific, Joe was planning to bring his journal up-to-date, to the day before when the two phone calls came. Setting his pen down, he raised the stereo earphones and fastened them over his ears. The music was midway through Rachmaninov's 3rd Piano Concerto. It stirred him deeply because he had first heard it played in the '30s by Rachmaninov himself.

A stewardess coming down the aisle broke his concentration. She was asking passengers to close their window shades since the movie was about to begin. Joe pushed on his overhead lamp and tried to recall everything that had transpired since Reardon interrupted his life a year ago. He believed now more than ever that Watanabe's story must not be forgotten, but he couldn't imagine how the story might end.

When the concerto ended, Joe again picked up his pen and wrote down this prayer: "O God, you have planted the writing muse in my heart. You know how much I want to birth this story. Don't let my efforts grind down to nothing. Give me the words. Help me conclude it so that I shall know it is finished."

With this prayer giving him a temporary sense of peace, Joe drifted off in slumber to the music of the engines' humming, wondering how God in His own time would bring closure to the story.

32

Behind a Prison Wall

At Lake Nojiri the Orimuras settled into their cabin. The rainy season had cleared. On cue the late-summer weather pattern took over and began its repetitive cycle of "sunny with some clouds followed by scattered heavy rain in the evening and throughout the night."

On August 5, the weather report repeated this same prediction, except for one difference, no thunderstorms, but only light showers a possibility. Confident of a restful night, Joe and Anita went to bed shortly before 9, fully expecting that August 6 would be a beautiful day, except for the inevitable cloudy memories of the A-bomb.

The next morning marked exactly one year to the day since Jack Reardon and Mei Li Ping had invaded Joe's privacy. The pre-dawn sky replicated that August 6th sky of 1996, the black archway of pines and cedars framing a shadowy Mt. Madarao waiting to toss up the first rays of daylight. The lake lay quiet beneath a blanket of fog. Nothing out there could distract Joe. Rather, the whole picture resembled a mirror reflecting back to him the events of the past year. He ached for the right words to end the story he was telling.

Writing for Joe was always painful. He struggled for the right words. Mental anguish bordered on a real physical agony, like the Psalmist's deer panting after flowing streams, making his psychic muscles taut. He pushed and pushed to say things right. His mouth would taste like desert sand. He would drink water; drink coffee, then more water and more coffee. If he could persevere, eventually, without warning, a swelling sensation from within would signal to him that the time to deliver the new creation had come.

That morning from out of nowhere Joe heard a familiar voice, smooth as olive oil: "Today, not tomorrow or the next day, but today you will end your story." The very second he heard these words, his inner vibrations ceased. Calm enveloped him. From the bushes at the end of the veranda, where tiny *shijugara* chickadees spent the night, a breeze rustled a whisper to him: "Wait, wait, wait, the time is now." The *Shijugara* shot up out of the bushes and raced over the pine tops toward the hills of Nagano.

Grasping for a sense of reality, he went to the back living room, the same place where Reardon had held their decision-making talks. The room hadn't changed, except now there was a computer with Internet access on the table. Joe recalled that memorable day a year ago and their high resolve to go forward.

Joe pushed the "On" button. Normally Anita checked for incoming messages, but for some reason Joe did it today. He pointed the mouse at "Netscape," then to the envelope icon to see if any messages had come in.

There was one, "From Maurene Liu." *Great! No wonder I checked the E-mail this morning...*

"What a surprise was in store for me," she wrote. "You recall the front of Truth Church facing the YMCA. Unbeknown to the general public, what everyone had assumed was repair work on a crack in the wall turned out to be a memorial to Pastor Watanabe.

"After I arrived, Mr. Reardon shared only that much with me — wanting to surprise me. He said a few close friends would attend the unveiling ceremony, but when we arrived, the sidewalk swarmed with people, spilling out two to three deep onto the road. Several foreign dignitaries arrived a few minutes before the festivity began. Later I learned that the Chinese deputy from the British Commissioner and the Commissioners from both Australia and New Zealand had come, as had the General Secretary of the Hong Kong Christian Council, who brought along a surprise visitor from the mainland. British TV filmed it. Josephine also shot it. Bless her. She and Helene have been wonderful. Helene's shorthand notes and Josephine's video have been invaluable to me as I describe what happened.

"Later, Josephine told me she spotted PeterYu looking down on the ceremony from the YMCA Restaurant on the 2nd floor.

"Truth Church's senior elder, Stephen Wong, presided. He opened by reading John 15:13: 'Greater love hath no man than this, that a man lay down his life for his friends.' In his prayer he gave thanks for Jesus and his faithful disciple Kiyoshi Watanabe, who like Jesus had offered up his life for his enemies. After the Lord's Prayer, the Anglican bishop of Hong Kong read a greeting, expressing the gratitude of the British Commonwealth and her allies for what Watanabe had done with so much love and bravery.

Next Bishop Arnold Walther of Stuttgart, Germany, who attended the recent Lutheran Assembly in Hong Kong, rose to say how proud he was of Watanabe. He said everyone that day was surrounded by a great cloud of heavenly witnesses. In closing, he touched on the heart of Watanabe's significance for the 20th century, by quoting from the last sermon the anti-Nazi Pastor Martin Niemoller preached at his church in Berlin, June 27, 1937: "We have no more thought of using our own powers to escape the arm of the authorties than had the Apostles of old. No more are we ready to keep silent at man's behest when God commands us to speak. For it is, and must remain, the case that we must obey God rather than man."

At that point, the Chinese churchman who had accompanied the General Secretary of the HKCC rushed forward and ascended the platform. He grabbed the MC's microphone and shouted loudly. "Forgive my boldness, but I can't stand idly by and not speak a word on behalf of the Christians of China. You probably don't know me. My name is Rev. Deng Jiayuan. I am the Executive Director of the Nanjing office of the China Christian Council. I feel very fortunate to be in Hong Kong today and attend this ceremony honouring Pastor Watanabe. May we all learn from him how to love. As our own beloved Bishop K.H. Ting always emphasizes, "Love never ends." Let us as Chinese, Japanese — as well as all people live bravely Jesus' love which reconciles us to God and to each other. He makes us brothers and sisters in Christ. Thank you for letting me speak."

"After that surprise, Mr. Reardon unveiled the memorial. None of us knew what to expect. When he pulled back the curtain hiding it, everyone gasped, speechless, then broke out in applause and cheers. A life-size painting of little Watanabe hung there. No matter where anyone stood, he gazed straight at you, with unbelievably compassionate eyes.

"The famous Hong Kong painter, Yang Chi-Ho, whom Andy had recruited to paint for the TV series, did the memorial, too. The biggest shock to me and to any of us who knew my husband was that the artist had made Watanabe look like Andrew. Afterward Yang confessed that Andrew had become so absorbed into Watanabe that he had created him to resemble Andrew. What I could hardly believe was that people who had known Watanabe claimed the painting looked exactly like him, too.

"We're shipping a copy of the TV video, the ceremony program and photographs to you. You decide whom the painting resembles most. Strange isn't it? Who else should get copies beside Gettysburg Seminary, Hiroshima Church, and the church headquarters? Can you E-mail your reply back to us ASAP, In Christ, Maurene."

Lowering his head to the edge of the computer, Joe broke the early morning silence.

"O God, praise be to you. You did not abandon us."

The date on the letter indicated she'd sent it on the evening of Monday, August 4th.

Joe started to go wake Anita, but thought better of it. He felt he needed time alone to let the news sink in.

Stepping out onto the veranda, he saw a rowboat far out on the lake, following a lone swimmer. He, or she, was headed toward the sacred Shinto island opposite Nojiri Village. *If only we could have a lifeboat always close by when we venture over our heads.* Joe sat down on his favorite chair to ponder that wish, letting his thoughts drift like clouds in the wind.

Remembering that he hadn't shut down the computer, he went back to click it off, but he was surprised to find another E-mail letter. It was from Josephine.

He skimmed through the first two paragraphs, since they repeated Maurene's account. Then the tone abruptly changed.

"The night watchman at the YMCA is an old friend by the name of Khong. When I went to meet Mr. Reardon, I entered the lobby through the side door and didn't see what had happened across the street. Khong blocked my way.

"'Stop,' he ordered me. 'I must talk with you. Let's go over to the sofa.'

"By his brusqueness I suspected something awful. His face looked contorted, and his hands quivered.

"'Last night,' he said, 'I was on duty. About 1:30 a gang of construction workers jumped off a truck over there in front of the church. They hoisted up a canvas and stretched it out on a frame. With hammers and crowbars they loosened the glass showcase window. Then they stuck in a plywood panel to hide the painting. In half an hour they'd plastered over the wood to match the rest of the building. By 2 o'clock they had wiped out the Watanabe Memorial, leaving no traces of what they'd done.

"Look for yourself. You'd never know that painting ever was displayed there in a glass-enclosed alcove."

"Damn!" Joe roared. "Damn!" That was the strongest word he could muster. He picked up a dishcloth lying on the table and flung it at the wall.

The letter continued. "That's not the end of the story. You remember Paul Kobayashi, don't you? He says he met you when you visited his book distribution office behind the church.

"Monday morning as he passed the church, he paused to pray at the Memorial. What had been so beautifully dedicated on Sunday was gone — vanished as in a dream. He could only guess who had smothered Watanabe's image under the plaster.

"Here's what he wrote to me. 'Not caring who might see me, I drew closer to the wall. The stucco covering smelled fresh and had not yet dried completely. On the right edge where the plaster began to overlay the puddy holding the wood paneling in place, some scratches caught my eye — not random ones. You could see them from six feet away. They were clear legible characters.

"'Someone, maybe one of the laborers, or some faithful soul standing watch, risked writing in Chinese the words Elder Stephen Wong had quoted in the dedication: Greater love hath no man than this, that a man lay down his life for his friends. (John 15:13) Those were the identical words which hung on the scroll next to the painting.'

"Paul told me he forgot about pedestrians and passing cars. He went down onto his hands and knees. He knelt with his forehead pressed against the sidewalk. People stared at him, but he didn't care. One old lady even mistook him for a beggar and pushed some coins under his outstretched hands.

"When I told Mr. Reardon about Kobayashi, he insisted on meeting him; so he took Mei Li, Eric and me over to his place, armed with a tape recorder and camcorder. Reardon bluntly asked him, 'What significance does Pastor Watanabe have for you?' He answered with no hesitation whatsoever...

"'He was the bravest. No, that's not quite right. Watanabe felt loved by Christ. He'd do anything for Jesus. He was a small man, unnoticed in a crowd, sort of like those barely visible scratches on the wall, which say everything. In utter simplicity, some unknown man, or woman, scraped that wall with a hidden message imaging Watanabe himself, and of course, Andrew Liu, too, a Chinese and a Japanese.'"

"Now, get this. He concluded his answer saying, 'Someone must write this story. Tell Orimura-san that he must do it. He knows it best.'"

Joe sat staring at the computer screen. Was this another answer to prayer? How could he not try to write it, and do it right.

But that wasn't all. Kobayashi's quote continued: "I am neither sentimental nor poetic, but as I climbed up the stairs to my office that morning, I paused at the 3rd floor landing to catch my breath. As I leaned my arm against the railing, *haiku*-like words came to me. I hadn't written a *haiku* since elementary school. I'm no good at it, but here's what came to me. Maybe someone can put my words into English that makes more sense.

"'*Yuri no hana*
Ishibei no ura
Sakaeru zo!'"
The Easter lily
Behind a prison wall
Blooms in glory.

"P.S. Maybe you already have heard," Josephine wrote, "but I think Mei Li Ping and Eric Gunderson have become more than co-workers. Co-workers don't hold hands all the time. Ha!"

Joe wanted to wake Anita, but he knew he must do it right this morning. He went to the bedroom and gently closed the door, making enough noise to wake her. She turned over to look at him standing in the doorway.

"Ani! Arise, shine! Pack your bags. Today, we're taking a plane trip. We're going to far-away Hong Kong to see some scratches on the wall of a church."

About the Author

George Olson is a native of Gary, Indiana. In 1950, the Lutheran Church sent him and his wife Miriam to serve as missionaries in Hiroshima, Japan, where later he headed the Lutheran Hour radio ministry in that area.

The Lutheran World Federation Broadcasting Service called him in 1965 to establish a new media liaison and research office in Tokyo. From that base he worked in Japan and Asia as a consultant for church media activities. This included being ecumenical Coordinator for Television Awareness Training in Asia, editor of the *Japan Christian Quarterly* and a founder of the Chinese broadcasting ministry called Kairos Communication Service International. In 1982, the Alumni Association of Augustana College, Rock Island, Illinois, honored him with their Outstanding Service Award.

The Olsons now reside at Pilgrim Place in Claremont, California, but they return every summer to their rustic cabin near Nagano City, Japan, from where the story of *Pre-emptive Love* begins.

Printed in the United States
6420